THE MALPAIS RIDER

Also by James Powell:

DEATHWIND

THE
MALPAIS RIDER

JAMES POWELL

DOUBLEDAY & COMPANY, INC.
GARDEN CITY, NEW YORK
1981

c.4

Library of Congress Cataloging in Publication Data

Powell, James.
    The malpais rider.

(A Double D Western)
I. Title.
PS3566.082M3   813'.54
ISBN: 0-385-17588-4   AACR2
Library of Congress Catalog Card Number 80-2978

THE MALPAIS RIDER

CHAPTER 1

Cam Stallings had no chance to gauge where the shots had come from, but he knew well enough where they hit. There were three in all, coming possibly from two different guns. The first shattered his saddle horn and put a burning crease in his left hip; the second and third struck the horse with dull, almost simultaneous thuds. The animal screamed, tried to rear, and before Cam could react properly, collapsed on its left side, pinning Cam's leg solidly between a thousand pounds of horseflesh and the ground.

The pain to his leg and hip was both instant and excruciating. For a few instants the horse struggled in its death throes, making both the pain and the predicament that much worse. Then, just as everything began to go black, Cam realized that he must have struck his head against something, for there was blinding pain there too. It seemed longer, but he lost consciousness only seconds after the fall.

The sun was almost down, the end of a warm day in late spring. Cam had ridden down out of Colorado hunting work, perhaps on a spring branding crew. But the Big Freeze that winter had ruined so many ranches up north and had sent so many otherwise regular cowhands south on the grub-line that his luck so far had not been good. Raton, Las Vegas, Santa Fe, Albuquerque, and everything in between were behind him now, and steady work had eluded him at every turn.

Someone had told him to follow the railroad west past the Indian pueblos, then cut south beyond the "malpais." Maybe in that country, or even on into Arizona, he would find something lasting. Surely he would.

He had struck the malpais—a thirty-mile-long stretch of inhospitable and generally treacherous lava land—near its northernmost extension. He had found a road of sorts leading down its east side, and on that he figured to eventually skirt the lava flow altogether. That had been early morning. He had ridden all day and was within a mile or two of what he thought was the southern tip of the flow when he had seen the other rider. Whoever it was had been moving furtively along in

Cam's direction, near the edge of the black rock vastness, but had ducked out of sight among the shadows of its breaks the moment Cam appeared.

Very shortly thereafter had come the shots . . .

Consciousness returned slowly, and so did the pain. Except the pain was slow only at the beginning; after that it came with a rush. His head, his leg, even a place in his side and his left arm were sore where he must have hit on rocks. He moaned, trying to raise his head so he could look around. His neck felt paralyzed at first and he could not seem to raise up even an inch. So he just looked at what he could see from where he was: his dead horse's neck and ears; his ruined saddle horn; his rifle butt and lariat rope; the ground; a little bit of sky; and, of course, the rim of the shadowy malpais.

One thing: it was still light. The sun was down now, but full dark had not yet arrived. Not much time had passed, perhaps no more than five minutes. So who had shot at him? Where was he (they?) now?

He heard voices—somewhere nearby, men's voices. Then came the shuffling hoofbeats of walking or nervously prancing horses. Coming closer. More voices. Cam relaxed his eyelids and became very still, trying not to move as he breathed, hard as that was.

"Who is he?" someone asked. Cam heard saddle leather creak almost directly above him. They had ridden up and were looking straight down on him. A horse snorted; another stomped an impatient foot.

Someone else said, "I dunno, but it ain't any of *them*. I told you it wasn't."

"I thought mebbe it was one of the Navvies. I could tell it wasn't the girl," the first voice replied.

"The girl was alone. How in hell could you've thought it was one of the Injuns?" This was a third voice, heavier and more raspy than either of the first two.

"The girl is never without her friends, señors," yet a fourth voice put in, its Mexican accent unmistakable.

"I reckon that's true," the gruff voice conceded. "But who in hell is this, then?"

"Just some drifter," the first man replied. "Somebody who don't count one way or the other, I'd expect."

"You reckon he's dead?"

"Probably. He ain't moved, that's for sure."

"Mebbe he's just out cold."

"That could be. Want me to check?"

More saddle leather creaked . . . someone stepping down. Cam's heart pounded crazily. Desperately he tried to remain still, to control his breathing. If they meant him dead, his only chance would be to make them think he already was. But could he do that? He was terribly afraid that he could not.

A footstep crunched in the rocks close by; a rough hand grabbed him by the hair and raised his head. Cam, determined to play it all the way now, let his jaw drop slack and his eyes roll partway open. The man, who he could see only as a blur, let go of his head and once again Cam felt blinding pain as he struck rocks again. It was all he could do not to wince or cry out.

"Looks dead to me," the man said. "Blood all over his head and the rocks. Want me to check and see if he's got any money on him?"

"Naw, hell, he's probably just some no-account grub-liner who can't even find work durin' the season. Just look at him. D'ya ever see such a down-and-out, half-starved case before?"

The man on the ground must have turned toward his horse, since his feet once again crunched rocks near Cam's head.

"Wait a minute," the gruff voice sounded. "His guns. He won't need those no more. See what he's got in the way of guns."

Cam heard his rifle being pulled from its saddle boot, then winced inwardly with pain as his gun belt was unbuckled and yanked roughly from around his waist.

"Winchester 'Yellow Boy,'" the man on the ground said, "and a Smith & Wesson handgun—looks like a forty-four. Not in bad shape, either one."

"Take 'em then. And come on. It's almost dark. Don't wanta get caught out here with them Navvies skulkin' around and us not able to see 'em."

Saddle leather creaked anew, spur rowels jingled, and presently hoofbeats faded in the distance. Alone once again, Cam for the first time in several minutes exhaled freely. It felt so good he almost made himself lightheaded and sick from just breathing.

Then the remaining seriousness of his predicament settled over him, and he became really sick. With his right hand he felt around at his injured head. Sure enough, his fingers came away wet and slippery with blood. He felt weak. And his now numbing leg was firmly pinned. Try as he might, he could not budge from beneath the horse's dead weight. It came to him that he could bleed to death, and if he didn't do that he would simply lie there and starve, and he wondered if he wouldn't have been better off taking his chances with his attackers. But no, he knew better than that. They'd shown no remorse for having shot at him in the first place; they'd likely not have left him alive if they'd known he wasn't already dead. For sure they hadn't sounded like the sort to *help* him!

But what was he going to do? It was indeed growing dark. He was not only alone but helpless. He could die before morning. Already he was weak and his senses were disrupted: vision blurred, tongue thick and dry and heavy, ears plugged and dimly ringing, consciousness once again on the wane.

He fought to remain awake, to think clearly. A coyote yipped, then howled, from somewhere off in the distance. Not enough distance, either, as Cam thought about it. Jesus, how awful it was to be so helpless! What a way to die!

Well, not many would miss him, if that was any consolation. In fact, probably no one would: his ma and pa having gone before he was ten, his foster parents back in Kansas having seen him for the last time less than three months after he'd been sent to live with them . . . no brothers or sisters. He had aunts, uncles, cousins, maybe even grandparents somewhere, but he didn't know any of them or particularly care to. That's the way it was when you had long been alone and had the feeling it was your destiny to stay that way. It was the way you grew to be.

There were just too few happy memories. His ma and pa had pulled up roots completely when they'd left Kentucky to come West, and they'd been all the kin he had ever known. And when they'd gone, it had been within two days of each other. Even the old sawbones who had come to tend to them couldn't identify what had caused their demise. Cam had been so devastated he'd decided even then that he never wanted to be close to anybody again. That's the way it had been with his foster family. He suspected later that he had disliked them from the start not because there was all that much wrong with them but because he'd just never wanted the attachment. He'd run away. He couldn't understand why his ma and pa had been taken from him, and he'd be damned if he would risk the same thing happening twice. It was a kid's way of looking at it maybe, but that's the way it had been. And still was, now that he was grown and had become used to going it on his own. Maybe what he'd come to wasn't much, but it was a way of life he knew and could handle; it had become his choice.

So, he ought to be able to die alone, too, then—right? Naturally that prospect wasn't inviting. Alone or otherwise, he didn't want to die. Who ever did? But what was he going to do? He couldn't budge the horse and he couldn't pull his leg loose. Hell, he could bleed to death while he lay there thinking about it . . .

Okay, he had to do something about that first, the bleeding. He twisted around so he could lie at least partly on his back, then fished in his pocket for his kerchief, which he seldom wore but always carried. He felt around his head until he decided exactly where the wound was.

His hair was matted and sticky with blood. He folded the kerchief and pressed it as hard as he could stand against the wound.

He lay there like that for maybe fifteen minutes, hardly moving at all, thinking and hoping the bleeding would stop and worrying that his leg might be broken. Darkness gathered around him and the coyote howled again, then was answered in kind from perhaps a mile away. Cam began to wonder what he would do, as helpless as he was, if a pack of coyotes showed up. He'd never considered being afraid of a coyote before—except maybe for that once-in-a-while possibility of one that was rabid—but then he'd never been in quite this situation before, either.

Oh, it wasn't the first time a horse had gone down with him, neither was it the first time he'd been hurt. But this time he was almost completely helpless. He began to think of snakes, scorpions, rabid skunks, even mountain lions. He might not make it through the night. And even if he did, how long would he have to lie there in the hot sun before someone came down the road to find him next day? Judging from the condition of the road and the last tracks made on it before his, he suspected it could even be a matter of days, perhaps a week.

As if this wasn't depressing enough, he got next to thinking about water. He'd carried a half-full canteen hanging from his saddle horn, but the horn was gone now and, he suspected, so was the canteen—at least it was beyond reach somewhere, for he could not find it by feeling around close. So he might not even have water. And where would that leave him?

Well, might as well face it. A man without water, a horse, or guns was in tough shape in this country; a man who added to all that the inability to get up and walk—or even crawl—was as good as dead already.

Presently, lying twisted on his back became too uncomfortable to bear any longer, and he rolled painfully back onto his side. Somehow he found his hat lying within arm's reach. He sort of wadded it up to put beneath his head, leaving the kerchief against the wound as best he could. It would probably be caked to his head come morning, but at least the bleeding might stay stopped. And he had to rest, perhaps even go to sleep. If something attacked him in the night, well, what could he do about it anyway?

But could he sleep? He was tired enough, no question about that. But there was still the pain all over, the numbness in his leg—which was now beginning to worry him because he knew the circulation was cut off, for all practical purposes, from hip to toe. A man could lose a leg that way, even if nothing else was wrong.

So, no, he could not sleep, at least not until exhaustion was so complete that he could no longer feel or care about the pain. All he could do was just lie there and try to wiggle his toes, endure the discomfort, and worry.

Perhaps no more than ten minutes passed—although it seemed an hour, at least—before he heard the sound. It would have been impossible for him not to notice it, for it stood out against the routine night sounds of crickets and coyotes like a shot inside a tunnel: the unmistakable sound of a horse clearing its nostrils, somewhere off in the darkness in the direction of the malpais.

Cam became instantly alert, trying despite the pain to rise high enough to see, straining his every nerve in an effort to hear. He heard nothing and saw less. Several moments went by. Had he really heard what he thought he had? Could it have been some other animal and not a horse, after all? No, he didn't think so. If he knew anything at all, it was every sound a horse could make. And there . . . again! The same sound, followed this time by low voices. Someone out there, at least two of them, and maybe more, closer now than the first time . . .

Who were they? Had those men for some reason decided to come back? Well, he doubted that. But who?

Suddenly he remembered the rider he'd seen briefly disappear in the malpais breaks only moments before the first shot had rung out. And those men who'd done the shooting, they'd talked of someone else— Indians, Navajos . . .

His thoughts were disrupted by the clank of bit shanks very close by now, the soft footfalls of a horse being made to walk very slowly, the clink of a spur. Finally words were called out in low but perfectly clear tones.

The voice was unmistakably feminine. "Jaz, Jozie . . . over here. He's pinned beneath his horse."

CHAPTER 2

Cam didn't know for sure how they got the dead horse off his leg. He suspected they had used their lariat ropes and horses to pull the body away, but there was no way to be gentle about it, and sometime during the process he had passed out.

He came awake again in the back of a moving wagon. It was still dark, and after his vision cleared he could see that the sky was cloudless above, for stars blinked brilliantly and there was a full moon. The wagon was moving at a slow, steady pace, but the road was rough and his head hurt blindingly with every bump; his whole body, in fact, seemed to hurt with each little jar. Still he imagined that everything possible was being done for his comfort. Some sort of pillow had been fashioned for his head and he was covered with blankets; and too, he realized now that someone was even riding at his side and on occasion bathing his forehead with a damp cloth. He didn't have to be told that it was the girl.

"Are you awake?" she asked as he moved his head to try to get a look at her.

"I dunno," he mumbled hoarsely. "I may be dead."

"Yes, you may," she said. He couldn't see her very well, but he thought he could see just the faintest flash of white teeth and imagined that she had a very pretty smile. "Do you want a drink of water?"

"Yes, please," he managed.

She produced a canteen from somewhere and helped him raise his head so the canteen could be held to his lips. The water was cool and immensely soothing to his now parched throat, despite the fact that he got about three times as much on him as down him.

"Enough?" she asked presently, holding the canteen with one hand while cradling his head carefully in her other arm. Cam almost hated to say that he was through, for the position she held him in was easily the best he'd known in a long time.

But he said, "Yeah . . . enough."

Very carefully she let his head back down. "I'm sorry I got you all wet."

" 'S okay. Feels good . . ." He wanted to say more but somehow he couldn't keep his thoughts straight for long enough to form the words. He wanted to ask who she was, where they were going, where they had got the wagon and how long it had taken them to bring it, who was driving it? But his tongue was thick and his mind sluggish. He was too tired, too groggy . . .

The girl seemed to sense this. "Don't worry. You're in good hands and we'll have you someplace more comfortable soon. Just rest. You'll be okay."

It was advice he could do little more than take. Even before she finished speaking his eyes were closed. Somehow he felt in good hands, and that was comfort enough for now. Within moments, he was asleep again.

The moon was still high overhead when next he awoke. They were trying to lift him out of the wagon. Cam never had been a heavy man and was even lighter than usual following his recent spell of hard times; still it was an awkward situation and they were not able to pull it off without waking him.

"Where . . . am I?" he mumbled. There were two of them carrying him—two men.

"You're at my ranch," the girl said from somewhere. "Just hang on; we'll have you inside in a moment." Then she addressed whoever carried him. "Take him to the store, boys. We'll put him on the cot in the back room."

She must have preceded them inside, for a lamp was already lit when they got there, and presently Cam felt himself being deposited on the cot. The room was dim and smelled of everything from burlap to leather goods.

"Take his leggins off, boys—let me get a look at that leg. I don't think it's broken, but if it is I'll have to set it."

Cam had already decided that she had a nice voice and had speculated about her smile; now, for the first time, he got a good view of what she really looked like. Perhaps his judgment was affected by the situation—hardly anyone could have blamed him if he conjured up an angel in her place, just then—but he certainly was not disappointed. Her hair was light brown and cascaded down around her shoulders. Her eyes were dark, her complexion even and clear and deeply tanned, her mouth strong but friendly, her overall countenance evenly molded. Her blouse was opened just enough at the throat to be modestly revealing, and her skirt was a divided riding skirt. She was an exceptionally attractive girl.

Cam dared look no further, for already she could probably see the degree of frank appraisal in his eyes. But he saw enough to know instantly that he was looking at quality among women, and that was not an everyday experience for him—a man who most days did not look upon any kind of woman at all.

She was standing looking down on him, but moved back as one of the two men who had carried him in came over to unbuckle his chaps while the other fellow stood watching nearby. It gave Cam his first real chance to study the two. On first glance they might simply have been a pair of lookalike, trim-hipped young cowhands like himself. But quickly he realized that despite their range-rider dress they were even more plainly Indian—the "Navvies" he'd heard mentioned by the men back on the malpais road, no doubt!

The girl interrupted his study of the two as she bent to inspect his injured leg. "Can you move everything?"

"What do you mean 'everything'?"

She gave him an impatient look. "You know what I mean. Bend your knee, move your foot . . . raise your leg from the hip."

He managed all of the required movements, despite, in each case, a good deal of mounting soreness. She examined him further, then declared, "Well, I think you're lucky on that score. But no question you'll be bruised to beat all, and you have a slight bullet crease on your hip. That's not even bleeding now, but the other will probably keep you from walking for a few days. And your head—you've got a nasty gash there. We've already cleaned and wrapped it and the bleeding had stopped even before we found you, so I think we can wait until tomorrow to bandage it properly if you want to get some more sleep."

"That sounds good to me," Cam said.

"Fair enough, then." She looked at the two Navajos. "You can turn in, boys. He'll be all right here." Then she turned back to Cam. "Can you undress yourself?"

He was a little startled. "I sort of figured I was all right like this . . ."

She shrugged. "Suit yourself—for tonight, at least. Tomorrow, though, you'll have to have a bath and get clean clothes on." She wrinkled her nose. "You must be half grown to the stuff you're wearing now!"

"It's all I have," he said self-consciously.

She paused at the door just long enough to give him a brief but sympathetic glance and say, "I'll be out front if you need anything. Just holler; I'll hear you. Okay?"

"Yeah," he said. "Okay."

And then she was gone.

* * *

He slept restlessly at first but well later. In fact, since there were no windows in the room to let outside light in, he slept past sunup for the first time in years. The girl woke him shortly past nine o'clock.

He could not believe how stiff and sore he was all down his left side and at first couldn't even remember what had happened to him.

"It'll come to you," the girl told him, "as soon as you try to move that leg."

. It came to him, all right. The leg was so stiff he wondered if he would ever move it again. "I reckon so," he said uncomfortably. It was almost as if the horse still lay on him.

"Well, you don't look much better," she said. "But it's obvious you're going to live. Except for a lot of moaning and groaning, you slept like a log."

She stood over him, a look of very faint disapproval on her face, and he could not honestly understand why she was being kind to him at all. One thing, though: he was glad to see that the reality of the morning had not caused his angel of the night before to evaporate. The girl really was something to look at. Which was just fine, when he thought how he at the moment must look in comparison. Just fine!

"You looked in on me, then," he said.

"A couple of times, yes. Why?"

Without answering, he struggled to rise, and despite a good deal of pain managed to work his legs off the cot so he could at least sit on its edge.

"I don't think you should do that," she warned, stepping back.

He shook his head. "I'm all right. And I don't want you to think the only way I ever look at anybody is from flat on my back. I'm not completely without pride, no matter how I look."

She cocked her head slightly but didn't say anything.

He went on. "Anyway, I owe you for what you did for me. I could've died out there under that horse—"

"Not could," she corrected, "would."

"Yeah, well, maybe. Anyhow, I want to thank you for it. Those fellows that shot at me left me for dead."

"I'm not surprised about that," she said levelly.

"You know them? Well, I reckon you probably do. The way they talked it was you they were looking for."

"It was. That's why we let it get dark before coming down to check things out. We saw you briefly and later heard the shots, but we had slipped back into the malpais by then and didn't know what had happened. We were really sort of lucky to find you, at night like that."

"Were *you* the rider I saw?" he asked, divining.

Again she nodded. "Yes. Those men were hidden in the rocks behind me, hoping to waylay either me or one of the boys. We saw them first and split up to slip past them, only I almost ran into you. I knew you weren't one of them, but I had to get out of sight and didn't have time to warn you. It never occurred to me they would lay down on you like that."

"They thought I was one of your Navajos," Cam told her. "But I got the impression they'd've just as soon it was you. Some country this is—where men go gunning for women!"

"You only know the half of it," she said grimly. "But it's not the country's fault; the country here is good and so are most of its people."

"If you say so." Cam wagged his head. "I came here thinking I might find a job; now I'm not sure what I'll do. I've lost my horse, my guns, and damn near got killed; I've got maybe two dollars to my name, and I don't know if I can even walk."

She studied him in a sizing-up sort of way. "You're a cowhand, I take it. Are you any good?"

Cam stared at her. It was a frank question, but as he thought about it he guessed he couldn't blame her if she was a bit skeptical. He knew he didn't look like much and quite plainly he was on the drift in a season when the demand for good riders was ordinarily high. A good man should already have a job, most times, and they both knew it.

But these were not most times. "I always thought I was pretty good," Cam told her finally. "But there're a lot more like me nowadays—at least since the Big Freeze up north and with cow prices having gone to hell the way they have. I reckon you must know that."

"Yes," she said thoughtfully, "I know that. And I'm sorry for what's happened to you here. I feel sort of responsible, in fact. Do you think you can walk on that leg?"

He looked dubiously down on the member in question. Hell, he couldn't even bend it at the knee! Nevertheless, he made the effort to get to his feet, and, had she not been quick enough to catch him by the arm, would have collapsed the moment he tried to put weight on the injured leg. To add to the problem, he was suddenly dizzy and weak. Even if the leg had held up he was pretty sure he would have passed out.

Slowly, with the girl's help, he sank back down.

"I was afraid of that," she said. "Look, you're going to be a few days before you can do much of anything. Let's get you something to eat, and a fresh bandage for your head. Then we can get you cleaned up and talk later about maybe a job, if you really want one."

"A job? Where?"

She straightened and stepped back. "Why, here, of course—my ranch. I need riders badly . . . But that's something we'll have to talk about in detail when the time comes. Right now, I'll fix you up some breakfast, and I'll have the boys heat and bring you over some bath water. And then some new clothes . . . Really, we must burn those you have on!"

﹨ He stared at her, dumbfounded. "New clothes? For chrissake, girl—I can't afford new clothes! And where are you going to get any to fit me, anyway? I mean—"

She shook her head and smiled. "This is a store you're in here, or did that part escape you last night? Dry goods right along with everything else. I'm sure we can find something . . . and believe me, it'll be worth it to me if you never pay a dime on them. You've just got to be cleaned up, and that's that."

He didn't say anything in response to this, so she said, "You just lie back down till I get back with your breakfast. Then we'll take it from there. Okay?"

He called to her just as she reached the door. "Wait! There's something you've gotta understand first."

She paused and looked back. "Oh?"

"I can't promise anything, miss. I mean, I want work and I can't think of a reason why here wouldn't be as good a place as any to get it. But we'll have to talk first. You understand that, I hope."

She looked uncertain. "Well, yes. I said that myself, I think—"

He went on. "It's just that I've never worked for a woman before . . . and there are some strange things going on here, like those four fellows yesterday. If nothing else, that may be a score I'll have to settle first."

"Yes . . . yes, of course," she said, albeit with a slight frown. "Is that all?"

"Well, yeah, I guess . . ." Again she turned to leave.

"Miss!" he called back again. "Miss, my name is Cam Stallings, if that matters to you."

She looked back, perhaps a little embarrassed. "Why, yes. Of course it does. And mine is Stacy Brightwood—*Miss* Stacy Brightwood, as you have already surmised. And this is the Stretch B Ranch. I'm sorry, I should have told you before. Now, I really must go."

This time she did leave, and for several moments Cam simply lay there, staring after her and thinking: Stacy Brightwood . . . *Miss* Stacy Brightwood, a very pretty young lady who owns a store—located, as far as he could tell, in the middle of nowhere—a ranch, and has four men trying to kill her . . .

He wagged his head. It was enough to set him to wondering a lot and deciding little, except that there was nothing ordinary about it. He would have to learn much, much more before deciding to go to work for her. But then, of course, he had always been one to want to know more.

CHAPTER 3

Cam had all but forgotten what a home-cooked meal was like, and he certainly couldn't remember what it was like to have two such feasts back to back. Additionally, a good hot bath, a clean shave, and newly bought clothes altogether served to make him feel like a new and different man.

By afternoon even his aches and pains had eased somewhat, and he no longer felt dizzy when he tried to rise. As expected, his leg was badly bruised from hip to toe. But it was mostly soreness in the knee that made the leg difficult to walk on and that, he now thought, would rapidly improve over the next few days if he would just use it sparingly. Shortly before noon, one of the Navajos—Jozie, he thought it was—had come in with a crutch fashioned from a forked juniper limb. A few minutes later the girl had brought over some lunch, then had left again. Finding himself still alone an hour later, Cam decided to get up and try hobbling around a bit, perhaps looking the place over as he went.

The store, he decided, appeared well stocked with food items such as flour, sugar, coffee, and various canned goods, not to mention dry goods and saddlery. It was built of adobe; its ceilings were high, as were most of its windows; and the building was surprisingly cool even during the heat of the day. It had two rooms—the back storeroom where Cam had spent his time so far, and the front or main room where business was conducted. Of course, Cam could only guess at how much business there was, for to his knowledge no one had come around since his arrival. Not much, he guessed.

Outside, he stood on the store's front porch, for a few moments simply letting his eyes adjust to the bright sunlight, then beginning to view the premises in general. To his left stood one other building, also built of adobe and looking to be the main ranch house. It was shaded by cottonwoods. Between fifty and seventy-five yards ahead and slightly to his right were corrals, several sheds, and a fair-sized barn. Still farther to his right and back a bit from the store lay another place of abode. It was low-roofed, likewise built of adobe, shaded by cottonwoods, and was probably a bunkhouse. There were four or five horses in the corrals, a milch cow grazing about a quarter of a mile away in a small pasture that connected to the corrals, and a couple dozen chickens pecking in the dirt over near the barn.

, Beyond the corrals, to the south and southwest, stretched a broad plain, light green with spring growth and all but devoid of trees. Southeast and east lay mountainous terrain characterized by tree- and shrub-lined hills and mesas that rose several hundred feet above the plains and seemed to grade into even more mountainous terrain farther south. Looking around one corner of the store, back to the north, he could see the southernmost tip of the malpais, several miles away and at this point little more than a low, dark bulge against the skyline. West and northwest were more mountains.

There was a bench at the porch's corner, and Cam, his leg hurting him again now, lowered himself onto it. For a while he just sat there, wondering where everyone else was. After a bit, a man he did not recognize appeared at the bunkhouse door and began hobbling across to the barn. He appeared to be an older man and was perhaps a Mexican. Reaching the barn, he disappeared inside, apparently without ever having taken serious notice of the stranger sitting on the porch of the store. The two Navajo cowhands were nowhere to be seen.

Cam turned his attention back to the broad expanse to the south and southwest. Strangely, little moved. He could see for miles, and it struck him that if this was any kind of ranch at all, the plain before him should have been dotted with cattle. It was as good a grama and wheatgrass country as he'd seen, and a vast area such as that should support hundreds, perhaps thousands of head. Oh, he did spot a few, mostly close in, but only peanuts compared to what it seemed to him there should be. It was only natural for him to wonder why . . .

A light step sounded on the porch to his left and broke his train of thought. Turning, he discovered Stacy Brightwood had just come around the corner. She was wearing a light gray divided riding skirt, dark blouse, kerchief, and a narrow-brimmed Stetson. Her long hair beneath the hat appeared even lighter brown than before. Although her outfit was not the usual women's garb of the day, he found it becoming.

"So you're up and around," she said. "Well, good. I thought maybe you'd feel better with a little food under your belt and a good bath. You certainly look better, I'll say that!"

"Thanks," Cam said, a bit grudgingly.

She came over to stand against one of the porch support posts. "Have you been looking the place over already?"

"Some, yeah."

"And what have you decided?"

He shook his head. "I dunno, for sure. Maybe I can't see enough from this porch to tell much."

"But you have observed *some* things."

"Well, yes, some things . . ." He was a bit hesitant, but decided to go ahead and be frank. "A store without any customers, a ranch with damn few cattle in sight, and a girl who claims to be its owner but who apparently has only two Indian cowhands and one old Mexican man for help . . . Have I missed anything so far?"

She looked at him sadly. "Not really, I'm afraid. You are very observant, actually."

"And yet you still say you need riders?"

"Yes. Yes, I do."

"But why? I don't see enough cattle to keep those two Navajos busy . . . or isn't that your range out there?" He motioned in the direction of the open plain.

"It's part of it," she said, "although some of our cattle run in the mesa country back to the east also. But you're right: there should be more in view."

"And there's more to it than just rough winters and poor cow prices, I take it," he observed intuitively. "Maybe even something to do with those four men last night?"

She nodded slowly, then sighed. "Do you want to hear the whole story?"

"If you want to tell it to me," he said. "Remember, I'm only a stranger."

She passed this off with a shrug. "I as much as offered you a job last night; you have a right to know what you'd be getting into. That is, *if* you're interested."

He met her gaze steadily. "I'm interested."

She came over and sat down on the bench next to him, her eyes drifting pensively out across the grassy plain. "Most of what you see out there is open range, of course. Still, it is traditionally Stretch B range, for my father, Amos Brightwood, was one of the first to settle here. He was also wise enough to obtain title to lands surrounding several of the best watering places around—this place here, where we have two good dug wells; what we call Paint Horse Springs, about three miles from here at the foot of Paint Horse Mesa; Bell Cow Cienaga, a natural marsh two miles west, where he dug out an earthen tank that never goes dry; and a narrow stretch along Loco Creek, ten miles farther south, which we have always shared with our neighbors down that way, no questions asked. Of course, there are others which are unpatented but are well within our traditional boundaries, and although my father never made any effort to refuse their use to anyone, Stretch B cattle have always been the primary customers for their water. It is a good range, and no one ever seriously managed to challenge my father's claim to any of it."

"But now something's happened to change all that," Cam guessed. "Something's happened to your father."

She nodded sadly. "My father died just over two years ago. He is buried not two hundred yards from where we now sit."

"And the ranch . . . you say it's yours now?"

"Yes . . . at least it's supposed to be." She hesitated. "You see, I have a half sister. Her name is Mala, and she is seven years older than I am. Her mother was my father's first wife. Unfortunately, Mala and I have never been the best of friends—to put it mildly—and we are now at odds over the ownership of the ranch . . ."

Cam frowned. He didn't say anything but could hardly hide the curiosity this raised in him.

The girl sighed. "It goes back to when Mala's mother died . . . when Mala was only three. My father was terribly saddened, of course, and was not quick to remarry. When he finally did, it was two years later to a woman several years his junior. It was a union, I suppose, that was never destined to succeed, and I was its only child. How it lasted as long as it did I will always be unsure, but when I was eight my mother ran off with a Kansas cattle buyer and never came back. You can imagine what a blow that was to me, as young as I was, but it was an even worse one to my father. At the time we were living in Texas, and somehow everything he'd ever felt for our little farm there left him completely when she disappeared. He tried and tried, but he just could not stand it there anymore. It was the basis for his decision, finally, to move farther west, which we did, eventually ending up here."

She paused, almost as if to catch her breath, then continued. "From the beginning it was clear that this place would be my father's salvation. He loved it here, and he right away went to work building up a good ranch and raising Mala and me the way he thought best. He did not remarry this time, however, and when he died we two girls were his only heirs—"

"And that is where the trouble comes in," Cam guessed again. "The inheritance?"

Again she nodded. "As I said, my half sister and I never got along. Mala always seemed to resent both my mother and me. I suppose because she forever considered us interlopers in her life. In fact, I think she hated my mother even before she ran off with that other man. Later, I think she transferred that hatred to me and finally, maybe because my father may even have appeared to favor me at times, I think she began to hate him too."

"Did he?" Cam wanted to know. "Favor you?"

"I don't think so really. I think many times he tried to defend me, even protect me, from Mala. I was younger, of course, and subject to abuse on occasion from a sister seven years older. You might know how that can be." Cam didn't, of course, but he didn't say anything. "But, no, my father was a fair man. He gave us each every opportunity. What eventually happened to Mala, I believe, she brought on herself . . ." A questioning look came to her eyes. "Am I making you uncomfortable with all of this?"

In a way she was, but all he said was, "If you don't mind telling it, Lord knows I should be willing to listen."

She didn't look entirely convinced, but she went on anyway. "Well, as I said, Mala brought much of what happened on herself. By the time she reached age twenty, she had become openly rebellious. Sometimes it was as if she would do things on purpose to hurt our father. And it did hurt him, terribly . . . perhaps because he loved his first wife so much and wanted so badly for Mala to be like her, which he always said she was not. As for me, I was all too frequently caught in the middle. Although I must admit there was no love lost between Mala and myself, I did love my father and did not want to see him hurt. Many was the time I even lied for Mala just so he wouldn't know the truth about her. But finally she did something he had to know about and could not forgive, something he believed—and so will I always— was done for no other purpose than to hurt both of us, but mostly him."

"And what was that?"

"She got married . . . which would have been okay, except she picked the one man in the world who my father never had and never would have any use for, a man named Gerd Terhune, a man who had set up ranching in the mesa country southwest of here a few years before, but who my father always considered no more than a common cow thief with an eye for Stretch B cattle and Stretch B range. My father could not help feeling that Terhune, who is a good ten years older than Mala, married her with that end in mind. He died convinced of it, in fact."

"If that's true, didn't your sister know it too?"

"Of course she did. That's what made it so bad. She did not love Terhune, yet she married him despite his designs on the Stretch B. I don't suppose there was ever any doubt in either of their minds that Mala would inherit the ranch—if not all of it, at least the best of it. She should have known my father better than to flaunt that in his face the way she did. She should have known what he would do."

"And what was that? Cut her out of his will?"

The girl nodded. "For all practical purposes, yes. He left her one hundred and sixty acres that fit better with Terhune's Cross Arrow country than the Stretch B anyway, and all of her mother's personal things—wedding dress, hope chest, items of family interest. But that was it. Not even any money, just the one piece of land and her mother's things. The rest all went to me, lock, stock, and barrel."

"And your sister never guessed this would happen? Never once?"

The girl shook her head. "I don't think so. She relied so heavily on the fact that she was the oldest, that she was the daughter of my father's first love, that she just never dreamed she wouldn't be his primary heir. Oh, she figured I would get something. Maybe about what she got except her mother's things and maybe some sort of income. I was the youngest, the daughter of a woman who had let my father down very hard. But for some reason Mala never understood our father, never realized that he was a man who judged each person on his or her own merits. When the will was read, she couldn't believe it. I guess I couldn't either, at first. Anyway, it was a valid document, and although we both had to go to Santa Fe and hire lawyers when she challenged it, the case was cut and dried. I won. Still, you can imagine: if she ever hated me before she really hates me now. She has openly claimed that the ranch should have been hers. She won't share it, and her husband, I'm afraid, is just what my father always thought he was and has vowed to somehow help her get it away from me in its entirety."

"And now they're having something to do with how many cattle I see out there. How many customers you have at the store."

She nodded sadly. "The first year after my father's death we had reasonably few problems. Then it became Stretch B hands being goaded into fights in town and winding up getting beat up so badly they were afraid to go in alone again; a cow or a calf occasionally found dead with a bullet hole in its head. For a while that was about it. After the fall roundup last year, we sold a reasonable number of two- and three-year-olds and shipped them on the railroad to points back East. But as winter came on I suddenly started losing hands. At first I didn't know what was going on. Most of them had worked here for years, yet all of a sudden they were quitting right and left. Then I learned that Terhune had begun hiring men that were known gunhands. Oh, they double well enough as cowboys, but several are outsiders and are known somewhere for having used their guns on more than just coyotes and snakes—"

"Like those four who laid down on me yesterday, maybe?"

She smiled feebly. "Yes, like those four. Suddenly our men were being threatened with more than just beatings. They were being shot at from ambush as they tried to ride the range. Finally, three months ago, even my foreman, a man my father had always placed utmost confidence in, disappeared from the rank like all the rest. His name is Dan Stanhope, and I learned only a few weeks ago that he was caught alone and beaten nearly to death before being warned to leave the country. I think he's over in Arizona now, but I've not bothered to look him up. I know he would never have left under any other circumstances than those he faced at the time, and he is a very proud man. It would do no good to shame him any more than he has already been shamed. Too, I have no doubt that those men might try to kill him if he comes back. I wouldn't want to be the cause of that."

Again she paused, then sighed. "Anyway, as you can imagine, it is pretty difficult to watch over a cattle range with no cowboys. All I had left, suddenly, were my two Navajos—the twin sons of my father's old cook and servant here until her death three years ago—and old Miguel, the Mexican you must have seen at the barn a few minutes ago. Jaz and Jozie are both in their early twenties but are smart enough to stay away from town and Terhune's gunnies. Miguel is in his seventies and rarely leaves the home place here. No one thinks he could possibly make a difference anyway. But they're all I have, and somehow we just didn't brand many Stretch B calves at the spring roundup this year. There just weren't that many Stretch B cows gathered. What happened to them I don't know, but some of them were simply passed up during the gather by Terhune hands, I'm sure. Others may have been run off altogether. Mavericks, I'm convinced, are being burned with Terhune's Cross Arrow as fast as they can be found, no matter where on Stretch B range they are discovered. And eventually, if I am left without riders as I am now, I will probably wind up without any stock whatsoever. I fully expect that next fall's roundup will be an even more miserable affair than this spring's by far."

Cam just shook his head. "You mentioned a town. Where is that? And the store. Isn't this a pretty isolated spot to be trying to run a store? And what about the law? Can't they do anything?"

She smiled thinly. "The town is Vera Velarde, twenty-five miles south of here. It is something of a business center but not a county seat. The law just doesn't venture into these parts much and perhaps won't as long as we're so isolated. As to the store, well, it was something my father built as a service to neighbors who found Vera Velarde and the railroad towns north of the malpais too long a trip. He built it for them and for travelers between the two points. At first people kept coming just as they always had. Then the neighbors—some of them admittedly homesteaders who have droughted out and given up over the years—mostly just began going elsewhere. And lately even the occasional traveler has begun to ride right on by."

"You mean what neighbors you have left have also been threatened, and maybe even the travelers?"

"I feel so, yes. And it is getting worse. Terhune's gunnies are becoming braver about it all the time. Yesterday, for instance, was the first time I myself ever felt in danger of physical attack. It may be that my half sister and brother-in-law have now decided that the easiest way is to kill me outright."

"And these neighbors . . . they'll stand for even that?"

Stacy Brightwood only shrugged. "Perhaps not. That may be the only thing that has kept me alive so far. I don't know. Maybe the Terhunes are just waiting until they have the whole countryside afraid of them. Maybe soon they themselves won't be afraid of anything or anybody anymore."

Cam gave a low whistle. "And you're offering me a job in the middle of all this?"

She eyed him unhappily, then dropped her gaze. "I suppose it's not much of an offer, all right. But that's why I told you what you'd be getting into. I wouldn't blame you if you said no, of course."

He was silent for a few moments, then said suddenly, "What's the pay?"

"Why, forty a month and found," she said, a little surprised. "Foreman's wages and ten dollars over the going rate for riders. About all I can do right now, or I guarantee you it would be even more."

Cam didn't know for sure why he said it—there would be plenty of times later when he'd think he had been nuts for sure—but he blurted out anyway, "I'll take it . . . but only on one condition."

"Oh?" She eyed him a mite suspiciously now. "And what is that?"

"I have to do something first. Those four men who waylaid me killed my horse, took my guns, and ruined my saddle. On top of that they left me for dead in a country where a man on foot most times wouldn't have a chance. If I'm to stay, I can't let that go by. I'll have to do something about it."

She frowned deeply. "What—exactly?"

"Well, soon as I can ride, I'll get you to loan me a horse and a gun and ask one of those Navajos to fetch in my saddle. Then I'll head over to the Cross Arrow spread and see if I can't get a little reimbursement for my losses. If it works, I'll come back here and see what I can do to help out."

She looked at him half aghast. "You would face Terhune and his men on their own ground? Alone?"

He nodded. "It's the only way. They've got to know that someone's around who isn't afraid of them. Any other approach and they'll run me off just as fast as the rest."

"And you'll not be afraid?"

He smiled thinly. "Scared to death, I imagine. But it's gotta be done. Will you loan me the horse and the gun?"

"I don't know. For your sake, I'm really not sure I should . . ."

"It's the only way I'll work for you," he said. "I'm not the bravest soul in the world and God knows I'm no gunhand, but a man shouldn't be gunned for no reason and left for dead like I was. I'd have to make that right, no matter what."

"You'll probably wind up dead for sure this time," she warned. "Those men are mean, and there are so many more of them than you. Why, you'll not have a chance!"

"Time will have to decide that," he said. "Just tell me—is it a deal or not?"

She studied him for several moments, then shrugged. "I feel like I'm sentencing you to death . . . Can't we both think about it for a day or so first?"

He looked down at his leg, then back at her. "Suit yourself. I guess I won't be going anywhere for a few days, all right. But I may back out; then what'll you do?"

"I don't know," she said earnestly, "but somehow I almost hope you do."

Nevertheless, a few moments later as she helped him to hobble back inside, he was saying, "About that forty a month . . . when would it start?"

CHAPTER 4

A week passed before Cam was finally able to cast aside his head bandage, don his hat without unreasonable discomfort, and find at last that he could walk freely without his crutch. He limped a bit—sometimes quite a bit—but that was okay. The bullet crease in his hip was now only a faint scab; the pain in his knee had become at least endurable; and he could, if careful with the leg, mount and ride a horse again—which, of course, was all Stacy Brightwood's newest and most anxious employee had been waiting for.

Not that he'd had no second thoughts about his decision to ride for the Stretch B. Sometimes he felt like a damned fool for ever having considered it. He had to be honest and admit that had it not been for the pretty face of his prospective employer, he might not have hired on at all. But that didn't matter now. Whatever his reasons, he'd said he was going to do something, and so he was. Whether he liked it or not, the first order of business was going to have to be that trip he'd planned to the Cross Arrow. It wasn't something he was looking forward to, of course. But as he'd told the girl, it was something that had to be done. He would not approach the job any other way.

So what he wanted now was to get it over with. He wanted to ride right up to the Cross Arrow headquarters, brace whoever was there, and demand both his guns back and whatever he figured he could get for his horse and saddle. He wanted them to know that Cam Stallings was not to be taken lightly. Trouble was, he would be risking a lot. If he failed, he could very well get run off or killed, and in either of those two events—especially the latter—his effectiveness would be rendered instantly nil. Certainly he did not want that.

So when he went he'd better be serious about it. He'd better be ready for anything and he'd better not back down. And for damned sure he had better not get killed!

Fortunately, this wasn't the only thing he had to think about during the week. On his second day at the ranch he moved into the bunkhouse with the two Navajos and the old Mexican, Miguel. He couldn't exactly say he was met with open arms—the two lookalike Indian boys were mostly quiet and maybe just a little suspicious of him, and Miguel hardly seemed to notice him at all—but at least he was tolerated. The Mexican did all of the cooking for the four of them, and Jaz and Jozie —Cam had about learned to tell them apart now—spent most of their time out riding somewhere. Stacy Brightwood explained that they were looking for Stretch B cows with unbranded calves, and Cam believed her. But somehow he suspected the two Indians were not straying very far from home in the process. They were too protective of their lady boss to leave her side for very long, or to get very far away while doing it. And undoubtedly the events up by the malpais of a few days before had made them nervous. Plainly they were not given to taking chances with Stacy's welfare.

Equally loyal was old Miguel. He had been with Stacy's father even back in Texas and, like the two Indians, seemed devoted to the girl. Early on Cam had noticed that none of them, including the girl, went unarmed anyplace he saw them go. He noticed, too, that he himself never went anywhere that at least the old Mexican was not somewhere watching—especially if he ventured near the main house. Apparently Cam was not yet to be fully trusted, but he supposed, given the circumstances the men had been experiencing, that their attitude was understandable. He did not feel insulted by it.

Toward the middle of the week he got Stacy—she insisted he call her that now rather than "Miss Brightwood"—to hand draft a couple of maps for him. One was a general layout of the surrounding countryside all the way to and beyond the town of Vera Velarde. It included the malpais to the north, the mesa country to the east, and the plains and mountains to the south and also west. The second map was more detailed. It included only the Stretch B range: watering places, roads and major trails, named canyons, and other landmarks Cam would need to know about in order to get from one place to another without getting lost, and generally which way and how far to the other ranches in the area, with specific reference being made to the Cross Arrow. Not surprisingly, the second map covered almost as much area as the first, differing mainly in detail.

The girl, saying she had never tackled anything like this before, labored over the two maps for almost half a day; but in the end it was clear that she knew the country well and, despite her lack of expertise as a mapmaker, the maps were good and just what Cam had wanted. Of course he watched her as she made them and quizzed her constantly about this and that—what was this distance, what did that mountain or canyon look like on the ground, was it easier to go one way or another to get to a place—and by the time she was finished felt like he knew the country fairly well already. Nevertheless, he pocketed both maps and spent a good deal of time the next few days studying each. He also vowed to carry them with him wherever he went until he knew the country as well as she did.

At the end of the week he approached her about the gun he'd asked for. There were a number available, inside the store. Mostly they were rifles and carbines, some used, some new. After some study, Cam selected a .44 Henry similar to, although older than, the Winchester "Yellow Boy" that had been taken from him. After carefully checking its condition, he took up a box of shells and went out behind the store to try it out. He shot up the entire box, and when he had finished he had determined what he needed to know: at two hundred yards the gun was reasonably reliable; at a hundred it was accurate; at fifty it was deadly. He could ask no more. Or could he . . . ?

"You are a good shot," Stacy told him when he returned to the store. "I watched you, you know."

"I used to shoot coyotes a lot. Coyotes and prairie dogs. With the right gun, I got to where I'd seldom miss."

"Coyotes and prairie dogs are not the same as people," she replied. "Especially when people are liable to shoot back."

"I know that," he said, placing the rifle back on the rack. "That's why the Henry won't do. I want something that will keep them from wanting to shoot back."

"*W-what?*" she asked, incredulous. "What are you talking about? That is a very good gun."

"Yes, it is," he said. "But it won't do. Over there in the corner. That's what I want. A shotgun."

She stared after him, then watched as he walked over to pick up the weapon he was referring to. It was a twelve-gauge Greener her father had taken in trade several years ago; he'd obtained it for a sack of flour. It was the only shotgun on the place.

"But that thing is no good," the girl protested. "It won't even shoot. One barrel is plugged and the trigger is broken on the other. There is no way you can do anything with it."

He broke it apart and studied it carefully. She was right. One trigger wouldn't move and the hammer was frozen in a cocked position; one barrel was plugged solid; there was rust on the outside of each barrel; he suspected the same was true of the inside. But the outer rust, at least, could be cleaned away. And from the business end of the bad barrel no one could tell it was plugged . . . He hefted the gun thoughtfully.

"This is the gun I want," he announced presently.

She stared at him, wide-eyed. "You're crazy! You are utterly crazy! Do you mean to tell me you would go to the Cross Arrow with nothing but *that* for your protection?"

"Yes, I reckon I do."

"There is no way of talking you out of it?"

"No."

She shook her head hopelessly. "When will you go?" She was well aware that he was getting around freely now.

"Tomorrow," he said.

At daybreak Cam threw his hornless saddle—brought in several days earlier by the two Navajos—across the back of a surefooted little sorrel that, according to its owner, had a good traveling gait and plenty of bottom for a long day's work. He rode out following the road south toward Vera Velarde, with which he stayed for about five miles before leaving it to slant to the southeast. Stacy had told him it was a good three hours to the Cross Arrow, and if nothing else he would get a plenty good look at the country along the way.

He saw no other riders and at first not many cattle. A few of the ones he did see carried a long upright B branded on their left ribs, but they were scattered and as he went, the predominant insignia increasingly became a shoulder-to-hip horizontal line with a cross made at one end and an arrowpoint at the other—the unmistakable Cross Arrow of the Terhunes'. Constantly he referred to his maps. There could be no question that he was still on Stretch B range, yet how few were the Stretch B cattle! Too, of the Stretch B cows with calves, less than one fourth of the offspring had been branded; yet most of the unbranded ones were easily old enough that they should have been gathered—and branded—during the spring roundup a month or more ago. It was more than enough to cause any man knowledgeable of range ways to wonder. More than enough.

The country, as he left the open plains behind, became one of piñon and juniper scrub, foothills and mesas. Canyon bottoms not unusually contained a few pine, and grama-grass turf seemed the order of the day everywhere. It was good country and Cam could see why folks would fight to control it. He didn't know if it was worthy of a sister-against-sister confrontation, but then, what was? He even found himself wondering what Mala Brightwood Terhune was like. Could she possibly be as vindictive, even treacherous, as Stacy's story had made her sound? Could she be as pretty as Stacy? Well, he decided, these questions probably had little to do with his current business on the Cross Arrow . . . He would probably do better concentrating on what those four gunnies who had waylaid him were like.

Unfortunately, he had heard much more than he had seen during his one contact with them so far. Stacy had got a clear look at them, however, and knew each by name. She had described them briefly for him.

First was the fellow with the gruff voice, a cold, deadly type who called himself Pit Emory, but whose real name was rumored to be something else entirely. Stacy didn't know what that name was, but she did know that the man was said to be from Texas, and that he had been on the Cross Arrow payroll for less than a year. It was also commonly accepted that he was a much better hand with a gun than with a horse or a rope, and that he was undoubtedly a dangerous man.

The Mexican Cam had heard up by the malpais but had not seen was a snaky little man named Lizard Guerrero. He had been with Terhune for quite some while now, was considered a good rider, but was known mostly for his terrible temper. The word was: *Don't cross him.*

The third and fourth men were Max Gruel, a big, ugly fellow who loved to fight with his hands, and Fern Carty, perhaps the most recent addition of the four to the payroll. Stacy didn't know a lot about Carty, except that he was one of those deceptively quiet sorts who some said might even be more dangerous than Emory, that he had been until recently a resident of Arizona, and was unquestionably a gunhand. Gruel, on the other hand, had apparently followed Emory over from Texas and was little more than a common thug.

Cam was still mulling over what he knew about the foursome when suddenly he came upon the ranch. He had been following a well-traveled road for several miles and had just rounded a curve along the point of a brushy hill when there it was. Based upon his maps, there could be little doubt that it was the Cross Arrow. Too, Stacy had described the place to him, and the description fit what he saw quite well. The main house was not big but was in the process of being built onto, and there were at least two bunkhouses, one on either side of the main quarters; there were also corrals, barns, chicken houses, woodsheds, all sturdily built and evidencing easily as much new lumber as old—a sure sign of growth and good times for the outfit. Which was interesting, Cam thought, since times really hadn't been all *that* prosperous of late.

He rode into the yard, causing little excitement. A couple of dogs barked and nipped at his horse's heels, while over at the corrals two men looked up briefly from their job of shoeing horses. But that was about it. From the porch of the main house, a fat Mexican woman scarcely paused over her broom to glance at Cam before returning to her sweeping. There was no one else to be seen.

Cam rode on up to the house, stopped at the porch, made no move to dismount. He called to the Mexican woman: "Is the boss at home, señora?"

She stared at him for a moment as if with limited comprehension, then turned silently and shuffled inside. While she was gone, Cam drew the shotgun stiffly from his rifle boot and placed the weapon across his lap. Moments later the door squeaked and a shapely figure with flowing black hair and a flawless face stepped into view.

When she spoke it was with a fine, full voice. "We're not hiring anymore, cowboy. I'm sorry but . . ." She stopped suddenly, as her eyes settled on the shotgun. "*What* are you doing with *that?*"

"I'm not looking for a job, ma'am," he said. "And the gun as well as this horse are borrowed, thanks to some of your men about a week ago."

Her eyes narrowed suspiciously, and for the first time Cam saw her resemblance to Stacy. But where the younger girl was fine-looking in every detail, this one was purely startling. In fact, he didn't know if he had ever seen such a beautiful woman before. For a moment he almost lost his train of thought, just from looking at her.

"You'll have to explain yourself, cowboy," she told him. "What have any of my men got to do with you borrowing horses and guns?"

"This is Terhune's Cross Arrow, is it not?" Cam responded. "And you do have four fellows by the names of Pit Emory, Lizard Guerrero, Max Gruel, and Fern Carty on your payroll, do you not?"

She eyed him sidelong. "This is the Cross Arrow and I am Mala Terhune. My husband is away just now. And you did not answer my question: What have those four men got to do with you?"

"They shot my horse and stole my guns," he said in level, purposeful tones. "They left me pinned beneath the horse, for dead—which I surely would be right now if someone hadn't come along to pull the horse off of me."

She looked at him in a way that said plainly that she did not believe him.

He went on. "They shot the horn off my saddle, too, ma'am. Ruined it, I figure. You can see for yourself, if you don't believe me." He reined the horse around slightly.

She appeared unimpressed. "Look, cowboy, I don't know what you want of me, but—"

"I figure someone owes me for my saddle and horse," he said stubbornly. "I'd like my guns back, too, if they're still around. And since it was your men who did it, I figure you oughta be able to help me."

She continued to eye him suspiciously. "How do I know you're telling the truth? Did you see these men? And how do you know their names? You're not from around here . . . at least I've never seen you before. What is *your* name?"

There was a hard, businesslike tone in her voice now, something he knew Stacy lacked. She seemed a complicated woman and it made him uncomfortable, but he did not retreat from her. "My name is Cam Stallings, ma'am. I'm from up north—Colorado, mostly. I was just passing through, looking for a job, when they waylaid me."

"But why would they do that? My men are not thieves who must go around stealing other people's guns."

"I figure they thought I was someone else," he said. "And I really don't care why they did it. I only want what's coming to me, what's mine."

"Where is this shooting supposed to have taken place?" she asked, still suspicious. "And who was it that pulled the horse off of you? Who loaned you that shotgun and another horse?"

"It happened up by the malpais, ma'am. And I don't think it matters who helped me. I don't think that matters at all."

She all but ignored this. "You didn't answer me when I asked how you knew they were my men. Did whoever saved you tell you that? Is that how you know?"

"Yes, ma'am. If it matters, that's how I know."

"And what if I still don't believe you? What will you do then?"

He had anticipated this, of course; he didn't have to think about the answer. "Why, I guess you and I'll just have to go on over to the bunkhouse where those fellows stay and look for my guns. I'm hoping they'll still have them. You would believe me then, wouldn't you?"

"Can you prove ownership?" she asked, a bit uncomfortably now. "You'd have to, you know. Just scraping up a couple of guns at the bunkhouse won't mean anything. There are always extra guns around."

"I can describe them beforehand easy enough. My rifle was a sixty-six Winchester 'Yellow Boy,' my handgun a Smith & Wesson forty-four, with holster, gun belt half full of forty-four shells, and my initials scratched on the back of the holster. Are you willing to look? Are any of those men on the place now?"

She jerked slightly at this, and her gaze switched ever so briefly toward the corrals, then swung back past the bunkhouse to her left before coming back to meet his. "I'm . . . not sure. I don't think so."

"Well, then, will you look with me?" He glanced off to his right. "Is that Emory's bunkhouse over there?"

She saw where he was looking. "Yes, that's the one. And yes, if you are determined, I'll go. But only to see you satisfied and off the place if you're wrong. You will go, of course?"

"I'm not wrong, lady. And I'll go when I've got what I came for. All I ask is what's due me."

Once again she glanced uneasily toward the corrals and Cam followed her gaze. One of the horseshoers had stopped what he was doing and was staring curiously their way now. Cam swept the place with his eyes. Still no one else had come in sight.

"Well?" he asked.

"I'm not in the habit of going into the men's quarters, cowboy. You'll have to let me call one of the horseshoers over to go inside with you."

He hesitated, then said, "Go ahead—call."

She waved toward the corrals, and presently the man who had been watching them came striding across the yard. He was not outwardly armed, and he eyed Cam and the shotgun cautiously. Cam was careful to keep his hand over the hammer that was frozen in a back position, knowing that only at the right time must anyone think the weapon cocked.

"This is Mike Cross," Mala Terhune said. "Mike, this is Cam Stallings. He says some of the boys shot his horse and took his guns from him. I've agreed to let him look through the bunkhouse for the guns. I want you to go inside with him."

Cross looked uncomfortably at Cam, then back at the woman. "Ain't nobody over there, ma'am. I sure do hate to be the one that has to go through someone else's things when he ain't there."

"You have my backing, Mike," she said simply, then looked at Cam. "Okay, cowboy. Get down and follow us. And for God's sake, don't point that shotgun at anybody!"

Cam dismounted and led his horse across the yard to the bunkhouse, following the woman and Mike Cross step for step. He carried the shotgun in the crook of his arm and very carefully made sure that Cross stayed in front of him as they mounted the bunkhouse steps. Mala Terhune remained at the foot of the porch.

"I'll have your man in there with me, Mrs. Terhune," Cam told her, "and this shotgun. Don't do anything foolish while we're inside."

She had been eying the shotgun somewhat strangely for several minutes now, but all she said was, "Don't worry, I won't. Just get on with it, cowboy."

Inside, he asked, "Which bunk is Pit Emory's?"

Mike Cross stared at him. "Emory's? Now look here, fella—you don't wanta go messin' with that one. Not Emory, you don't."

"He's one of the men who shot at me," Cam said steadfastly. "He's also the one who told them to take my guns as they were leaving me for dead, and it's his bunk I wanta look at."

The other man sighed and pointed over toward one corner. "On the end there. That one." He stood by quietly while Cam searched the bunk and looked through Emory's gear.

When Cam looked up, having found nothing, Cross said, "You're lucky, cowboy. Damn lucky."

Cam ignored him and turned his gaze to the other bunks. After a few seconds he spotted something a few bunks away. "Whose is that?" he asked, pointing. "The one over there."

Cross thought a moment, then said, "Gruel. I think it's Max Gruel's."

Cam nodded. "I think he's another of them. Come on, let's look."

This time Cam found what he was looking for—or at least part of it. Hanging from one bunkboard was his gun belt and six-shooter. Quickly he showed the back of the holster to Cross. "My initials, right there. Do you see?"

Mike Cross peered at the holster. "I see a C.S. scratched in the leather, if that's what you mean."

"Cam Stallings. That's me. My gun belt, holster, and gun. Only what have they done with my rifle . . . ?"

He was still looking around a few moments later when suddenly they heard voices outside—men's voices mixed with that of the woman. Cam looked at Cross, then said sharply, "Come on—outside. You lead."

As they stepped out the door, Mala Terhune was addressing two men sitting their horses on opposite sides of Cam's sorrel.

She said, "Gerd, Pit—meet Mr. Cam Stallings!"

CHAPTER 5

Gerd Terhune was a handsome, gray-templed man whose clear gaze was both steady and commanding. Pit Emory was hawk-faced, dark, and sullen.

Cam stood on the porch alone. Mala Terhune stood on the ground just to one side and Mike Cross had stopped beside her.

"I believe I've already met Mr. Emory," Cam told the woman, and with his left hand he held out the gun belt and six-gun he had just found inside. "You can ask Cross here—my initials are on the back of the holster. I couldn't find my rifle."

The woman bent a stern gaze on the gunman. "Is he telling the truth, Pit? Did you and the boys leave this man for dead up by the malpais?"

Pit Emory peered hard at Cam. When he spoke, all doubt was removed that his was the same gruff voice Cam had heard that day a week ago. "Could be him," he said frankly. "Cleaned up and with a good meal or two under his belt, yeah. We thought he was dead. That's why we left him."

"Did you shoot his horse out from under him?"

Emory shrugged, apparently unafraid to admit to just about anything. "We thought he was one of them Navvies. You remember, you told us—"

She cut him off sharply, with a warning look at her husband as well. "That's enough about that. I just want to know about this cowboy. Did you also take his guns?"

Again Emory shrugged, only this time impatiently. "Like I told you, we thought he was dead. Didn't figure he'd need the guns."

"Who has his rifle?"

"I dunno—Guerrero, I guess."

"And where is he?"

"Christ! I dunno . . . town, I think. Him and Max talked about goin' in early this mornin'. I haven't seen either of 'em since."

Mala Terhune turned to her husband. "The cowboy wants his guns back and to be paid for his horse—"

"And my saddle," Cam put in. "They ruined my saddle when they shot the horn off, remember?"

"And his saddle," the woman said with a sigh. "Anyway, I think we should give it to him, Gerd."

Cam was genuinely surprised. He didn't know what he had expected from her, but somehow it had not been this. Gerd Terhune, on the other hand, looked torn between a mild sort of amusement and a not too mild irritation. Pit Emory seemed not at all amused.

"Now just a minute," the gruff-voiced gunny said. "I don't see how this drifter oughta get anything atall. He's lucky to be alive. He ain't got no call to come ridin' in here demandin' things."

Cam sensed, then saw, the man's hand ever so slightly easing toward his six-gun. He knew the action might have been more instinctive than overt, but he wasn't about to assume that. Quickly he raised the double barrel of the shotgun and drew back its good trigger. The sound this made was both loud and unmistakable.

"Don't do it, Emory," Cam warned. "I'll blow you all the way to Mexico if you try."

Emory blanched. For a moment he looked as if he might go for his gun anyway, but Gerd Terhune put out a cautionary hand that seemed to dissuade him.

The rancher looked hard at Cam. "I wouldn't get rough, cowboy. My wife is willing to be generous; maybe Pit and I aren't. Between the two of us, we just might take you."

"There are two barrels on this thing, Terhune," Cam replied, trying to keep his voice steady. "All I want is what's mine. Don't be a fool and die trying to deny me that."

Mala Terhune said, "Gerd, he's right. And Pit admits to what they did to him. I say pay him and let him go."

Terhune twisted uneasily in his saddle, his eyes settling on Cam's horse. "Where'd you get the animal?" he asked.

"I borrowed it," Cam said.

"And the shotgun?"

"I borrowed that, too."

Terhune looked back at his wife, who shook her head silently but meaningfully.

Terhune sighed and reached inside his shirt pocket. He fished out a couple of coins and handed them down to his wife. "Forty dollars," he said. "For damages done to one horse and one saddle. Give it to him."

She came to the porch with it, but Cam shook his head. "My horse and saddle weren't much to brag about, Terhune . . . but I figure sixty at least."

Terhune glared at him. "Now, look, cowboy—"

"Gerd," his wife said. "It's not worth it. Just pay him."

For a moment the rancher looked as if he might take heated exception to his wife's advice, but then it was as if a subtle something in her tone convinced him otherwise. Grudgingly, he drew out another gold piece and flipped it to the woman.

She handed the money up to Cam, who fingered the coins for a moment then pocketed them. "There," she told him. "I can do nothing about your rifle just now, since it is apparently in town with Guerrero. But you've got what else is coming to you, and I advise you to ride on out while the riding's good. You have my word you'll not be harmed if you do."

Cam looked questioningly at the two men flanking his horse.

"Don't worry," she told him. "Pit, Gerd . . . move back and let him go."

The two men exchanged glances. Terhune nodded, then backed his horse away a few steps. Pit Emory followed suit, growling as he did, "You've pushed your luck here, cowboy. My advice to you is don't try it again. The next time we leave you for dead, there won't be any question whether you are or not."

Cam ignored him as he led his horse away a safe distance, slung his gun belt across his saddle, and mounted. At no time did he take his eyes off the two men, and once settled he held the shotgun with its butt resting on his right thigh in a ready position. To the woman he tipped his hat with his left hand.

"My thanks to you, ma'am." To the two men he only said, "Good day to you, gents. See you around, probably."

"You better hope not," Pit Emory growled.

Cam rode away without looking back, but was around the bend and out of sight before the tension and the barely resistable urge to kick his horse into a gallop relaxed. At no time in his life had he ever felt such a baleful stare as the one Pit Emory had leveled on him as he rode away, and he promised himself that never again would be put his back to such a man as that. Never.

Behind, in the ranch yard, Gerd Terhune turned to his wife and said, "Why did you let him get away with that, Mala? Why?"

"He's got sand, Gerd," she told him simply. "To ride in here the way he did—that took sand. We could use a man like that. We really could."

Terhune stared at her in disbelief. "Am I crazy, or didn't you see? That man was riding a Stretch B horse, for chrissake!"

"I saw," she said.

"And you realize he may very well have hired on with your sister already . . . you *realize* that?"

She nodded. "I'm almost certain of it. And I am equally certain that as much as anything else that's the reason he came here—to show us that someone on the other side has sand. And that is why the next time you or I see him we are going to offer him a job . . . Better he rides for the Cross Arrow than for the other side, don't you agree?"

Pit Emory harrumphed loudly. "You let me put a bullet in him, you won't have to worry about him ridin' for the other side."

She answered this with a hard glance. "You put a bullet in him, Pit, and *you* won't have to worry about riding for *this* side anymore."

He stared back, only slightly daunted. "Yeah . . . okay. But I'll only be pushed by him once. Job or no job, I won't let that happen again."

She knew he meant what he said, and because of this was smart enough to take a more moderate tack the second time. "Well, try it my way first, okay? Both of you. My way first."

Terhune sighed. "All right. But don't be too impressed with that guy, Mala. He might not have shown so much sand if it hadn't been for that shotgun—"

At this, Mala Brightwood Terhune laughed outright. "Oh, but that's just the reason he did show it, Gerd. I recognized that old gun even before you showed up, and I'm sure he got it from Stacy. My father took it in trade one time . . . and do you know what he gave for it? A sack of flour. That's right, *flour!* And do you know why only that?"

Again she laughed, this time at the quizzical looks she got from the three men. It was beginning to dawn on them, but still they did not quite understand. "Fellows," she said, "that gun was long ago ruined beyond repair. That cowboy came in here alone and braced the four of us—and he did it with a gun that no way in the world can be made to shoot!"

Cam Stallings, already out of view from the ranch, had no idea that the woman had recognized the shotgun; the possibility never once occurred to him. Had he heard her championing of him, he would have been flattered. What he had done had worked, and he was sort of proud of that already. But he was not about to be fooled by it. He had gone to war with an empty gun and got away with it. He knew perfectly well that he could be pushing his luck with what he had in mind to do next. Still, he was determined to proceed on with what was now step two of his plan.

He rode steadily until reasonably assured that he was not being followed, then he reined to a halt and fished out his maps. He was wondering if there was a shorter way to town than going all the back to the main north-south road leading to and from the Stretch B. After a moment he decided that there was; his map indicated, a short distance down the road he was on now, a good trail branching to the southwest, one that eventually should intercept the main road about five miles from Vera Velarde. It was that way he would go.

It wasn't all for the sake of a shortcut, either. He wanted to see as much country as he could, and he wanted to see as many cattle as possible while he was about it. So far he was still seeing three Cross Arrow cows to every one that carried the Stretch B or any other brand. And, as before, rarely was he seeing a branded calf with a Stretch B cow. As he rode on, he finally stopped seeing Stretch B cows altogether, and he decided that he must have passed beyond even the extremities of Stretch B range.

Stopping only around noon to rest his horse and eat a portion of the jerked beef, day-old biscuits, and canned fruit he had brought with him from the Stretch B, he had struck the main road to Vera Velarde by two o'clock and by three had come upon a low hill that overlooked the town.

It wasn't a big place, but it did seem to be prospering. Nestled within the mountain footslopes he had been seeing in the distance all week, the town consisted of two principal streets, one lined for about two blocks with stores and various businesses, the other lined mostly with houses and shacks. There appeared to be at least one livery stable, on the near edge of town, and about a quarter of a mile beyond the opposite edge was a sawmill. Smoke rose lazily above the mill, so it appeared active, and not surprisingly most of the buildings in town were built of wood plank rather than adobe.

Cam rode on into town and stopped to talk to the first person he'd seen since leaving the Cross Arrow that morning. Said person turned out to be the town's lone hostler and blacksmith and was full owner of the livery stable Cam had spotted from the hill above town.

The man seemed a friendly enough sort—which was a good thing, for he was as big and muscular as any blacksmith Cam had ever seen. His name was Blake Stoddard.

"Any place around here a man can buy a decent saddle?" Cam asked, after a few pleasantries had been passed.

Stoddard eyed Cam's ruined pommel and said, "Looks like you could use one, all right. Sam Edwards down the street makes 'em himself. He might have a new one or two. If you're more in the market for something used, I can make you a good price on any one of three or four here."

Cam thought about it, unsure whether he would rather break in a new one or take his chances on a good fit with a used one. Finally he said, "Will you take what's left of this old hull in trade?"

Stoddard walked around Cam's horse, ostensibly studying the saddle. "Where'd you get the shotgun?" he asked offhandedly.

"It's a long story," Cam said, not wanting to go into it. "How about the saddle?"

"I might give you a couple dollars on it," the blacksmith finally said. "Come on inside, see if you see anything you like."

Half an hour later, and after a bit of haggling, Cam had parted with his old saddle and fifteen dollars and was just finishing the cinch tightening and stirrup adjusting on his new one—"new" only in the sense that it was different, for if anything it was even older than his "old" one. But the tree was solid and the rest in good shape, so he figured he hadn't done badly—especially since he still had forty-five dollars of what Gerd Terhune had been more or less coerced into giving him. Of course some of that was for a new horse, but for now, since he had a job riding for an outfit, he figured he'd do like most and stick with company horses. If and when he got ready to leave, he'd look into buying one of his own.

"Anything else?" the smith asked.

"Well, just one thing," Cam said. "You wouldn't have happened to see a couple of Cross Arrow riders in town today, would you?"

The man peered at him. "I might. Why?"

"A Mexican called Guerrero, he's the main one. Did you see him?"

"Yeah . . . I reckon I did," the big man said slowly. "But why? What d'you want with him?"

"He has something of mine," Cam said simply. "Where would I look for him?"

"Well, if he's still in town, probably McKenzie's Saloon. Other than that, I don't know. He was ridin' a bald-faced bay horse, if that's any help to you."

"Thanks," Cam told him, starting to mount. "It might be."

"Something I gotta ask, though," Stoddard said.

"Yeah, what?"

"Well, I couldn't hardly help noticin' the brand on your horse. I ain't seen you around before, so I reckon you'll understand . . . It's just that Stretch B riders have been pretty scarce around Vera Velarde recently . . ."

Cam eyed him. "I didn't steal the horse, if that's what you mean."

"No," the blacksmith said. "No, I didn't mean it that way. I wouldn't accuse a man like that. It's just that . . . well, the Stretch B and the Cross Arrow ain't exactly . . ."

Cam waved him off gratefully. "I know. I know real well. But thanks, Stoddard. You've been a real help to me. I'll be seeing you again, I'm sure."

He rode on down the street until he found McKenzie's Saloon and, tied to a hitch rail out front, a bald-faced bay horse with Cam's Winchester "Yellow Boy" snugged away in its saddle boot. For a few moments he just sat there, wondering if what he had in mind to do next might really work. When he finally decided that at least it was worth a try, he dismounted and tied the sorrel to the rail next to the bay. Then he reached over, withdrew the Winchester from the boot, and with the shotgun carried loosely in the other hand stepped onto the walk in front of the saloon.

CHAPTER 6

Lizard Guerrero looked up from the table where he, Max Gruel, and two others sat drinking. Long ago his eyes had adjusted to the dim light of the saloon, but the back-lighting of the doorway leading outside made it impossible for him to identify the cowboy who had just entered. All he could tell was that the man was slender and of about medium height, and that he carried what looked like a rifle in one hand and a shotgun in the other. This alone was enough to rivet his attention on the doorway, to cause him instinctively to suspicion this man and whatever it was he had in mind.

The cowboy's eyes roved around the room, adjusting, searching, and settled presently on Lizard's table. This was not surprising since the Mexican and his friends were the only customers in the place and naturally might expect to draw his attention first. Nonetheless, Lizard stared resentfully back. Who was this man? Why was he armed like that? And why was he staring like that? Did he want something or didn't he?

Lizard was self-conscious about being stared at, always had been, because of his looks. He gave the appearance of being a smaller man than he really was, due mostly to a congenital deformity of the spine that had so twisted him he had never been able to stand or walk fully upright. He thus resembled a slumped and wizened old man even though his fortieth birthday was still more than six months away.

But his was one of those cases in which looks are deceiving. Seldom was there a man who could move more swiftly than Lizard (some said he could produce and fire a previously holstered six-gun faster than any man around); and his upper body strength was just short of spectacular for a man of his build. He couldn't help it that he was ugly and that the way he walked was with a peculiar sort of unattractive grace, a sort of slither, which was of course why they called him Lizard. He couldn't help it and he accepted it—just so long as people didn't stare at him. He'd once wound up killing a man who had stared; most people who knew him were aware of that.

Not that Lizard's skill with a gun and his strength were his only claims to fame. He might not be the best man in the country with cows, but he had few equals with horses. That was one reason he had been kept on all this time at the Cross Arrow: he was all but irreplaceable at the breaking corral and everybody knew it. He was among the very, very best.

If they wanted to stare, let them do it admiringly or not at all. That's the way he looked at it. So who in hell was this cowboy? And what was it about that rifle that looked so familiar . . . ?

Leron Hardwick, the man behind the bar in McKenzie's place, was also wondering who the cowboy was. He had a better view of the newcomer than did Guerrero and his pals, and he knew he had never seen the fellow around before. Like Guerrero, however, he had noticed the two firearms and was instinctively alert for almost anything.

The cowboy stood in the doorway for nearly a minute, then moved toward the bar. He was wearing a six-gun holstered at his right side and, Hardwick was quick to notice, favored his left leg when he walked.

When he finally spoke, the cowboy's voice broke the silence in the saloon like a whip being cracked. "I'm looking for a Mr. Lizard Guerrero of the Cross Arrow Ranch," he said. "His horse is outside, and I just took this rifle from his saddle boot. I wanta thank him for finding it for me."

It was a startling statement and was so completely unexpected in content that the bartender had no idea what to make of it, except that this cowboy had walked up to Lizard Guerrero's horse and lifted a rifle from its saddle boot and was here now to tell Lizard about it to his face. That, and the obvious fact that there was yet a whole lot more to it, made it a startling statement indeed.

Instinctively, Hardwick looked over at Guerrero. The Mexican just sat there with his eyes glued to the cowboy. He didn't say anything, so neither did Hardwick.

The cowboy went on. "You see, I became separated from both my rifle and my handgun up by the malpais about a week ago. I heard some Cross Arrow punchers had found them, so I visited the ranch this morning and had the handgun returned to me by Gerd Terhune himself—him and his wife. They were real nice about it, in fact"—just a little lie—"and they told me Mr. Guerrero was carrying my rifle with him, for safekeeping, I suppose"—a somewhat bigger lie—"until he found me to return it to me. Now you don't have any idea how much I appreciate that, and I sure do wanta thank him for it."

The cowboy had laid the Winchester on the bar now, but had done a particularly subtle job of keeping the shotgun in a handy position without being overtly threatening with it. Likewise, although he addressed the bartender, he never once took his eyes off the table where Guerrero sat. The Mexican, it was plain, had noticed this just as Hardwick had. Problem was, he seemed so completely taken aback by the whole thing that he didn't know how to respond to it.

"One of you fellows Guerrero?" the cowboy asked. Since three of the men at the table were Mexicans—Max Gruel being the only exception —it wasn't a stupid question.

"I am Guerrero," Lizard finally answered. He did not, however, make any move to get up. Obviously he still didn't know what to make of the situation and was yet unready to commit himself to anything more than the giving of his name.

The cowboy said, "Well, I sure do wanta thank you for taking care of my rifle for me. I really favor that gun, and I don't know what I'd've done if you hadn't found it and kept it for me. I sure don't."

Guerrero just went on staring at him. Leron Hardwick suspected that the little Mexican was being had somehow, and if so, Guerrero should know it. But those two barrels on that shotgun had to look mighty big from less than fifteen feet away, and the bartender suspected that each of the four men at the table was keenly aware that one hammer was at full cock already. One blast could put all four of their candles out and they knew it.

The cowboy picked up the rifle again. "Well, now that I've thanked you, I guess I'll be going." And for the first time he did something that demonstrated all was not what he had made it seem to be: he *backed* toward the door. What would later prove to be the most startling part of all was that Lizard Guerrero sat there and *let* him do it.

At the door the cowboy paused. "You know, this old shotgun is really one more gun than I've got room to carry now, and since I've got my rifle back I guess I don't need it anymore. I could buy you a drink or something, but how about I give you this old gun instead, Guerrero? You know, as a sort of token of my gratitude." With no more warning than this, he tossed the weapon in the direction of the table. Two men ducked, another dove, and only Guerrero was quick enough to come to his feet in time to catch the shotgun while it was still in the air. By the time any of them looked toward the door again, the cowboy was gone.

For a moment the Mexican just stood there. Then Max Gruel blurted, "For chrissakes, Lizard—you gonna let him get away with that?" Quite plainly both men had long since figured out who the cowboy was.

"Shut up," Guerrero growled.

"But goddammit—he took the rifle!" Gruel persisted. "He took that damn rifle right out from under your nose!"

"*I said shut up!*" Lizard snapped, louder this time. "Besides, you got no place to talk. He took that handgun right off your bunk at the ranch."

Gruel's expression clouded as this bit of deduction struck him as most likely true, then he frowned angrily. Almost as one the two men headed for the door. Out of curiosity the bartender followed, but by the time any of them got there, hoofbeats had long since sounded and died away outside. The street was empty. The cowboy was nowhere to be seen.

"Who was that fellow, Lizard?" one of the other Mexicans asked.

At first, Guerrero did not answer. He had broken the shotgun apart and was examining it curiously. He looked down both barrels, slammed it shut again, and tried to pull the trigger that should have worked the one cocked hammer. Nothing happened. He looked up, then after a moment swore loudly and slammed the weapon hard against the sawdust-covered floor.

"A dead man," he muttered with a little hiss. "That's who that fellow is. *A dead man for sure!*"

This time, Cam was not too proud to leave the scene of adventure at a gallop. Looking back on it, he figured it might have been the only smart thing he'd done all day. He had left Lizard Guerrero perhaps too stunned and confused to react immediately, but he did not doubt that full realization would soon come to the wizened little Mexican, and when it did, the man's anger would not be mild.

At first he had meant only to retrieve his rifle and further establish to everyone's satisfaction that he was unafraid of the Cross Arrow. The way he had gone about it had at the time seemed a cute way to avoid a real confrontation. But that last act of leaving the ruined shotgun behind just might have been a bit too cute. He had made a fool of Guerrero, just as he had made a fool of Pit Emory that morning. That, as a result, he had made enemies of both now went without saying. In retrospect, it was not good business . . . not good business at all.

But there was no use agonizing over it now. What was done was done; he couldn't change any of it even if he wanted to, and at least he would know where he stood with the two men from here on out. Which was just as well. In a war, he figured, a man should know who his enemies are, and if what he'd signed on for between the Stretch B and the Cross Arrow wasn't a war, Cam didn't know what was.

About three miles north of town he decided to leave the road and head west. He knew he could not make the Stretch B by nightfall, and he had no desire to camp overnight along the main road. And for good reason. While no one yet seemed to be following him, he knew he might just as well get in the habit of not taking chances. Besides, he had been studying his maps again; if an extra day was going to be necessary, he might as well do a little exploring while he was at it. He could ride west a few miles to make camp, then tomorrow strike north across the plains. On his way he might also visit a couple of those Stretch B waterholes Stacy had told him about—the stretch along Loco Creek and Bell Cow Cienaga in particular striking his fancy. If he was to find significant numbers of Stretch B cattle anywhere, a major watering place ought to be the place.

He made camp beneath a towering square-topped mountain with a spring at its base, and for supper boiled a pot of coffee over a small fire and ate about half of what was left of his jerky and biscuits. A little while later he unrolled his bedroll, kicked dirt over the fire, and went to bed.

Next morning, he awoke with a shiver. Quickly building a new fire, he began to reheat what was left of last night's coffee. By sunup, he had finished off not only the coffee but his jerky and all but two biscuits, and was ready for the day ahead.

He saddled the sorrel and, after several moments spent studying his maps, decided to set out in a northerly direction. Although it was unclear to him from the maps just whose range he was now on, it seemed unlikely that Stretch B cows would wander much farther south than this unless allowed to drift ungathered for an extremely long period of time. On the other hand, it seemed too far west for Cross Arrow range, and the nearest ranch on the maps was about five miles south and west of where he had camped. According to Stacy, that would be the Circle R outfit of a man named Mitch Ressler. West of Ressler about six or seven miles was Lester McNaab's Dot M. North and west of McNaab lay Reece Crawford's Railroad Slash, and Crawford's was perhaps the largest outfit of the three.

Riding along at a comfortable pace, Cam saw mostly Circle R cows for the first mile or so; then, as he began to leave the mountains for the plains again, a fair mixture of Circle R, Dot M, and even Railroad Slash stock took over. He was well out onto the plains, however, before he saw his first Stretch B cow, and it came as no surprise that she had at her side a calf with no brand at all.

But of course that was only one cow; he still hoped to find more nearer to water. Once more turning to his maps, he decided that he was not far now from Loco Creek. Off to his left, perhaps two miles away, he could see a long narrow depression and a few trees that he'd just bet was the area he was looking for. He reined the sorrel in that direction.

He had ridden maybe half a mile when suddenly he noticed what looked to be a small herd of tightly bunched cattle coming up out of the creek. They were headed generally southeast on an angle more away from than toward him. But something about the way they were bunched and moving cause him to pause to watch them further. Sure enough, behind them now, appeared one, two, then three moving figures that he was sure were horses with riders. He could tell this mostly by the way they were moving, for the distance was too far to be certain otherwise. He watched them for a moment more, then got to wondering if they would notice him. His position was completely in the open, and there wasn't a tree or anything else to shield him for a quarter of a mile in any direction. He decided to dismount and see what happened.

Apparently they either never saw him or assumed he was nothing more than a harmless dot on the landscape, for he watched for almost fifteen minutes as they drew away and never once showed any sign of having detected his presence. Pretty soon they went out of sight among a low grouping of hills in the distance. After about ten more minutes of waiting to see if they would reappear, Cam finally decided they weren't going to and remounted his horse.

Although he suspected that by now it should not have, what he found when he reached the creek surprised him. The water alternated between a fair-sized trickle and mere damp sand but did have pools here and there that were large enough to serve several cows at a time. And there were plenty of cows. The creek drained from south to north and seemed to play out in the distance, probably going underground somewhere out on the plains never to surface again. All along its length that he could see, however, cattle were gathered, despite the fact that many, having had their fill of water now, were moving off to graze for the day. It was here that Cam had counted on finding his first representative delegation of Stretch B cows. And it was here that he drew only puzzlement.

Save one old longhorn bull, maybe half a dozen cows and one or two calves, he found no Stretch B stock to speak of. Plenty of Circle R stuff, Dot M, Railroad Slash, even a few carrying the Cross Arrow, but easily as poor a showing for the Stretch B as anywhere he'd been so far.

He rode up and down the creek for over an hour. He found another Stretch B bull, a couple of two-year-old steers, and one yearling heifer to add to his previous count. But that was all. The Stretch B, supposedly the biggest ranch around, might just as well have been the least of the four represented.

He got to wondering about the three riders he had seen driving the small herd of cattle away earlier. How many cows could there have been in the herd? Thirty, forty at the most. And whose riders were those? Whose cattle?

For a few moments he considered following their trail, but then he discarded the idea. They were long gone by now and no telling what would happen if he did stumble onto them. After all, they were three and he was only one, and anyway, their business was probably legitimate. Loco Creek was surrounded by open range; those cattle could just as well have been Circle R or Dot M or Railroad Slash stock as Stretch B . . . couldn't they?

Well, he was curious, even suspicious, but he would just have to let it go at that for now. If he was going to make it back to the Stretch B by nightfall and still see anything on the way, he'd have to get on about his business.

He consulted his maps briefly, then reined his horse in what he thought was the direction of Bell Cow Cienaga.

CHAPTER 7

As a little girl, Stacy Brightwood had never ceased to be fascinated by the beauty and serenity of the western sunset. It was something she had always known and something, as she grew older, that she might have been expected to take strictly for granted. Many days, she did. But times remained when she was just as fascinated, just as drawn to sit out on the porch and watch that early evening sky first glow brightly then fade into twilight, as she had ever been as a child.

Lately, it had come to mean even more to her. The stresses and strains of the past two years were at times almost more than she could endure, and somehow on her very worst days, stopping late in the day to simply sit and contemplate the sunset was the only thing that would relax her.

Not that she was normally a moody sort; certainly she was not. But there was just so much a person could stand, and lately a feeling of utter hopelessness had become difficult to dispel.

This particular day had been especially hard. She didn't know why, except that maybe when what has looked like an unexpected bright spot on the horizon suddenly dims, things just naturally look even worse than before. That's how she guessed it was with the way Cam Stallings had ridden into and then right back out of her life. For that one brief week, she thought she detected in him something that could really help her. Oh, she knew he was just one man, but God, how she needed someone to lean on for a change. Sure, she had Jaz and Jozie and old Miguel; she loved each of them deeply for their faithfulness. And they were of help to her, for without them she could not have hung on even this long. But when it really came down to it, they were just as dependent on her as she was on them. The boys were too young (not that they were any younger than she, for they were not) and the old man too old for it to be any other way. But Cam Stallings was different. Or at least she had thought he was. In him she might have had someone on whom *she* could depend without being depended upon, someone who could actually help and maybe more . . .

Well, she was young enough herself yet to have been caught dreaming. That's all it had been, a romantic dream. She had let him ride off on that fool's errand to the Cross Arrow, and she had actually believed that he would be back that same day. But he had not come. She had waited well into the night and then had been up early next morning, down at the bunkhouse checking to see if he had come in after she had finally given up and gone to bed. He had not been there.

All day today she had thought: maybe . . . maybe he'll still come. To no avail. The day had passed slowly and here it was, sundown, with still no sign of him.

Of course several things might have happened to him. At best, he had perhaps got himself run off from the Cross Arrow the minute he started making demands. At worst, he might have got himself shot. In between somewhere was the possibility that he had simply taken the horse Stacy had loaned him and hit the trail for healthier climes. Somehow she doubted this, but who could say? Did she know him well enough to place any real confidence in him? Had she simply been gullible?

Well, in a way she almost hoped she had. At least he wouldn't be dead or whatever else might have happened to him to keep him from coming back. Certainly she didn't have so many good horses that she wouldn't miss the sorrel; but she could stand that. To have something really bad happen to the young cowhand, to have that on her conscience, would not be a burden so easily borne.

Just the thought of this had off and on during the day tempted her to saddle up and ride straight over to the Cross Arrow and find out for herself what had happened. Fortunately, reason had thus far won out over this idea. She wasn't really afraid to go to the Cross Arrow; at times she felt like doing just what Cam Stallings had set out to do—brace the lot of them right there in their own ranch yard, demand a showdown once and for all. But she knew that's just what they would want her to do; she had no chance of winning in such an encounter, and if she herself forced the play and came out dead for her trouble, then she would simply have played into their hands and Mala would have everything.

Not that Mala wouldn't eventually have it all anyway. Stacy knew that the deck was already so stacked against her that she could never win. She had known it all along, perhaps—certainly after Dan Stanhope had left. Cam Stallings had represented nothing more than a brief but futile flurry of raised hopes; now even those were dashed, and she did not know if she would ever be able to raise them again.

Maybe she should just sell out to Terhune; maybe that way she would at least wind up with something. But even that might not be an option anymore. Mala probably wouldn't stand for it, and why should she? It was her contention that the Stretch B should have been hers all along, and now that Stacy was all but brought to her knees, why pay for something a little patience and skulduggery might get you for free anyway? Why indeed!

Stacy sighed disconsolately. The sun was half behind the horizon now, and the sky there varied from brilliant orange to pink, then purple. Long shadows stretched across the ranch yard. The milch cow bawled for her evening milking down at the barn. A dog barked. Old Miguel was just leaving the bunkhouse with his bucket. A bull bugled from somewhere off in the distance, causing Stacy to wonder idly if it was one of hers. And then a form materialized beside her, standing at the foot of the porch. Her reverie had been such that she had neither seen nor heard him approach.

It was one of the Navajos, wanting to tell her something but as always waiting until spoken to before addressing her directly.

"What is it, Jozie?" she asked in a voice so tired it surprised her to hear it.

The Indian pointed toward the open plain, west and just south of where she had been looking yet still somewhat into the setting sun. Stacy squinted hard; she could just make out a lone horseman coming toward the ranch. She looked questioningly at the young Navajo.

"The cowboy with no horn on his saddle," the Indian said simply. It was the way the two Navajos had referred to him ever since that first night near the malpais.

"Are you sure?" she asked, marveling at how he could tell who the rider was at such a distance, and completely unsure if to really hope.

He nodded. "I'm sure."

Stacy joined the men for supper at the bunkhouse cookshack that night. She didn't do this often, but she did not hesitate to do it whenever the urge not to be alone in the main house struck her, and at no time had it ever seemed to her an unseemly thing to do. They were a family here on the Stretch B, what there was left of them. Stacy saw no impropriety in the boss lady eating side by side with her hired hands, any more than she did working alongside them or living alone on her ranch with them. To think otherwise would not have been like her at all.

"I never thought about you going into town," Stacy told Cam from across the table after having listened intently to his story. "And I still can't believe what you did to Lizard Guerrero."

Cam smiled weakly. "I've had my own second thoughts about that, believe me."

"I should think so," Stacy said. "That Guerrero is a touchy man. He won't forget."

"Yeah," Cam had to agree. "And neither will Pit Emory or Gerd Terhune. But I'm not sorry for what I did. There's something bad going on between the Cross Arrow and this outfit, and if I'm going to work for you there's no use expecting to be friends with them. So far, I haven't run into any of them I'd trust anyway—except maybe . . ."

Stacy's eyes narrowed. "Except who?"

"Well, your sister, I reckon. I mean, she seemed decent enough about things. I probably wouldn't have pulled it off at the Cross Arrow at all if it hadn't been for her."

Stacy felt herself instinctively grow cool at this. Mala was a beautiful young woman and Stacy supposed it was natural for men to resist thinking bad of the older girl. Of course maybe Stacy herself was too biased, maybe Cam Stallings' reaction to Mala was by far the more objective of the two. Still, she was disappointed. She had hoped Cam would be one of those who saw through her half sister from the beginning.

Cam seemed to sense her feeling and sort of shrugged. "You know her better than I do, Stacy. I'll reserve judgment on that basis, okay?"

She shrugged, passing it off. "Tell me what you learned on your ride back. You say you rode past Loco Creek and Bell Cow Cienaga?"

"Yes. Yes, I did. But let me ask you a question. How many cows were there on the Stretch B when your father died? Do you know?"

Stacy frowned. "Well, I don't know how reliable such estimates are, but my father always said about three thousand total, cows, bulls, yearlings, and older. He tried to keep it at about that, although he always maintained that had Stretch B cows alone populated what we thought of as Stretch B range, four thousand would not be too many. He said the country could handle that many even in the not-so-good years and was conservative about bringing in more because he was afraid of what overgrazing might someday do."

Cam nodded approvingly. "I think I would have admired your father. From what I've seen of the country, I wouldn't have been surprised if you'd said five thousand."

"But you had another reason for asking, I'm sure," she said perceptively.

He smiled. "Yeah, I reckon so. I wanted to know how many there should be, for I sure didn't see anything like three thousand yesterday or today. My guess would be more like three hundred . . ."

Stacy's eyes widened. "Oh, come now . . . no more than that? Surely you are mistaken!"

He shook his head sadly. "I wish I was. Of course I didn't ride the entire range—probably no more than a fourth of it at best, and some of that was along the fringe. But I rode what you say are your two best waterings, and believe me, hens have a lotta teeth compared to how many of your cows were at either place. One hell of a big loss since fall, wouldn't you say?"

"I knew it was bad," Stacy admitted, "but I had no idea it was that bad. And there is no way we lost that many to the storms over winter. It was nothing like we heard it was up North. What on earth could have happened to them?"

Cam wagged his head. "Nothing natural, I'm sure." He looked over at the two young Navajos, sitting on either side of Stacy. "Don't either of you fellows have any ideas? Haven't you seen anything going on that might explain it?"

Jaz and Jozie looked simultaneously at Stacy, then past her to each other. It was Jaz who finally spoke. "Dunno for sure. White men drive 'em off, I think. Little bit at a time, drive 'em off. We can't catch 'em, dunno where they go with the cows. We find tracks, differ'nt times, differ'nt places . . . try to brand calves we find. Can't do much else."

It was a long speech for either of them to make, but was of surprisingly little help. Cam looked in exasperation at Stacy. She said, "Don't blame them, Cam. They do all they can, but I know they are afraid to stray very far from the ranch with Miguel and me here alone. I've gone with them a time or two, even helped them brand what calves we found. And they've told me before that there are not enough cattle out there. We just had no idea how many were missing—or what happened to them. I mean, you can't just drive off two or three thousand head of cattle without making some dust, can you?"

Cam shook his head. "Not hardly. And I don't think anybody did drive off that many—at least not at one time, they didn't. I think we've got something a little slicker than common cattle rustling going on here. As a matter of fact, I think your cattle are still in the country— somewhere; they're just not where they belong, is all."

Stacy frowned and just stared at him in her puzzlement.

"Look," he went on. "It's easy enough to explain what's happened to leave a lot of this year's Stretch B calves unbranded. You yourself recognized that. You didn't have enough hands at the roundup to properly represent you, and maybe the Cross Arrow riders just didn't bother to gather Stretch B cows. Most everything that got branded had to be something you yourselves, or some of your other neighbors, brought in. Could be those other neighbors didn't help much either. Who knows, maybe they were threatened like your own cowboys who quit. But it's a cinch only a token of your calves have ever seen a branding fire, or ever properly will, if we don't bring them to it ourselves. The problem is, where have the vast majority of your cattle gone? That's what we don't know."

"Well, yes . . . but I think we already knew what the problem was; we just didn't know the extent of it."

"Of course you didn't," Cam acknowledged. "And maybe we still don't. But I can tell you it's bad, and I had a chance to do a lotta thinking about it while I was riding around yesterday and today."

"And you came up with something?"

He smiled. "I can't swear to that, but I do have ideas. First, your sister and her husband probably figure to put you out of business the quickest way possible, and leaving you with no cows would do that pretty quick, I'd say. Probably, too, any cattle they can get their own brand on in the process would be just as well and good for them. Now, it wouldn't seem likely they'd try to make off permanently with your grown, already branded stock—that Stretch B brand of yours should be fairly hard to change to much of anything else, and certainly into a Cross Arrow. And as we've said, driving off large numbers at a time would be just a little too out in the open for them to get away with. So I think your cattle are still around, maybe scattered to high heaven, maybe being held in various places outside your range—unlikely as that may seem when you first think about it. And although I don't know how they're going about all this, I do think we've got to find out pronto where the cattle are and start getting them back if we ever want to at all. And we've got to get brands on your calves and maverick stock. I think if we don't, that's exactly what someone else is going to do, and then you really will have lost."

Stacy took all of this in with rising incredulity. "Do you mean to tell me my sister and her husband will brand *my* calves with *their* Cross Arrow if I don't get it done first? Calves sucking Stretch B cows? My God, Cam, you're a cowhand; surely you don't think they can get away with *that* in range country!"

He shook his head. "Think about it. Once those calves are weaned and are no longer following their mamas, who's to know the difference? And if they never show up at the fall roundup this year, if the cows or the calves either one are never gathered for outsiders to see, how will anyone ever know to point out the crime? Think about it."

Stacy did, but still she could not conceive of anyone trying such a thing. "Cam, we're talking three thousand head of grown and half-grown cattle, at least two thousand of which are mother cows and at least half or better of those with this year's calves. How on earth can they keep so many from showing up at the roundup?"

"I don't know. But somehow they've already caused an awful lot of them to disappear, and we've got to find out where that is and get them back."

Still Stacy was not convinced. "I just don't see how they could be doing something like that. How are they moving my cattle? Why haven't we seen them doing it?"

"I don't know," he said. "I just don't know."

Stacy leaned thoughtfully back from the table. They were long since finished with their meal, and Miguel had already begun clearing away the dishes. The two Navajos squirmed uneasily in their seats as if ready to leave. All three spoke fair English and had undoubtedly understood everything Cam had said, but it was unlikely any of them could be made to comment on it now. Stacy herself needed time to mull it over.

She pushed back her chair. "Well, that gives me a lot to think about." She rose from the table. "But it's about all I can absorb at one sitting. Miguel, that was good cooking tonight."

The old Mexican characteristically only grunted, but she knew him well enough to know that he was pleased with the compliment. He was keenly aware that he was no longer much of a hand, which made him all the more proud of what he could do around the cookshack.

Cam rose too. "It's dark out. Will you let me walk with you?"

"Why, yes . . . I suppose so. But you don't have to. I've walked that walk after dark many times. I am not afraid."

He smiled. "I'm sure you're not. But I'd feel better about it if you'd let me. Besides, there are still a few things I think we should talk about."

"Oh?" she said. "Well . . ."

Outside there was no moon at all, and away from the bunkhouse, no light. Stacy knew the way by heart, however, and could negotiate the path that led behind the store toward the main house without so much as a stumble. Cam was less fortunate, but they walked slowly and he made only a few missteps.

"Have you had any customers at the store while I was gone?" he asked as they passed the darkened structure.

She shook her head sadly. "No, not a one. I am beginning to think I never will again."

"What will you do about it?"

She looked at him. "Why, nothing, I suppose. I have an inventory that fortunately is paid for. Some of it is perishable, but most is not, at least not immediately. I suppose I will sell what I can when I can and not replenish the supply. What else can I do?"

He wagged his head. "Well, if it's paid for, I guess that's about it. You're lucky on at least that score."

"Meaning I'm not so lucky on some others, right?"

He nodded just perceptibly, there in the darkness. "I'm afraid so. Unless you've got a lot more money than I think you have to buy back

cattle and hold your own against your sister and her husband, I think
that's exactly the case."

"You don't think we can regain the cows you say I've lost but are
still around somewhere? You don't believe we can salvage this year's
calf crop if we do?"

"Well, I'm not saying we can't," he said. "We can sure enough try,
and we might be able to pull it off in pretty good shape—*if* we can
locate the cows. But that's one of the things I wanted to talk about: we
need more riders. Even without the Cross Arrow to shoot our horses out
from under us and threaten the neighbors and try to scare us off, we
simply don't have enough bodies to watch over that many cattle."

Stacy stopped walking. "I can't get any more riders," she said evenly.
"I told you that the Cross Arrow has run all I had off, and I doubt if
any of them will come back. Besides, I doubt if I could pay them for
long anyway; I'm really pretty short of cash . . ."

"Oh?" He seemed surprised.

She resumed walking, feeling obligated now to explain further. "As
I told you before, I sold a fair number of cattle last fall, but the price I
received was very low. I stocked the store over winter using cash and I
paid off all my hands who quit with what little profit I had from the
cattle sales and store receipts from last year. Expenses have a way of
showing up after the fact, and on top of everything else, I had to pay
that Santa Fe lawyer a small fortune to handle the inheritance and to
represent me in court against Mala. She wound up with the other court
costs, but I still had to pay my lawyer. My father left me some operating capital, but not nearly as much as you might imagine. Mostly it was
because of the times, I guess. Cows haven't made us any real money for
two years, and right now I am just about caught up with. I was counting on the store to kind of hold things together, but now it looks like
I'll do well to pay your wages and keep us all in food till fall."

"Don't you pay your Navajos and the old Mexican anything?"

She shook her head. "To my shame, they won't take anything. All
they ask is a place to live and their meals. I can't just run them off, so I
let them stay and rationalize that I will someday make it up to them
when times are better."

Cam whistled softly, and once again Stacy stopped. "Look, if you're
having second thoughts about staying on, don't feel obligated. I won't
blame you if . . ."

"I never said that," he protested. "I want to help you now maybe
even more than before, and I reckon I'll hang around even if I have to
do it on the same basis as your two Indians and the old cook. It's just
that I didn't know . . ."

"I don't want to be a complete charity case," Stacy replied, suddenly steadfast and prideful despite herself. "And you don't owe me anything. I'll pay you what I said I would or I'll not have you. And I won't have you trying to do the impossible, either. If you don't think you and I and the two Indians can do the job, well, I'd just as soon not put any of you to it."

He wagged his head. "Well, maybe if we try hard enough even the impossible can be overcome. And I figure I do owe you something. You and those boys of yours pulled that horse off of me; I'd be dead if it wasn't for that. I want to stay, and one way or another I aim to help. I hope you will accept that."

They once again resumed walking and soon arrived at the porch of the house. Stacy mounted the first step and turned back. For a moment she was silent, thoughtful. "Okay," she said finally. "But where do we start? How do we go about trying hard enough that we overcome the impossible?"

CHAPTER 8

Cam knew only one answer to Stacy's question: apply the seat of one's pants to the seat of one's saddle, dawn till dusk, for however many days it takes to get the job done. He didn't really know the odds against success; he didn't even know if success was possible for them to attain. But he did know that difficult achievements require difficult efforts, and he was determined to at least give it a try.

What he didn't figure on at first was Stacy's own determination to help out. He had thought he and the two Indians would do the riding while the girl and old Miguel held down the store and the home place. He was soon to find out that Stacy would have none of this, however. She said she could ride and she could rope, and she could heat and apply a branding iron, and she could cook over a campfire, and since it was her ranch and they were already short-handed, she wasn't about to sit by and watch.

Cam argued only long enough to see that he wasn't going to win—and to realize that at least if she was with them he wouldn't have to worry about leaving her alone at the ranch for several days at a time—then gave in. Too, he found out quickly enough that she could do everything she said she could. She wore men's breeches, had her own made-to-fit leggins, and in a day when other women did well to hang on sidesaddle, she rode astride without the slightest hint of impropriety. She could heel a calf almost as well as Cam, and she never once flinched when it came time to apply a hot iron to one's side or the knife to a bull calf's testicles. Not that they had her doing the latter two jobs much (Cam or one of the Indians usually handled these chores), but despite dust-caked face and manure-encrusted boots, the girl was always there helping, and never once did she complain.

Not to say there were no problems. Naturally the matter of the night camp (distances alone made it imperative that they stay out for several days at a time) caused some. But she handled these problems one way or another, and because she did, so did the men. At times they even forgot she was a girl . . .

But not many times. After all, she was a very pretty girl, which made the fact of her sex just that much harder to forget. But somehow this still did not matter, for there was always a dignity about her, no matter how undignified the circumstances she had to deal with might become. Her bedroll was always placed discreetly across the campfire from the men's, her absences from camp to disappear behind a bush in the mornings and evenings went by almost without notice, and her ability to simply not hear the not so occasional cussword so inherent in many of the jobs at hand was nothing short of remarkable. Cam really marveled at her, in fact. She was like no other female he had ever known—except maybe her half sister, Mala . . . and he had no idea why he kept making *that* comparison. He had made his choice of sides and had every intention of staying with the one he'd chosen, regardless of how hopeless their cause seemed to be.

And it did seem hopeless at times. For a solid week they stayed out, taking with them needed extra horses and supplies, setting up camps first near Bell Cow Cienaga, then Loco Creek, and finally working their way across to wind up the last two days near Paint Horse Mesa. They worked long, hard days, overworked their horses, and in all branded only fifty-one calves, fifteen yearling or older mavericks that they were pretty sure were the offspring of Stretch B cows, and carefully tallied just over four hundred grown or half-grown animals already carrying Stacy's brand. Considering they figured they had seen three fourths of the Stretch B range outside the mesa country in the period, it wasn't much of a showing for an outfit that should count three thousand head. It confirmed what Cam had been saying was the problem, but in no way did it explain why or how it had come to be.

If anything, this latter was the most discouraging development of all to Cam and Stacy. They had hoped that perhaps they might stumble upon something that would help provide the answer, but only twice all week did they even see other riders and both times from long distances and under circumstances that were beyond determination. Oh, a couple of other times either Jaz or Jozie reported observing a lone rider or two, but again distance was a factor and at no time were they able to confirm anything suspicious.

Perhaps the only clue to anything occurred near Paint Horse Springs. It was here, at the most peripherally eastern of the major Stretch B watering places, that they encountered the largest single concentration of Stretch B cattle—over a hundred cows, more than not either without calves or with calves already branded—which fact caused Cam, at least, to do some wondering.

It was on the morning of the eighth day, as they were saddling up to head back to the ranch, that he turned to Stacy and said, "Tell me something. Is it usual for your cattle to use this mesa country heavier in the spring and summer than they do in winter?"

She met his gaze curiously. "Why, no. Just the opposite, in fact. Following the spring roundup, I would say two thirds to three fourths of our cattle have always stayed on the plains right though till the fall gather. The mesa country is best for winter, since it provides so much more protection from storms, and my father always insisted it be used that way. Ordinarily only a small percentage of the herd ever summered there."

"But it worked out mostly because the cattle were always *driven* onto the plains for the spring roundup," Cam said. "They were worked there and most of them just naturally stayed until pushed east again in the fall—isn't that right?"

"Well, yes, I suppose so. But why?"

"It's simple," he said. "Just recall what you told me about this spring's roundup. Very few Stretch B cattle were ever gathered—and now we're finding as many as anywhere right here on the east side. Of course we're only on the edge of the real mesa country, but I saw the same thing in my travels last week—more cows east than west and not a whole lot in between. Now, isn't it possible a lot of your cattle, being ungathered, simply haven't worked their way onto the plains yet? That they might still be to the east of us?"

She thought about this a moment, then said, "Yes, that's possible, but I'm not sure it's likely. Our cattle, the older stock at least, have summered on the plains too long to break the pattern that easily. I believe most of them would have drifted west long before now on their own, regardless of the gather. Certainly a lot more than the four hundred or so head we've seen this week."

Cam considered this and decided that probably she was right: cattle are creatures of habit; a lifelong pattern like that would not be easily broken—not to this extent, anyway. But as he thought about it, he also realized that the conclusion only led to another question.

"Okay," he said. "But what if someone has done more than just fail to help gather them? What if someone is actually pushing them east and holding them there, for the very purpose of making sure they don't show up on the plains? What if most of these cows here were simply left where they were because they either had calves already branded or had no calves at all?"

Stacy's eyes grew wide. "But why? By who?"

"You know by who as well as I do," he said. "And I think you know why, too, if you'll just think about it."

She finished tightening the girth on her saddle, then turned to lean against her horse, studying Cam. "Mala and her husband," she said, "intent on breaking me, and perhaps putting their Cross Arrow brand on as many of my unbranded calves as possible in the process."

Cam nodded. "I don't see what else."

Stacy wagged her head. "I don't know. Somehow it seems too raw even for Mala . . . but I guess it's possible. What do we do about it?"

Cam looked around thoughtfully. The two Indians were finished with their own saddling, the camp gear was packed, and already the extra saddle horses and their one packhorse were haltered so they could be led back to the ranch. A hundred or so yards away, eight or ten cows hung around the water at Paint Horse Springs. Others had scattered overnight and only a few were to be seen in the distance. Some were even Cross Arrow stock, but most of the Stretch B animals they had seen yesterday would not be far away.

He turned back to Stacy. "Well, I say we start by pushing everything around here that's yours on west, maybe as far as the main ranch itself. At least that way they'll be where we can look after them."

"And then?"

He looked back to the east. "I'm not sure. Some of these cows of yours are outright wild, and I'm pretty positive no big lot of them have ever been gathered by four riders—not from country like that anyway . . ."

She gave him a reproachful look. "I thought we had talked all we were going to about hiring more riders."

Cam shrugged. "Yeah, I know. But it could sure make a difference if we could get some of your old riders back."

Stacy did not look encouraged. Still she said, "Well, you get any that are still around to come and you're welcome to them, even if I have to mortgage something to pay them. But I've already tried hanging onto them once. In fact, even if you do get one or two, I'd be willing to make you a little bet on your chances of keeping them, once Terhune and his gunnies find out. I really would."

Cam studied her for a moment, thinking about it, and as he mounted his horse, said, "I just might take you up on that, boss. I just sure as heck might."

They spent two hours gathering some sixty-five cows, bulls, yearlings, and two-year-olds, and finally gave up on finding any more. All were somewhat wild, but once out onto the plains went easily enough in a bunch. As much trouble as anything were the extra horses and the packhorse. At least two riders were occupied most of the time with them, so it was fortunate that once they were started in the right direction the cattle took to the plains as if that was where they wanted to go anyway. Of course, to Cam, this seemed to bear out what Stacy had said earlier. It was not within the Stretch B herd's nature to stay in the mesa country this late in the spring. Something had to have kept them from making the move, or at least delayed them. Something or someone . . .

As he rode, he just couldn't help wondering if there was any hope of picking up even one or two more riders—ex-Stretch B hands who knew that mesa country well. He was convinced this was going to be necessary before they could ever hope to locate the main Stretch B herd and gather them. He got to thinking about Stacy's ex-foreman . . . what was his name? Stanhope? Yes, that was it. Last heard of over in Arizona, the girl had said. Certainly Stanhope would be the ideal one to start with, but was there any chance? Had the Cross Arrow run him off for good or not? And if not, what would the Terhunes' gunhands do if he came back? Stacy had implied that they would not stand for it. Cam supposed she was right, but then, for that matter, who was to say they were going to stand for Cam Stallings hanging around, either?

Well, time would tell. Right now it was a case of first things first. They had these cattle to get home, then they could worry more about obtaining additional riders—and the Terhunes. Cam wasn't sure what the latter would do anyway. For certain, he hadn't seen hide nor hair of any of them since that day over a week ago in town—which caused him to wonder: Even if Stacy could not lure back any of her old riders, what was going to be the Cross Arrow's way of dealing with Cam Stallings? It had to be some way. And when was he likely to find out?

He got a pretty good hint a couple of hours later when they rode wearily up to the ranch—and discovered Mala and Gerd Terhune, Pit Emory, Lizard Guerrero, and the one called Fern Carty, waiting for them in the yard before the main house.

CHAPTER 9

By the time they realized they had company, then got close enough to tell who that company was, there was precious little they could do but ride on in to the ranch. Cam sent the two Indians to the corrals with the extra horses; he and Stacy rode on up to the house.

"If they're here to fight it out," he told her, "we've probably had it anyway. No use getting the Navajos killed too."

"I don't think they've come to fight, Cam," Stacy said.

"How do you know that?"

"I don't," she said. "I just think it." Plainly she was more puzzled than sure; there really was only one way to find out.

They reined up at the front porch, facing their visitors. For some reason the Terhunes and their men still sat their horses, and although they apparently had arrived only shortly before Cam, Stacy, and the Navajos had come into view, it seemed odd that they had made no move to dismount. But then Cam spotted old Miguel sitting in the shadows of the porch, rifle in hand, and knew instantly that the visiting party had been invited in no uncertain terms to stay where they were. A toothy grin spread across the old Mexican's face the moment he realized that Cam had spotted him.

"Not a very neighborly way to welcome guests, Stacy," Mala said coolly as the younger girl dismounted and tied her horse to the porch rail.

"What makes you think you're welcome guests?" Stacy answered, just as coolly.

Mala shrugged. "Nothing, I suppose. Anyway, it's not a social call."

"I didn't figure it was." Stacy swept a contemptuous glance over the group. "Social callers don't bring bodyguards."

Mala's eyes snapped, and as far as Cam was concerned, never had he seen a woman more beautiful. Even in riding clothes and with her hair drawn back in a tight bun, she was utterly striking. And those eyes. Somehow Cam felt like a bird being charmed by a snake, yet he just could not bring himself to equate this woman with anything reptilian.

"They are not 'bodyguards,'" she replied stonily. "They are my husband and three Cross Arrow riders. They are here on Cross Arrow business, just as I am."

Stacy mounted the porch, eyebrows arched. "Oh, really! Armed to the teeth and fifteen miles from Cross Arrow range—and they are here on business. Well, well. Isn't that interesting!"

Mala looked impatient. "I didn't come here to trade insults with you, Stacy. As a matter of fact, our business isn't even with you."

"I see," Stacy said, meaning she did nothing of the kind. She addressed Miguel, "Might as well put that rifle down, old friend. These people are here on business, can't you see? And it isn't even with us!"

The other woman, doing her best to ignore this, shifted slightly in her saddle. She looked directly at Cam, who still sat his horse several yards away. "Our business is with you, Stallings. We've come to offer you a job."

The effect of this was something similar to an explosion in their midst. "Now just a minute—!" Stacy blurted, but Mala continued to ignore her; the woman kept her eyes strictly on Cam.

"I am dead serious, Mr. Stallings. Gerd and I brought these men along to prove that there are no grudges held for what you did a week ago. We want you to come to work for the Cross Arrow."

Cam was almost too astounded to think clearly. If she had said "We've come here to pay you back in kind for what you did," he might have believed her. But to tell him there were no grudges and offer him a job to boot—that was just a little beyond an ordinary man's comprehension.

"Well?" she went on. "What do you say? We will pay you twice whatever you are earning here—assuming that is anything at all. Can you turn that down?"

Cam glanced at Stacy, who likewise did not seem to know what to say, then from one to the other of the four mounted men. Gerd Terhune did not meet his gaze and did not in fact seem especially interested. The one called Carty, a man of medium build but with bushy eyebrows and a lionlike mane that made him appear larger, seemed either bored or impatient with the affair, and if anything was even less interested than Terhune. Pit Emory, on the other hand, looked just the opposite. He might have been trying to hide it, but his anticipation (of what Cam was afraid to guess) was plainly keen. Lizard Guerrero's eyes darted and shone, and if he'd licked his hungry lips Cam would not have been surprised. No grudges, eh?

What he did not understand was the woman. Why was she offering him a job like this? From somewhere a tiny, desperate voice warned him not to be flattered.

He finally said, "I already have a job, ma'am. And it seems to me you have plenty of riders already. How could you possibly need me?"

"She doesn't need you, Cam," Stacy warned from the porch. "She knows I do and is only trying to get you away from me."

"Shut up, Stacy," the woman said, without once taking her eyes off Cam. "I simply like the sort of man you are, Stallings. We always need good hands. Besides, it's your chance to work for a good outfit—not a down-and-out operation like this."

Cam looked at Stacy, this time unabashedly for help. She met his gaze and shook her head. "It's your decision, Cam. I can't tell you not to do it." But there was a tightness in her voice, and Cam could sense that her anger was barely under control. She *was* telling him and he knew it.

He returned his gaze to the Terhunes. Gerd Terhune said, "Make up your mind, cowboy. You won't get the offer twice."

For Cam there really was no choice. Throughout the conversation he had known this. Whatever else he had or had not picked up while riding for different outfits over the years, one thing had taken hold in a light that had no exceptions; a sort of unwritten code, it was. A man rode for the brand; loyalties counted. When there was conflict, changing over for money alone broke the code. A man had to have a better reason than that, and Cam had none. He was the kind of man who had always abided by the code.

"I'm sorry," he said. "I appreciate the offer, but for me it wouldn't be right. I think you know that. I signed on here and here is where I reckon I'll stay. Thanks just the same."

Mala Terhune looked disappointed but not surprised. She said, "You won't reconsider?"

"No . . . no, I reckon not."

"Very well, then." Her voice was cold and full of dismissal. She looked over at Stacy. "It won't do you any good, you know. He and ten more like him won't do you any good."

"Why?" Stacy asked angrily. "Are you going to run him off like all the rest? Are you going to sic your goons there on him like you did on Dan Stanhope?"

Mala never flinched. She only said, "I don't have to answer that, Stacy. I never did have to answer to you."

The girl's eyes were suddenly appraising. "No," she said, "I guess you never did. You always assumed the right to be perfectly rotten and I see that you are still assuming. But this is the worst ever, Mala. You come here knowing that I am down to only three full-fledged riders, and you offer to take one of *them* away from me. I think it proves that what Father finally came to think of you was true, that—"

"That is enough, Stacy!" Mala's voice cracked like a whip, for the first time exhibiting that hard quality Cam had observed back at the Cross Arrow. "I won't listen to that from you. I warn you, I will not!"

"Of course you won't," Stacy said coldly. "You don't want to hear the truth. You won't admit that half of this ranch could have been yours, that you *drove* Father to change his will when you—"

"*Stacy . . . I told you I will not listen!*" Mala's voice grew almost shrill, and suddenly Cam honestly could not tell if it sprang from anger at an accusation fairly made or from anguish at just the opposite.

Stacy's eyes virtually smoldered. "And you aim to have it all, too—right, Mala? You and that cow thief of a husband of yours. You will stop at nothing. You will run off my hands, my cattle, frighten away my neighbors—anything to get it."

"*Stacy, don't say any more, I'm warning you! Don't say any more or—*"

"Or what?" Stacy demanded. "What, Mala?"

Suddenly Cam realized that he had been sitting there half mesmerized, as had the other men present. The spell was broken when Gerd Terhune moved his horse up alongside that of his wife and took her by the arm. She tried to shake loose, but his grip was firm. "Enough, Mala," he said. "We're only wasting time here. The cowboy has said no, and that's all we came for." Then he looked sternly at Stacy. "I don't take kindly to you calling me a cow thief, girl. I'd advise you to retract that."

"And I would advise you to go to hell," Stacy spat back. "You are what you are. And now that I've told you to your face, get off my ranch! Do you understand? Get off and don't come back!"

Terhune stiffened; there was a dangerous glint in his eye. It must have been instinct that his hand slipped down toward his gun butt, for Cam couldn't believe the man would draw on a girl. Or would he? Quickly he became aware of a tension among the other men, and was shocked to see other hands upon their guns as well. For several moments the situation hung in precarious balance. Cam knew there was little he himself could do and he had no idea what would happen if the others were provoked further.

Then the unmistakable sound of a gun hammer being pulled back caused them all to freeze. All but forgotten in the porch shadows, old Miguel had suddenly leveled his rifle. The old man was standing, his sights placed squarely on Gerd Terhune's heart. More unexpected yet, from behind the group, a shell was jacked into yet another rifle chamber, and all heads turned to find Jaz and Jozie quietly sitting their horses about twenty-five yards away, rifles trained on the group.

How they got that close undetected no one else would ever know, but they were there just the same.

Cam did not move to draw his own weapon. He only backed his horse away a few steps and said, "I think you'd better go, Terhune."

The rancher looked from the barrel of one gun to the barrel of another. There was not much to be said for his position. With a cautious nod to his men, he said to his wife, "Come on. We're leaving."

Mala shot a somewhat strange, indecipherable look at Stacy, then said to Cam, "I'm sorry you chose no, Stallings. Believe me, I was trying to do you a favor."

. They reined their horses away from the house and filed out across the yard, each riding more or less past Cam, each paying him a different notice as they passed. Terhune ignored him; Fern Carty simply glanced at him curiously and rode on past; Pit Emory grinned maliciously; Mala only nodded. Only Lizard Guerrero paused to say something, and that was a barely whispered, "I am glad you are still an enemy, señor. It would be such a shame to want so badly to kill someone who is on my own side!" He laughed then and rode on by.

Cam, unable to help a little inward shiver at this, watched steadily as they moved off; then he dismounted and walked over to the porch. "That was close, Stacy. If it hadn't been for the Navajos, I'm not sure what those men would have done."

She considered this solemnly. "For your own sake," she said, "you probably should have accepted my sister's offer."

He doubted that she really meant it, but he told her anyway, "There are at least two of those men who hate my guts, Stacy. Even if I'd had the notion, I don't think I'd want to try to work alongside of them. I sure don't."

"I don't blame you for that," she said glumly.

"Well, that part came as no surprise. Your sister's job offer—and Gerd Terhune letting her make it—did. I would never have expected that in a hundred years."

"I told you why they did it. They wanted to get you away from me."

"I suppose that's right, but why do it that way? Why not just run me off or turn Guerrero loose to shoot me? Seems to me that would be the surest way."

"Yes, and it might well be what they *will* do now," she warned seriously. "In fact, it might very well be what's in store for all of us, after this. Jaz, Jozie, me, even Miguel."

Cam looked around. The two Indians had gone on back to the corrals to unsaddle the horses now, and Miguel had sidled off the porch and was heading for the barn. Not unusually, not one of them had so much as uttered a word during or after the affair.

"Stacy," he said suddenly, "is there a place you can go in case of real trouble? I mean, if it really gets rough—is there someplace besides here?"

She gave him a quizzical look. "I won't leave the ranch, Cam. I won't run and just leave it to them."

"That's not what I mean. I just mean someplace on or near the ranch where you might go temporarily in case your life really is in danger. I know that sounds extreme, but if things get completely out of hand I don't think here at the headquarters would be the best place for you to be."

Understanding showed on her face. "A place to hide? Is that what you mean? You would actually want me to hide from them?"

"Only if it's necessary. Come on, think. Isn't there a place? Someplace where no one would know to look for you, or at least would have a hard time finding you?"

"Well," she said, "I guess there is the malpais. I suppose I could go there."

"The malpais." Cam recalled vividly that wicked stretch of inhospitable lava he had observed so closely over two weeks ago. "You know a place on the malpais? A way to get there?"

"Yes, there is a place. I have never been there, but the Navajos know it, my father knew it. It is several miles into the main lava flow, but there is a trail of sorts if you know how to find and follow it. What's called an ice cave is there, enough water to keep a small party and their horses alive, and a sort of tiny valley with soil enough to grow a strong stand of bunchgrass for feed. It would be an ideal hiding place, and back when the Apaches roamed this country, I think it was used for that."

"How long ago was that?"

"Not long at all. They were all over the place when we first came here; only in very recent years have they been fully confined to reservations. We never had any real trouble with them that I know of, but my father always said the malpais would be our last resort if we did."

"And you say Jaz and Jozie know the way? Are you sure?"

"My father told me they did, yes."

Cam sighed. "Well, there is no use worrying about it a lot just now. But it's good to know there is a place. I'll have to talk to Jaz and Jozie about it, first chance I get. Right now I guess I better go on down and help out with the horses. Will you be coming to the cookshack for supper?"

"Yes," she said. "Yes, I think I will. It is not one of those nights when I want to eat alone, of course."

He smiled. "Of course." Then he turned to leave and was almost off the porch when she called to him.

"Cam, please . . . I don't want to forget to tell you how much I appreciate what you did today—staying on here that way. You didn't have to, you know."

He had already turned back. "I know. But I ride for the brand, and right now you're it. You don't have to thank me."

Nevertheless, she smiled gratefully, and as he turned once more to go he was scarcely aware of the soft gaze that would follow him all the way to the corrals.

CHAPTER 10

A hard two days' ride from the Stretch B Ranch lay Round Valley, center focus of the upper reaches of Arizona's Little Colorado watershed, and Springerville. An early-day haven for outlaws, rustlers, and horse thieves of all stripes, the area had since been colonized by Mormons and was now a fast-growing trade and cattle-raising center.

Cam rode into the town late one warm June afternoon and dismounted in front of Julius Becker's store. He had done a lot of hard thinking before deciding to come here, and he knew he was taking a chance on wasting several days of his time. He could have gone north, to the railroad beyond the malpais, might even have enjoyed better odds of finding men who would hire on. But those men would not be Stretch B hands, and it was Stretch B hands that Cam wanted.

Not that he wouldn't take help anywhere he could get it. He would. But he had more than one reason for figuring that ex-Stretch B riders would be the best he could get. Naturally he wanted someone who already knew the mesa country well enough to operate effectively within it; that much was obvious. But, too, he figured that anyone he could get to come back would likely do so out of loyalty—especially if they knew it might be a while before they were paid. Cam knew it would be difficult at best, but he planned to appeal to that loyalty and he planned to start at the top—with Dan Stanhope, ex-foreman.

Actually he couldn't even be sure Stanhope was still in or around Springerville. Stacy had heard he was here, but that had been less than a month following his departure from the Stretch B. The man could be almost anywhere by now. Cam had simply decided to take the chance that if he did not find him here, at least he might be somewhere not too far away.

The first person he encountered, a gray-bearded old-timer standing on the walk in front of Becker's store, directed him to a saloon down the street. Yes, he knew Stanhope; and yes, if you wanted to find the man, you had to look behind the nearest bottle. Dan Stanhope was a "down-'n'-outer," sure as there ever was one.

He wasn't in the saloon, but the bartender there knew where he had been living: a run-down shack over by the river. Any time he wasn't in this or some other saloon, he would most likely be at his shack. He had a woman living with him and rarely was he sober. And no, he wasn't working anywhere, not that the barkeep knew of.

• It was almost sundown by the time Cam found the shack, a pathetic-looking hovel situated along one bank of the Little Colorado about a mile above town. A couple of mangy curs met him at the yard gate, and out back a half-fallen corral contained a single horse. Whiskey bottles littered the yard, and only a brief inspection was needed for Cam to conclude that the place—at least on the outside—was a wretched mess. He was unsure if he even wanted to look on the inside.

But he had come too far to turn back now; he entered the yard and headed for the door. One of the dogs tried to bite him, and he sent it tumbling with a strong boot to the ribs. It yelped loudly and raced around the corner of the house, the second mutt tearing along behind as if it too had been kicked. From inside came voices, one slurred and grouchy, the other feminine and clearly filled with mixed surprise and anger. Cam knocked on the door, then had to stand there for over a minute before anyone answered.

When the door finally opened, it was the woman who stood there. She was Mexican, neither pretty nor young. Her clothes were in disarray, as if hastily donned. The room behind her was so poorly lit that Cam could not make out a thing, and the expression on the woman's face was not a pleasant one.

"¿Quién es?" she asked in harsh Spanish, then added in English, "Who are you? What do you want?"

"I am looking for a man named Dan Stanhope. Is this his place?"

She turned and rattled off something Cam couldn't understand to someone inside. A husky voice replied in halting words that were again beyond Cam's comprehension, Spanish being a lingo he had never learned up North the way Anglos did here in this southern country.

The woman turned back. "What is your name? What do you want with Stanhope?" Her English was not good, but at least it was understandable.

"Tell him I am Cam Stallings. He doesn't know me, but I am from the Stretch B Ranch. He'll know where that is."

Again the woman spoke in Spanish, into the darkness. There was a startled "Huh?" then a sharp command. The woman stepped aside and pointed into the room. "He is over there."

Cam lowered his head as if to move through the doorway, then was startled as the woman darted past him and disappeared around the corner of the shack without a backward glance.

Inside, he let his eyes have a moment to adjust and soon made out a solitary form sitting slumped on the edge of a bed across the room. The place reeked of liquor and was so stuffy it almost made Cam sick to his stomach. He left the door open as much for the fresh air as the light. His eyes adjusted a bit more; the figure on the bed became a man dressed only from the waist down, hair tousled, a week's growth of stubble further darkening his already darkened face. He was thin, almost emaciated, and although Stacy had said he was somewhere in his early thirties, from where Cam stood he could have been forty-five.

The man seemed to be staring at him, yet he made no move to get up off the bed. "You think I'm drunk?" he asked abruptly in a thick but no longer slurred voice.

Cam looked around, then back to the man. "From the smell of things, I'd say anything in here must be drunk."

"Not funny," the man said, then added, "What d'you want of me?"

"You are Stanhope, aren't you?" Cam said. He went over to a nearby chair and, throwing one leg across it, sank down slowly to sit with his arms resting against the back.

"I'm Stanhope, shame to say. Who'd you say you are?"

"Stallings. Cam Stallings. I work for Stacy Brightwood. I reckon you remember her."

Stanhope jerked at this, then peered. "Look, man, the dark spot in my life is what I did to Stacy Brightwood. You'd better have a good reason for bringing her up to me. If not, make it quick and get out."

"I rode all the way here from the Stretch B," Cam said in level tones. "I don't figure it was for a poor reason."

"And you're tellin' me you did that just to see me?"

"I did."

"Well, you didn't find much, did you?"

Cam shook his head. "No, I can't say I did. But it's still you I came to see. I haven't failed yet."

The man continued to just sit there, seemingly perplexed but not intensely curious. "Why? What do you want of me?"

"I want you to come back to work for the Stretch B. I want you to help me round up some more of the boys who quit. We need all of you that we can get."

Stanhope stared as if he had not heard right. "You want *me* to come back *there*? Man, you must be crazy! You must not know what I did!"

"I know," Cam said quietly. "I know that you and all the others were run off by Cross Arrow goons and gunnies—"

"But that's just it, for chrissake!" Stanhope cried out, impassionate now for the first time. "What makes you think any man in his right mind would go back for more of that? Do you really know what happened to me? Have you ever seen that man-monster they call Max Gruel? Do you know what he can do to you with his hands alone? It's dark in here and you can't see the scars on my face; you don't know what he did to my ribs and my gut. Man, I'm still sick from it at times, and you want me to go back for more? And do you know the one they call Carty? Do you know what he told me would happen if I went back? Do you have any idea what that man can do with a gun—him or Guerrero or Emory, any one?"

Cam maintained his level gaze, albeit sympathetically. "I know them all," he said. "I've had run-ins with them myself already and was almost killed by them the day I came to Stretch B country. But do *you* know what's happening to Stacy Brightwood? Do you know that she right now has only her two Indians, her old Mexican cook, and me for a crew? That she is in danger of losing all if she doesn't get more help?"

The man looked at the floor. "I can imagine," he said, almost inaudibly.

"Well, then, you know why I've come. We need men, good men who know the Stretch B range, especially the mesa country to the east. Men like you and the others who have left. The Terhunes will have it all if something's not done soon."

Even in the poor light Cam could see the agony etched on the man's features as he looked up. "But I told you, man: I am no good! I ran. Do you hear me, *I ran!* You don't need such as me."

Cam studied him for a moment. "Look, Stacy has told me you are a good man. You were her father's foreman. You know cows and you know the Stretch B like a duck knows webbed feet. I wouldn't waste my time if I didn't think you could help us as much as anyone can."

"And you waste your time totally if you think I ever will!"

"But why? Why won't you, knowing that the need is so desperate?"

"I told you. I am no good. Look at me, man. Can't you see what I've become? I am a drunk. I don't work—I live off that woman you saw here. I am no good, I tell you!"

"Make up for it, then," Cam countered. "Can't you see the chance I'm giving you? Leave all this behind and come back."

Stanhope only shook his head. "Don't plague me, man. I am no good, and I can't go back. There is no hope, don't you understand that?"

But Cam would not give up. "If there was no hope, you couldn't be plagued," he persisted. "Sure, I can see you're down just now. But it's from shame, not fear; I can see that too. And I figure that proves there's hope. All you have to do is come with me. You have it in you, I can tell you do."

For the first time the man looked susceptible to persuasion—just barely, perhaps, but a crack had been made in the armor.

Cam went on. "Do you know how many calves Stacy branded at the spring roundup? Can you guess? A couple hundred at best—on a ranch with over two thousand mother cows. And have you any idea how many Stretch B animals can be counted on the plains right now? Four, maybe five hundred—counting yearlings, two-year-olds, and bulls. Something's bad wrong in all that, of course; and I think you know who's behind it."

The man nodded slowly. "The Terhunes."

"Right. And I think I know what's going on; the cattle are being held somewhere, but we've tried and tried and can't locate them. We've got to have more help—four or five men at least . . ."

"You need gunhands, not cowboys," Stanhope said. "I know Mala Terhune and her husband, and I know some of the men they've hired. You've got a war on your hands, whether you know it or not."

Cam shook his head vigorously. "I don't know any gunhands. And anyway, I need cowboys first. We've got to find those cattle and get them back. That'll take good men who know what they're doing on a horse. Stacy may not be able to pay any of you just now, but I think you all owe her something anyway. And don't let the word gunhand fool you. Most of their type would rather shoot from ambush than face you any day. I figure I can use a rifle as good as most of them and I figure you can too. Now, what do you say? Can you find me a few more men like yourself? Will you do that and come back? For Stacy?"

Stanhope wagged his head in misery. "I can find the men, but I don't know if they'll come. I don't know if I will come!"

Cam sensed that here was a point in which he must not be merciful. He said sternly, "You have to, Stanhope. I'm going to say it to you plain. If you don't you will have gone to hell for sure. That is, unless you actually want to go on like this, unable to bring yourself to do anything for anybody or yourself, living off that woman until you drink yourself to death. Is that what you want? Do you want Stacy Brightwood to go under because you wouldn't help her? That's your choice, you know. You either pull out of it now, or you never will."

Cam stood up, knowing that he had called for the cards now and that if he did not win with this hand he never would.

"Well? What'll it be? Answer me now, for I won't ask again."

Dan Stanhope stared at the floor for almost a minute, then he very slowly straightened and stared Cam in the eye. "Give me five days," he said. "You go on back and give me five days to find some of the boys. My word is good. I'll be there."

Cam did not go straight back to the Stretch B. He felt good about what he'd done with Dan Stanhope, and as had been his wont before, success only spurred him on to further adventure. While he was at it, he figured, he might as well enlist whatever other help he could get. He knew this effort might not produce the results he thought he had achieved with Stanhope, but he felt he had to do something to stir up Stacy's neighbors if he possibly could. If it ever came down to an outright confrontation, his only hope might be them.

He stopped first to see Reece Crawford of the Railroad Slash; then came Lester McNaab at the Dot M and finally Mitch Ressler of the Circle R. In each case he was received openly and, when he told them who he was and where he worked, with some embarrassment as well. They had all heard of his confrontation with Lizard Guerrero in Vera Velarde, and it was plain that they were inwardly amused, even pleased, at the outcome. But they were ill at ease with him too. Underlying their initial friendliness was the fact that they must know all was not right on the range these days; they were almost surely aware that it was through no fault of theirs the situation had got no worse than it already was. Cam wisely chose not to emphasize this; in fact, he rather adroitly pretended ignorance on the point. He would not accuse them outright of being afraid of the Cross Arrow and thereby put them on the defensive unnecessarily.

What he did do was to explain what he thought was going on with Stacy Brightwood's cattle. He did not appeal directly for help; he simply let it go without saying that he assumed good neighbors would not do otherwise when the time came, once they were properly apprised of the situation. He had only stopped by to let them know how things were, and that is how he left it. Each rancher in turn accepted the information with proper nods of concern and expressions of appreciation that he'd come, and whether this was sincere or not Cam did not care. He had put them on notice; he figured their consciences would have to do the rest.

It was late the second day out from Springerville when he prepared to leave the Circle R, and it was Martha Ressler, Mitch's wife, who pressed him with the ordinary ranch country courtesy of asking him to stay the night. He declined, saying he needed to get on back to the Stretch B even if it meant riding into the wee hours to get there, but he did consent to take supper with them.

An hour later Martha Ressler once again came somewhat tentatively up to him as he was getting ready to leave. "Something I feel I should tell you, Mr. Stallings. I hope you don't mind."

"Why, no. Of course not," he said.

"I've known Stacy Brightwood since she was quite young. She's a good girl, and I would be the last to say she was anything else. But things do have a way of looking bad sometimes, if you know what I mean . . ."

, Cam stared at her. "No, ma'am. I'm sorry . . . I reckon I don't know. Exactly what is it that looks so bad?"

"I'm only saying this for the girl's own good," she said, a bit defensively. "You see . . . I mean, well, it's just her living on that ranch with nothing but men around her. Like I say, it's only the way it looks . . . but you do see what I mean, don't you?"

Cam frowned, then nodded somewhat uncertainly.

"Get her someone to stay in that house with her, a woman, a housekeeper or something. Do that for her, will you?"

Cam stared at her. The woman was right: only a fool would have failed to see what she was pointing out a long time before this. That's what comes of not being around females much, he told himself—you don't notice a damned thing that's out of the ordinary because you don't even know what ordinary is.

The woman smiled. "When you get home, send one of the Navajos over to the reservation. He'll likely find just who you need there, maybe even one of the younger women or girls who can speak English. You won't regret it, believe me."

"Thanks," he said. "I'll do that. I sure will."

He was serious about it, and it was one of the many things on his mind a few hours later when he rode into the ranch well past midnight. Actually, though tired, he was highly pleased with his accomplishments over the past few days and his mood was as light as it had been in a long time. He had every intention of making a housekeeper for Stacy one of his top priorities.

He was surprised, however, to find a light in the bunkhouse when he rode up to the barn . . . and he forgot all about housekeepers and the like a few minutes later when, inside, he found everyone hovering over one of the bunks.

It was Jozie, just brought in. They had found him out on the range, where according to a tearful Stacy he had been caught alone and beaten senseless. To Cam, he looked barely to be alive.

CHAPTER 11

The young Indian's face was a mass of purple splotches and raw red cuts. They had wiped away the blood, but his eyes were puffed shut, his lips were swollen three times their normal size, and there were cuts over both eyes and Cam would have bet inside the mouth as well. The boy was unconscious, had been ever since he had been found.

Cam shook his head in angry exasperation. "Whoever did this damn sure didn't care if they killed him . . . What was he doing out there alone, anyway?"

Stacy had a troubled look on her face as she said, "It was my fault. I talked them into going back, to see if we couldn't find and gather a few more cows from the mesa country. As usual, pickings were pretty slim, but we did find about twenty-five head just east of Paint Horse Mesa. We were driving them toward the plains when about ten of them broke away in some brush. Jozie went after them and became separated from Jaz and me. We got the rest of the bunch as far as Paint Horse, and when Jozie didn't show up with those that got away, we went back to look for him. Jaz found Jozie's tracks near where we had last seen him, and we followed along until we found him, about an hour later. This is how he was."

Cam frowned. "Yet you saw no one else? You don't even know who did this?"

"I know," Jaz muttered without the slightest trace of uncertainty. "It was the big ugly white man from the Cross Arrow. I know it was him."

Max Gruel, Cam thought. Of course. Still, he asked, "How do you know that?"

"Tracks, all around," the Indian said simply. "Big boot, heavy man. Other mans there too, but I know who done it. He just wait, get one of us alone. I know 'im, I kill 'im someday mebbe."

Cam frowned even more heavily than before at this. All he needed was an angry Navajo setting out to exact retribution for Cross Arrow sins, and perhaps getting even worse than his brother got in the process. He wagged his head and looked at a still miserable Stacy.

"Look, don't blame yourself," he told her. "I wish you hadn't gone, but we can't hide inside the house all day either. We'll just have to stay together from now on, that's all. Maybe when Stanhope gets here and there are more of us—"

Her eyes widened with surprise. "*Stanhope?* My God! I forgot all about that. Dan is actually coming back?"

Under happier circumstances Cam would have smiled. "I didn't get a chance to say so yet, but yes, he's coming. Not only that, he's bringing some others with him. I look for him in about five days."

"I can't believe it," Stacy murmured. "Are you sure? Do you really know he's coming?"

"He said he was, and I believed him. He's a good man, Stacy, the kind whose shame would have ruined him if he never made it up to you. I think all he needed was for someone like me to show up and give him the chance."

The girl cast weary eyes down upon the unconscious Jozie. "Well, I just hope he doesn't come back to wind up like this," she said sadly. "He did once, you know. I don't know if I can stand it if it ever happens again, to any of you."

Cam didn't say anything more. He knew how she felt. It was hard not to be apprehensive, always having to resurrect hope in the face of such things . . . But that's just what one had to do, wasn't it? Keep on resurrecting. Otherwise, he told himself, you give up—and now was no time to be doing that. Whatever happened, they must not give up.

Next morning, however, he was still worrying about the two Navajos. Brother Jozie was conscious again and looking much better, but Jaz had remained dangerously sullen over the whole thing. Cam was more concerned than ever now that the boy might go off half-cocked in search of vengeance. That could end in disaster for Jaz, he knew. At least he thought he did. Ordinarily he would consider either of the young Indians capable of taking care of himself. Chances were Jozie had been surprised or Max Gruel and his buddies would never have caught him to beat him up. But caution and good sense were the qualities that would normally keep them out of trouble. Throw especially the caution part to the winds—which was just what Jaz might do—and no telling what might happen.

Cam remembered his brief conversation with Martha Ressler and wondered if an errand such as bringing Stacy back a housekeeper-companion from the reservation might not be a good diversion. *If* he could just get Jaz to go; *if* he could get Stacy to accept the girl or woman when Jaz got back; and *if* he could convince himself it was any way wise to send someone out alone again . . .

Stacy was almost a bigger problem than Jaz.

"I don't care what Martha Ressler says," she declared hotly. "I don't *need* a housekeeper."

"It's mostly for looks, Stacy," Cam argued. "Besides, I don't like you living alone up there in the main house. I'd think *you* wouldn't like it."

"I do not need a companion, Cam Stallings. And I don't give a hoot about looks. Those things are the least of my problems right now—you should know that."

"Yeah, I do," he said resignedly. "But look, I need something for Jaz to do, something to get his mind off going over to the Cross Arrow and trying to collect Max Gruel's gizzard, or something equally foolish. Right now, short of tying him up in the barn, this is about all I can think of."

"What makes you think he'll go? If he wants Max Gruel so badly, why should he even bother with your errand?"

"If you tell him, he'll go. Too, the reservation is in the opposite direction and is well removed from the Cross Arrow. It'll take him four days at least to get there and back. By then Jozie should be better and Jaz will have cooled off some."

She eyed him skeptically. "And maybe Stanhope will be here—is that it, also?"

"Well, yeah," he admitted hopefully. "As a matter of fact, yeah."

Finally she relented; Jaz was given his instructions and convinced that there was nothing he could do for Jozie at the ranch. He left that night, going under cover of darkness just in case the Cross Arrow's *"un*welcoming" committee should be lurking about again, and Cam and Stacy saw him off.

They watched until the young Indian was gone in the night, then Cam said, "Maybe he'll get a medicine man to do some kind of dance for Jozie while he's gone."

Earlier in the day they had considered sending Jaz for a medical doctor instead of to the reservation. But the nearest physician anybody knew about was over a hundred miles away, and now that the injured boy was conscious again and seemed to have suffered neither broken bones nor serious internal damage, they had decided against sending for the sawbones. The main thing was to occupy Jaz, and Cam really was determined to have someone to stay with Stacy. He was convinced that Jozie would be long over the hump before a doctor could be found and brought to the ranch, anyway.

"I still feel rotten about it," Stacy said, as Cam walked her back to the main house. "If I hadn't taken them back out there, Jozie would never have had that happen to him."

"The blame rests on whoever did it, Stacy, not on you; I keep telling you that."

"Yes, and it keeps being only half true. As long as I keep trying to hang on here, anyone who works for me is in the same or worse danger. Oh, Cam, don't you see? They are not going to let us win. The harder we try, the meaner they will get. We will finally be forced to fight them or give up, you know we will."

"And you're not willing to fight for what's yours?"

* She shot him a look he could better sense than see there in the dark. "I *have* been fighting, or at least trying to. But I'm not sure I'm willing to get innocent cowhands like yourself shot up by a bunch of hired guns over it. Someone will be killed for sure, and I think you know where the odds lie on who it will be."

He didn't want to argue with her; he only said, "Have a little faith, will you? Even a bunch of cowhands can put up a good fight now and then. Give Stanhope a chance to bring us some men, then we'll see . . . okay?"

Three more days passed. Jozie was doing much better, and although he was still in pain and looked a mess, he seemed clearly headed for recovery now. The boy was tough, no doubt about that. Late the fourth day Jaz returned. He had with him a Navajo girl of about sixteen—the daughter of his mother's cousin, he told them. Her name was Juana, and she could speak some English. She was very shy around the men, but seemed to take to Stacy almost immediately.

As the fifth day came and went, Cam carefully and somewhat dejectedly noted on his bunkhouse calendar that it was the seventh now since his visit to Springerville. Dan Stanhope had not shown up.

"I was afraid of that," Stacy told him that evening after supper.

Cam shook his head stubbornly. "He'll come, I know he will. He's been held up somehow, that's all . . ."

"Or something's happened to him," she added meaningfully. "That's possible, you know."

He couldn't argue with that, and when two more days passed without Stanhope's arrival he couldn't bring himself to discuss it anymore. Fortunately, things otherwise were going almost better than expected. Jozie was up and around some now, and Stacy actually came around to thank Cam for sending for the girl, Juana. The two of them were getting on famously, and Stacy didn't mind admitting now that a companion was not such a bad idea after all. It *had* been lonely up at the main house and another female around was a luxury Stacy had missed more than she'd realized. Too, the Navajo girl somehow contributed to a spirit of normality around the ranch that Cam was quick to note had been missing ever since he had arrived. It was hard to believe the difference one little girl could make.

But this was only partial compensation for the problems that remained. Stacy Brightwood's ranch was suffering through stormy times. Her store had no customers, the great majority of her cattle were missing, and still Dan Stanhope and the men he had promised to bring with him failed to show up.

Cam rode out early on the tenth day, alone. He had waited around all he was going to. He was restless; he needed to get on with the problems at hand. Time and again he had taken out his now well-worn maps and studied them, his thoughts inevitably coming to rest on Cross Arrow range and the missing Stretch B cattle, a continuing intrigue that he could no longer put off investigating.

Stacy had begged him not to go alone, and he supposed he knew better than to do so. But on this occasion at least he wasn't about to take her with him; and if he left her, then he felt he had to leave Jaz as well. With Jozie still recovering and Miguel so old, only Jaz was fit protection for the place and the women. Maybe there was and maybe there wasn't any real danger, but that's the way he saw it. Too—and maybe more the reason anyway—he wanted to be alone. The disappointment of Stanhope not showing up had weighed on him most heavily because he had promised Stacy that the man would come. It was a failure he was already sick and tired of facing, and at the ranch that seemed about all he could do—sit and face it. Not his way at all.

Astride that same smooth-gaited sorrel he had ridden to the Cross Arrow on the one earlier occasion, he struck out across the edge of the plains, rode past Paint Horse Springs and the towering sandstone mesa of that same name, and finally turned southward amid the juniper-cloaked hillsides that formed the imaginary boundary between Stretch B and Cross Arrow range. He was well armed and at all times alert. He had no intention of winding up like Jozie, and he knew he might not go unwatched. Still, though he saw more and more cattle as he went, not once did he see any other riders.

He rode slowly, and along about noon stopped to rest his horse and to eat lunch. There was no water save for that in his canteen, and for the latter he was particularly thankful. The day was perhaps the hottest of the year thus far, and the summer rains had not yet arrived to cool things down.

But it wasn't just hot; the country was becoming alarmingly dry. As a result, in some areas forage was already in short supply. Compounding the problem, on the Cross Arrow what grass there was appeared to be seriously overgrazed. This seemed a waste, for on the lightly grazed plains country to the west, spring growth remained faintly green and plenty of dry feed still existed from the year before; cattle there could go yet a month or more and never suffer, rain or no rain. Here, things were already going from bad to worse and before long would represent real trouble if the rains did not come.

Cam wondered several times if the Cross Arrow practiced such overgrazing as a matter of habit but decided after a while that there were no signs of such a history. The grasses here were good and had not been replaced by those inferior species typical of a range long overgrazed; the area was admittedly overstocked, but this was not, Cam was convinced, a routine practice.

So what was going on? Certainly this was the farthest he had ever penetrated Cross Arrow range, especially from this direction, and he'd had no idea how many cattle would be here.

He consulted his maps again. He wasn't exactly sure where he was but thought he was yet eight or ten miles from Cross Arrow headquarters—mostly to the south and some west of his present location. This was far enough away that he was beginning to hope his little sojourn might actually go undetected, although whether it did or not made little difference to his decision to go ahead. His curiosity was whetted more than ever now; he had no intention of turning back.

Contributing to this was the fact that he had begun to observe more and more Stretch B brands, mostly on she-stock without calves, on yearlings, and only rarely on a cow with an unbranded calf. At first this seemed odd, here deep within Cross Arrow range. But then he thought: *Didn't I expect this? Isn't this the reason I came here in the first place? The Stretch B herd has to be someplace, doesn't it?* Trouble was, he still had not found enough of them. He was looking for two thousand, not a hundred or two hundred, and the latter was the most he had seen so far.

About two miles from where he'd eaten lunch he came out upon a high juniper- and piñon-clad ridge. He had been climbing for some while, a gradual incline that suddenly culminated in a high point that then ran off to the east to form a ridge. The south side was very steep and overlooked a lower country that was vast in its many hills and tiny valleys and occasional isolated mesas. Cam didn't know much about geology, but if he had, he would have described it as a crazy mixture of sandstone and basalt and even limestone, the lower areas open, the hills and ridges tree-dotted or lined. For a while he simply sat and looked, his eyes narrowed in an attempt to scan every visible part of it.

Presently he picked out a long rift in the landscape, not immediately distinct from his view, but upon some study recognizable as a narrow valley running west to east for a matter of several miles. He wished he had a glass with which he could get a closer look, but even without such an aid he was fairly certain of what he was looking at. He had studied the maps in his saddlebags so many times, had asked Stacy so many questions about the area, that he hardly needed to consult anything more than his memory now. Without a doubt, this had to be what Stacy had labeled the valley of Red Creek, where Terhune ordinarily wintered a large part of his herd. According to the girl, the valley was perhaps eight miles long and two miles across at its widest point; a live creek ran throughout much of its length; and it had good grass that was almost never used in summer. Also, it was more or less enclosed, quite isolated from other ranches, and intrigued Cam no end. He would very much like to get a closer look . . .

But even as he thought this, something else caught his eye: a drifting dust cloud coming from someplace near the head of the valley. Distant low hills blocked his view in such a way that he could not have told what was causing it even with a glass, but this did not reduce his curiosity in the slightest.

Carefully he studied the slope to his immediate fore, looking for a way down. It would not be easy, but after a few moments he thought he had discovered what he was looking for; he spurred the sorrel in that direction.

CHAPTER 12

Red Creek had as its source three large springs that never went dry. A small but perennial stream was formed that snaked eastward for almost ten miles before joining a larger drainage yet, its waters by then disappearing in the thirsty sands of the second streambed, this one normally being dry the year around except for an occasional violent summer flood.

About a mile downstream from the head of Red Creek spread a broad, grassy flat. The creek trickled innocently down its center, and canyon walls reared on its either side. A quarter of a mile below this the canyon narrowed into a box before opening out into the valley Cam had observed.

Across the mouth of the box stretched a barbed-wire fence, one of the few thus far constructed in the area. Its materials were new; it had been installed only recently.

Near the center of the flat a group of riders encircled a herd of about 150 dusty, milling, bawling cattle, while two other riders moved carefully among them on well-trained cutting horses. Off to one side a smaller herd was forming, composed of animals cut from the first herd and driven there one or two at a time by the two riders. Another group of riders were charged with holding the second herd and keeping them from bolting back—not an easy task, to be sure.

Sitting her horse comfortably back from the action, beneath a lone but well-branched ponderosa pine, Mala Terhune was watching. Her husband Gerd had just ridden up to stop beside her.

"How many Stretch Bs do you figure?" she asked.

Terhune shrugged. "Hard to tell. I'd guess maybe half the herd. The rest are Cross Arrow and maybe a few Circle Rs."

"And how many in the valley?"

"Last count, just over fifteen hundred head, not counting calves."

She considered briefly. "That's around half of my sister's total herd—but is it enough?"

"Depends. Half is half. Half again is scattered across Cross Arrow range and the mesa country north of here. Your sister and her men have been working, trying to get all they can out onto the plains. That's Stallings' doing, I reckon. But, yeah, I'd say half is enough for the valley, especially when the half we've got includes three out of four of her cows with this year's calves. Too, the valley probably won't hold many more. Like I've been telling you, we'll be short of grass there by fall just as we already are everywhere else. If it doesn't rain this summer, we'll be completely out long before that."

"I anticipate having Stretch B range to run on by fall, Gerd," Mala reminded him crisply. "I wish you would remember that."

Gerd Terhune ground his palms uncomfortably against his saddle horn. "That's all well and good to say," he muttered, "but it's a bad plan that doesn't allow for something to go wrong. I know that as well as I know anything—and you ought to."

"But what can go wrong, Gerd? Just tell me, what?"

"Well, Stallings, for one thing. I went along with you trying to hire him when I knew you couldn't; you should've gone along with me when I wanted to let Guerrero or Pit get rid of him. Mark my words, you damn sure should've!"

"But what can *he* do?" she insisted, irritated that he had found a way to bring it up again. "He is only one man, Gerd. Surely one man against this big tough crew of yours isn't going to upset things."

"He can if he finds out too much," Terhune warned stubbornly. "And believe me, Mala, this deal is shaky when it comes to dealing with a real cowman. Which is just what Stallings is. I've had the boys watching him off and on. He knows something's up, I know he does. And if he ever sniffs out exactly what it is, well, the only thing going for us then is he doesn't have a crew. Just him, the girl, and the two Navvies—and one of them has been out of commission lately, thanks to Max." He sort of chuckled at this last thought.

For once, however, Mala's own expression was one of serious concern. "What about the other ranchers, Gerd? They are cowmen. Are you sure they won't interfere?"

He shrugged in uncertainty at this. "They haven't so far, only because they're too scared to even want to know what's happening. But I have to warn you, Mala, if they ever do, if they ever get together on it, this deal will turn the Cross Arrow into an outlaw outfit for sure." He paused. "I want the Stretch B as much as you do, but there are risks. You've got to understand that. And as far as I'm concerned, that Stallings is the guy who's most likely to put it all together for the other side."

"But how? You said yourself he has no crew. How can he do anything?"

"By being curious, mostly. By letting the cat out of the bag if he ever stumbles onto the valley and all those Stretch B cows, that's how!"

Mala's eyes were wide with concern now. "But you have the valley guarded at all times . . ."

He shook his head vigorously. "Not fully, we don't. We've fenced both ends, but we only guard this end and certainly not the whole thing. It would take a hundred men to do that. There aren't many ways the cows can get out, but there are any number of ways a smart rider—or even several—can get in without passing our guards. Any number of ways."

The concern on the woman's face deepened; still there was doubt.

"Look," Terhune said, "it's one thing for Stretch B cattle to be scattered some away from Stretch B range. Without a crew, no one's surprised when their outfit has a poor spring gather. But for fifteen hundred head to be found all in one place, well, that's no accident and only a fool would assume so. Lucky for us, that valley is square in the middle of Cross Arrow range; it's an out-of-the-way place for anyone but us to go to. And we're counting on that, for all we have to do is hold the herd till fall, wean the unbranded calves, then push the cows gradually back onto their own home range. We brand the calves and every maverick we find with the Cross Arrow and scatter them among our own. Next year or the year after we sell them as ones or twos. In the meantime, your sister goes begging once again and hopefully broke. It's our ticket to the ranch, of course. But let the word get out what we've done and those other ranchers may not be so scared anymore. They'll realize we can do the same thing to them, and then's when they'll band together and maybe even bring the law in. We can't stand that, Mala. We can't stand for your man Stallings to find out and spill the beans on us. Do you see what I mean?"

"Yes." She nodded slowly now. "Yes, I do see."

"Well, then?"

"I don't want Stacy to have the Stretch B, Gerd. You know that."

He looked hopeful. "Then you'd be willing to let Guerrero or Pit handle Stallings, like I say? You'd be willing to see him dead if necessary?"

For a moment it appeared she would not answer. Her eyes seemed glued to the grassy flat before them, as if some strange inner conflict plagued her desperately. But actually her decision was predetermined. If it meant risking the one thing she wanted most—full share in the Stretch B—then nothing or no one was too good to be sacrificed. Gerd Terhune was sorely aware of this and for once was even glad to have it to bank on.

Not surprisingly, when she looked up, her expression was once again a steady one.

"I am willing to do whatever has to be done," she said simply. "When and if the time comes, whatever needs to be done."

Cam sat his horse atop a far ridge. He was concealed by brush and had been sitting patiently that way for a good half hour, studying the grassy flat below. From his vantage point, everything down there was antlike; he had no way of telling who was who, and he didn't even see the two riders located off to the side and shielded by the shade of the pine tree. But he could tell well enough what was going on otherwise.

It explained the dust cloud that had attracted him in the first place: cattle being worked; two bunches, one smaller but growing, the other larger but shrinking as certain animals were being cut away and removed to the second herd. All very intriguing indeed, as far as Cam was concerned.

From the first, he had realized that there were some good cowhands down there. Already the two herds had become approximately equal in size and were being quietly milled by the riders, who were making sure that each calf was properly "mothered" with its rightful mama before anything else was done. When this was completed, what was left of the original herd were then allowed to wander off as they pleased, while the second bunch was driven on down the creek toward a narrow, straight-walled box in the canyon. Cam watched wonderingly as these cattle disappeared from sight beyond the box entrance, then as all but three of the riders who had driven them there a few minutes later reappeared on their way back to the grassy flat. Following this, the two observers Cam had not seen before emerged, and the entire party rode off and disappeared in the trees to the south.

For a while Cam stayed where he was. Mostly he was studying the mouth of the box. He knew the valley of Red Creek opened out beyond somewhere, and he was fully aware that three riders had remained at the entrance. Why? Well, he was almost certain they were guarding it. Again—why? Cam had to know, for certainly there was nothing normal about it. But how was he going to get past those three guards?

As it turned out, there was nothing spectacular to be done. He was forced to spend the time it took to circle out of sight back to the north, then curl again eastward until he approached the valley rim at a point well below the box. Here he had an excellent view of the valley and could see quite large numbers of cattle scattered along its base. The Stretch B herd, perhaps? Cam never doubted that it was . . . but how was he going to get down there to make sure? He looked around. A way could probably be found, but at most he had two hours of fading daylight in which to make his way down and get back out again. Was it worth it? Could he possibly be wrong in what he thought? Could he in any way afford to leave without making absolutely sure that he was not?

Presently, he made up his mind. He searched around until he found a trail, then without further hesitation proceeded to wind his way down into the valley.

Shortly past noon the following day, he rode back into the Stretch B. Stacy met him at the corrals and quickly became absorbed in the news he had to tell.

"Apparently the Cross Arrow has been running a gather of their own ever since early spring," Cam told her as he unsaddled his horse. "Only they've been concentrating on *your* cows, especially those with unbranded calves. I didn't have time to ride the whole valley, but I know I saw over five hundred head, and my guess is that's no more than a third of what's down there."

Stacy's mouth formed an O as she stared at him in disbelief. "Why, that could mean as many as fifteen hundred head! Oh, Cam, can it really be?"

"At least that," he affirmed. "And maybe more. The Terhunes are overgrazing some of their own range to make room for them, but I figure they've been gathering your stuff since well before the spring roundup. I know because I saw them doing it just yesterday."

"Do you think that could be what those riders you saw over near Loco Creek were doing? Driving off Stretch B cattle?"

"At the time I doubted it," he said. "But now I wouldn't be surprised. It's pretty brazen, but I have a feeling they figure as long as they're dealing with small bunches of mixed Cross Arrow and Stretch B stuff, they can explain their way out of it if anyone stumbles onto them. If no one does, so much the better, of course."

Stacy wagged her head. "How can they possibly hope to get away with it? And what on earth do they think they're going to do with Stretch B branded cows? They can't just sell them as their own, can they?"

Cam dumped his saddle on the ground and pulled the bridle headstall over the weary sorrel's ears. "I have no idea about the cows, but like I've told you before, I think the calves will eventually be weaned and branded Cross Arrow, then mixed with the rest of the Terhune herd for the winter. Any unbranded yearlings or two-year-olds they've managed to bring in will probably be branded and sold this fall. By next year, this year's calves will be sold right along with other Cross

Arrow beef of the same age. And you, of course, will be all but out of business."

"Won't they be selling an unusually large number of cattle for the size cow herd they have? Won't people wonder how they managed to have so many calves in one year?"

"Probably, they won't sell them all in one herd, and who other than themselves will have a complete count anyway. Besides, I have a feeling their aim is to have you off the Stretch B and gone before they ever sell a one, and if they succeed, this ranch too will be theirs. I doubt if anyone outside the Terhunes would ever know the difference."

Stacy leaned back against the corral fence in a dejected pose. "As you say, it's brazen. Horribly, horribly brazen. And Red Creek—almost no one outside Cross Arrow people themselves ever goes there."

"I have a feeling they're counting on that, all right," he said, then thought for a few moments before asking, "How well do you know that valley, Stacy? Have you been there many times?"

She shook her head. "Only once, and that was before Terhune came to settle the Cross Arrow. But I remember it as steep-walled and very long, with access mostly on each end. A box in the canyon on the west, an open-mouthed valley to the east, and tough going to get out just about anywhere in between."

He nodded very slowly. "That's my impression, too. Except, as I said, I didn't have time to ride it from end to end. I was sort of hoping there would be a good way to drive cattle out besides one of the ends."

She looked up curiously. "Why? What difference does that make?"

"Well, I don't know about the east end, but the mouth of that box on the west is guarded and, I think, fenced. It'll cause us some problems because it's beginning to look like the only way for us to come out with the cattle."

"Come out . . . ?" She thought about the words as she said them. Then she asked, "Fenced? Did you say fenced?"

"I couldn't swear to that, but I thought I could make out a line of posts . . . I figure barbed wire."

"Barbed wire!" Again she looked thoughtful. "Well, I guess I'm not surprised. Is it likely they've fenced the other end, too?"

"Probably. Chances are ninety percent of those cows will never leave the valley if they can't go either of the two easy ways. And no use us driving them east. I figure we'll have to bring them through that box to get them out and back to the Stretch B . . ."

Her eyes widened. "We? Did you say we are going to bring them through the box?"

He gave her a patient look. "The Terhunes are not going to just deliver them to you on demand, Stacy. And since they haven't actually branded any of your calves with their Cross Arrow yet, I doubt if we could get the law to help even if we could get the law to come here. So, yes, I think *we* are going to have to bring them out."

"Just go and bring them home like so many milch cows, right? You, me, Jaz, and Jozie . . . just like that?"

He shook his head. "We'll have to drum up some help first, of course. I haven't given up on that. Naturally we can't do it with just the four of us. Fact is, I still have hopes that Dan Stanhope will finally show up. I . . ."

Something in her expression suddenly caused him to break off, and Stacy looked away as she said, "That's something I haven't had a chance to tell you about yet, Cam. Something that happened while you were gone."

He frowned. "What? What's happened? Did Stanhope come?"

She shook her head sadly. "Not exactly. But it has to do with him." She paused, then went on. "Yesterday a man stopped at the store, a rider passing through on his way north. He had just come from Vera Velarde. He had a message from Blake Stoddard—you remember him, don't you? The blacksmith who sold you the saddle? Anyway, Blake had asked the man to stop here with a message for you."

Again she paused, and Cam said, "Go on."

"Stanhope is in Vera Velarde, Cam. Blake found him passed out in an empty horse stall two nights ago. He'd been drinking, and he was alone. He mentioned your name, but then wouldn't tell Blake why. Blake thought maybe he should let you know. He thought maybe you'd want to come and see him for yourself."

For a moment Cam just stared at her, then tiredly he reached down, picked up his bridle, and started looking around the corral for a fresh horse.

CHAPTER 13

Cam rode into Vera Velarde just after dark and went directly to Stoddard's livery barn. The town seemed quiet enough as lights blinked innocently from house windows and street traffic was all but nil. Stoddard was in the process of shutting down his forge and looked as if he was just about ready to leave for the night.

The big smith ushered Cam directly inside and pulled both of the big double barn doors closed behind them. The place was dimly lit by a single bull's-eye lantern hanging near the forge.

"You got my message, I reckon," the blacksmith said, somewhat relieved. "I've been looking for you all day."

"I came straight here the minute I got the word," Cam explained. "Where's Stanhope?"

Disappointment claimed Stoddard's expression as he said, "He's not here. I haven't seen him since noon and my guess is he's down at McKenzie's trying to drink himself unconscious again. I'd've dragged him back here a long time ago, but he's a grown man and I didn't figure he'd stay anyway."

Cam wagged his head sadly. "You're probably right. Didn't he tell you anything about why he came back?"

Stoddard nodded. "At first he was mum as hell, but finally he did tell me you'd gone to Springerville to get him and that he'd promised to be back on the Stretch B within five days. Said he was supposed to bring some men with him. Best I can tell, that's why he never showed. He's looked up every ex-Stretch B man he could find between here and the Arizona line and nary a one would come with him. Imagine that, nary a one!"

Cam removed his hat and plopped down wearily on a bench located against a near wall. "They're that scared, I guess," he said.

Stoddard only gave a little grunt of disgust. "I don't know exactly what's going on out there, but I've known the Brightwoods for a long time and they were always good to their hands. I figure Miss Stacy deserves something better for it than a bunch of people running scared on her!"

"Not only deserves," Cam said, "*needs*. She is in desperate need of better than that right now . . ."

Stoddard's expression of concern deepened noticeably. "What *is* going on out there, Stallings? Exactly, I mean—between Stacy and the Terhunes?"

Cam met his gaze. The man's demeanor showed more than just a passing interest. "You really want to know? The whole story?"

"Anything you want to tell me," the other man said sincerely. "Anything at all."

Cam studied him. This was an honest man here, a good man whose concern was obviously very real. Something in his tone, too, told Cam that the man might potentially be more than just a talking ally, perhaps much more. Without further hesitation, he went on to relate everything from the strange disappearance of the main Stretch B herd to what he'd found only the day before along the valley of Red Creek. He made it clear, also, what he thought the Terhunes' game was and did not stop short of calling it outright rustling, or at least the intent to do so.

Stoddard, listening intently throughout, gave a low whistle and wagged his head when Cam was finished. "It's not saying much for the onetime neighbors and friends of Amos Brightwood, that they'd sit back and let such as this happen."

Cam shrugged. "Well, to be fair, most are like you—they just didn't know. Of course they may have looked the other way on occasion, I can't deny that—"

"And you don't have to accept it," Stoddard inserted quickly. "You can give them a chance to make up for it now, just like you did Dan Stanhope—and me. You can make sure they know the whole story. You can make sure that if they really wanta help they've got the chance."

Cam smiled thinly. "And relieve them of all excuses at the same time, huh? Yeah, I've thought of that. I even made it a point to visit Ressler, Crawford, and McNaab on my way back from Arizona, although that was before I knew what I know now about what's going on at Red Creek. But you've seen what success I've had with Stanhope, and what success he's had with his old crew. Why should I expect any more from anyone else?"

"You haven't failed with Stanhope yet," Stoddard said in a positive tone. "And as for the ranchers, they may not know it yet but it's in their interest to help; it's in all of our interest, townspeople too. It's just that not many have ever realized how big the problem is. And if what you tell me is so—and I'm sure it is—then the Cross Arrow has become an outlaw outfit if ever one existed. If they're gonna swindle and steal and get away with it, then we'll all suffer, for they'll be just that much harder to stop the next time. They'll decide why not do it again with such as Lester McNaab or Reece Crawford or even Mitch Ressler. And why not start pushing their way around Vera Velarde?—as if they weren't already, in some ways. Why not elect themselves a marshal, a town council, a mayor they can call their own? Why not buy out this business and that? Why not just run everybody and everything? Which makes it more than just the Stretch B in trouble, you see. We all are—we've just been too damn big a bunch of scared-sightless fools to see it."

Somehow Cam couldn't imagine Blake Stoddard as ever having been "scared sightless," but in general he was quick to see the depth of the man's insight. He also thought he detected something else. "Are you saying you would help us? *You?*"

Stoddard never hesitated. "That's exactly what I'm saying. I've done a bit of cowboying in my time, and if you wanta go drag Stanhope over here, I'll help you sober him up and then be the first volunteer for your new crew. And if you wanta go straight out to Red Creek to bring back those Stretch B cows, why, I'll strap on a gun to boot—just in case good old Cross Arrow shows up for a fight. How about that?"

"What about your business here?" Cam asked, grateful but at the same time trying to think of the other man first.

"I can always get somebody to watch over things around here for a few days," Stoddard said. "You just say when you want me, and I'll go. A day at the most is all I'll need to get ready, less if necessary."

"Well, I'll be damned!" Cam breathed. "Look, as long as you understand what you're letting yourself in for, there's no way I can turn an offer like that down. And if it's decided that we're in business, why, I'll start right out by taking your advice and going after Stanhope. It may not do much good, but I hate not to try one more time. We need every man we can get, if you know what I mean."

Stoddard gave him an understanding nod. "I know. What's more, I wouldn't give up on Dan too quick, either. If you ever do get him back on the Stretch B and can keep him sober, then I think he'll be as much help to you as one man can be."

"What should I do with him for tonight? Can he stay here?"

"Sure. I have a couple of cots in the back. You can stay, too, if you like. It's not quite a hotel, but it's not much worse than the one we've got, either. Tell you what, you go on and get Stanhope; I'll tend to your horse and a few other chores and still be here when you get back. Then we'll talk and make plans. How's that sound?"

"Sounds great," Cam said. "Purely great."

* * *

Great, however, is not always as great as it sounds. Even before he reached the place, Cam could tell that the crowd inside McKenzie's was going to be nothing similar to what it had been on his first visit there. That had been in midafternoon when things were slow. Now, loud voices, laughter, and the tinny pitch of a poorly played piano carried to him from half a block away. There was life in the old place tonight, no doubt about that.

As he drew closer, he noted that directly across the street from the saloon was the town's lone hotel—one of those ten-room tinderboxes that by policy required doubling up to get a bed—and that a certain amount of foot traffic between the two establishments was occurring. This seemed natural enough to him, and perhaps because of this and the number of people about, he failed to recognize at least one individual he should have, who preceded him by a full minute inside the saloon. Cam took immediate notice, however, of the sudden cessation of the piano music and hush of voices that occurred inside even before he himself reached the still lightly swinging front doors.

An inner caution caused him to hesitate and peer over the batwings before entering. The place smelled like beer, cheap whiskey, and sawdust, and was indeed filled to capacity with patrons. Hardly a table seemed empty and tobacco smoke formed a thick haze throughout the room. Many of the customers were in their chairs, but many more were on their feet, crowding more or less against the near end of the bar and looking toward the back of the room. Those nearest Cam had formed a tight knot and were effectively blocking his view. The bartender—not the same one who had been there during Cam's earlier visit to the place —was looking around apprehensively, as if for help. Someone beyond the pack of onlookers was talking, but Cam could not see who it was or make out what was being said. All others were breathlessly silent.

Quietly, Cam pushed his way through the doors. Nobody seemed to notice him. For a moment he just stood there, unsure what to do next. Then a crashing of tables and chairs sounded from beyond the crowd and someone called out:

"Aw, c'mon, Max—he's not even sober. Let him alone."

Cam froze. *Max!*

"Who is it? Who said that?" The voice from beyond the crowd was an angry growl. No one answered, and the voice went on, justifying its owner's actions perhaps needlessly. "You know who this is? It's Stanhope, by God! I told him not to never come back . . . by God, I told him!"

Cam edged his way in among the crowd, trying desperately to see. No one challenged him and with little trouble he achieved a position looking between two heads and over another. What he saw was the broad back of big Max Gruel, and just beyond, a rumpled, unshaven Dan Stanhope just coming to his feet from amid a pile of overturned chairs. There was blood on his mouth, and he appeared dangerously unsteady on his feet.

"You're a bastard, Gruel," Stanhope said bitterly. "You were then and you are now."

The big man, instead of reacting angrily, seemed almost pleased as he turned to face the onlookers. An evil-looking grin spread across his face as he growled, "Now did you hear that? Did you hear what he called me? Anybody expect me to stand here and take that? Anybody atall?"

No one said a thing. Gruel grinned a little more broadly and bobbed his head in an I-thought-so manner, then started to turn back to Stanhope, who now had the look of a man who had just signed his own death warrant and knew it. Cam, sensing a moment in which something must be done, looked quickly around the room. He had no way of knowing if Gruel was the only Cross Arrow man here, except there were none he himself could identify. No Guerrero, no Emory, no Carty. But there could be others he wouldn't recognize—a chance to take, he knew.

When he spoke, his voice almost seemed as if it had come from someone else, another bystander. He was tense and was surprised that the words came out at all.

"*What's that?*" Gruel whirled around. "*Who said that?*"

"I did," Cam said, and the two men on either side of him stepped away as if burned. Those to his front and back reacted the same way and quite suddenly Cam found himself standing there all alone.

"You're so interested in beating up on Stretch B riders," he said again, "why not take on one who's not drunk or being held by your cronies while you work on him?"

Max Gruel stared at him, at first unbelievingly and without recognition. Then, suddenly, his eyes lit up and his smile began to return.

"Well, I'll be," he said. "If it isn't our Mr. Malpais Man! Big shot with a shotgun, right? Oh yeah, I remember you!" He advanced a couple of steps menacingly.

Cam knew this was crazy. Although he was virtually the same height as Gruel, at no time in his life had he ever weighed more than 170 pounds. Gruel weighed 250 if he weighed one. And although Cam had had his share of fist fights over the years, it was plain that his opponent had all but made a living of it, might even have fought professionally at some time or another. Certainly the scar tissue over the eyes and the telltale flattened nose would seem to attest to the fact. And those huge shoulders and trunklike arms—a single bear hug alone could crush a man Cam's size into soup.

"Well, Mr. Mouth," the big man said. "I been kinda lookin' forward to a shot at you. You gonna try to take me, are you?"

Cam looked around the room. The onlookers had cleared back now and were eying him with anticipation. He couldn't tell if they were for him or against him, but they expected him to fight, that much was clear.

"Don't do it, Stallings!" Dan Stanhope cried out, leaning against the far end of the bar for support now and just able to stay on his feet even with that. "He'll kill you, man! Don't do it!"

But Cam was trapped. He'd bought his way in and he knew there was only one way to buy his way back out; he would either whip or get whipped, no two ways about it.

"Are you gonna take your gun off?" he asked Gruel, somewhat less forcefully than he would have liked.

The big man never hesitated; quickly he unbuckled his belt and laid the gun atop the bar. Then he looked expectantly at Cam, who much more slowly and with less relish followed suit. The bartender offered a sympathetic glance as Cam laid the gun on the bar, but looked as if that was all the support he was brave enough to offer otherwise.

Cam squared his shoulders, knowing that any time he had to plan an attack was severely limited. His one advantage, he figured, was his size. Not because of his speed—although he did suspect that he should be a good deal the faster of the two—for that could be worn down eventually by superior firepower. No, it was something Cam had always held to: if you are David and some Goliath presumes to take advantage of your smaller stature in a fist fight, then all is fair for David to do whatever he has to do to win. And if Max Gruel wasn't a Goliath and Cam Stallings a David, he had no idea who ever had been since the original pair! Trouble was, where this time was David's slingshot going to come from?

Gruel moved toward him, grinning, his fists upraised. Cam kicked a couple of chairs out of the way and started to move around, assuming likewise a pugilist's pose but playing for time more than anything else.

Not surprisingly, it was Gruel who struck first, or at least attempted to—a lunging right hand that whistled over Cam's head. Cam didn't have a chance to counterpunch; he just ducked beneath the man's arm and came up behind him. Gruel whirled with surprising speed and threw another punch, a left this time that likewise drew air above his opponent's bobbing head. Cam got in a left to the ribs, felt as if he'd belted a tree, and was propelled backward by a lumbering right that caught him squarely on the left shoulder. He hit the bar and managed to roll away just in time to avoid being pinned there by the other man's weight.

"C'mon and fight," Gruel snarled as they squared around once more.

Cam took a quick glance around. The crowd was on its feet almost to a man now. Tables had been pulled back out of the way and the fighters were almost completely encircled by onlookers. Dan Stanhope had somehow become lost in the crowd, and Cam felt even more trapped than before.

Gruel came at him again, this time flailing away wildly with both hands. Cam tried again to duck beneath the blows, but it was almost inevitable that the ploy would eventually cease to work. He caught one blow in the ribs, another atop the head, and yet another on his still numb left shoulder. He went down under the onslaught, and Gruel stumbled over him and fell just beyond.

Somehow Cam got to his feet before the big man could come back to cover him. The smell of sawdust from the floor was thick in his nostrils and he knew it was all over him as well now. A terrible pain sliced through his ribs; the top of his head felt as if someone had hit him there with a hammer. But he was not groggy, and something inside told him move fast, move fast . . .

Gruel came again, head down, swinging viciously in an effort to bludgeon Cam back to the floor. This time Cam darted to the side at the last moment and the man charged past him like a bull beneath a matador's cape. When Gruel tried to turn back to see where his opponent had gone, Cam hit him a solid left to the eye and followed with a quick right to the mouth. The big man bellowed as Cam danced hastily back out of reach.

He had drawn blood now; the man's lips were split and teeth probably had been loosened. And there was a swelling beneath the right eye —the first hopeful sign yet to Cam. Maybe, just maybe, it would swell enough to hamper Gruel's eyesight. Maybe . . .

But the bigger man only seemed to grin through the blood, as if pain was what it took to really warm him up to the fight. And this time he moved in more slowly, more with the purpose in mind of cornering Cam against the bar or the crowd. His breathing had grown heavy and air seemed to whistle between his mangled lips as he sucked in, but still he came on.

Cam attempted to dance first to one side then the other, hoping to confuse his man. But Gruel proved that he had been in more than a few fights with adversaries cagier than Cam. He feinted with a right as Cam tried to go left, then caught him a crunching left hook to the side of the head as he tried to go the other way. Cam reeled, took a glancing right to the jaw, and crashed into the bar, the room suddenly spinning, lights flashing, and his eyes fogging.

He would have gone down except Gruel moved in and caught him by the shirt front, holding him up. Groggily and in pain, he felt himself being spun around toward the crowd, and vaguely knew that he was being measured for a blow that would send him to the floor.

Dazedly, he told himself: *One more punch and you're helpless, Stallings. You are gonna get pulverized, beat into meat, maybe even killed . . .*

He flailed away desperately at the other man's head. It was no good. Gruel held him at arm's length and only laughed. The crowd yelled— Cam had no idea whom they were favoring, if anyone—and he steeled himself for the blow he knew was coming.

And come it did. He didn't see it, but he would have sworn he heard that big, hamlike fist swishing through the air. Pinpoint lights flashed and he felt as if airborne for a moment before landing on a table and hearing its legs crash out from under him as the whole thing went down.

He lay there, somehow not unconscious, trying desperately to clear his head yet fully expecting the next blows to come before he could do so.

But then, from somewhere off to the side, he heard Gruel cursing. Hazily he saw the big man struggling with someone who had apparently come at him from behind. Somehow, from somewhere, Dan Stanhope had reappeared and was now attached as firmly to the big man's back as a black bear cub to a tree limb swinging in the wind.

For a moment it was almost comical; the crowd hollered and hooted. But then Gruel managed to get a grip on the smaller man, and presently Stanhope went flying. He landed in a heap against the footrail of the bar, apparently hitting hard. He did not immediately get up.

"I'll . . . be back for you . . . in a minute . . . you bastard . . ." Gruel snarled between heavy breaths; then he turned back to his first opponent. "I'm gonna . . . bust you good now, Malpais Man. Bust you good . . ."

Cam tried desperately to get to his feet. He knew he must not let Gruel get to him while he was down. But his legs gave way as he was almost up, and he collapsed back on the fallen table top. Then Gruel was standing over him, apparently debating whether to reach down and maul him senseless with his hands or kick him to death.

Once again Cam steeled himself, and as he did so his hand closed around something: a broken table leg, a weapon, the proverbial equalizer—*David's slingshot!* He gripped it only a split second before he felt the first crunching blow from Gruel's heavy boot to his ribs. He groaned and doubled up in pain, pulling the table leg under him as he did, then felt another blow, this time obviously aimed at his groin but glancing off his right hip instead.

But he still had the table leg. Whether Gruel had seen it or paid it any attention he did not know. It didn't matter. Another kick would be coming. He had to act fast . . .

Summoning all of his remaining strength and quickness, he suddenly swung a backhand, coming around level with the floor, and both felt and heard the heavy crack of wood against bone as the table leg contacted a shin.

Gruel screamed and sank to his knees, cursing. Cam scrambled to his knees, somehow dropping the table leg but not caring now. With all his might he swung a left for the jaw, catching Gruel hard and sending him over backward. Then Cam was on top of him, raining blows to the head, thinking of Stanhope, of Jozie, of himself, of the Stretch B, not caring if he actually killed the man or not. He just wanted to beat him, beat him into total submission, punish him as he had punished Jozie and Dan Stanhope and all those others before . . .

But then he was being pulled away and a familiar voice was calling in his ear: "Stallings—*for chrissake, Stallings!* He's out cold, man!"

It was Blake Stoddard. "C'mon, man. You've whipped him. No one around here has ever done that before, even with a stick!" He seemed to be smiling, and all around men were talking and laughing, and one even slapped Cam on the back in apparent congratulations.

The blacksmith was no longer smiling, however. "I came as soon as I heard. But look, you're lucky Gruel was in here alone tonight. No telling what would've happened if he wasn't. We've got to get you out of here."

Cam just stared at him. His ears were still ringing, his head throbbing, his eyes not yet fully focusing. His hands hurt all the way to the wrists and his knuckles were bleeding; his ribs felt caved in and it hurt just to breathe; he even felt sick, like he might throw up at any moment. Who cared what would have happened? Who gave a damn?

But Stoddard was insistent. "Hey—are you okay? Do you understand what I said?"

Cam looked around. Stanhope was on his feet by the bar, looking wobbly but somewhat sobered from before. Others were straightening up the furniture and a couple were evidently checking Gruel to see if he was alive.

"Yeah, I'm okay," he mumbled. "I understand."

"Good. Can you ride?"

"Ride? Why?"

"Because we've gotta get you and Stanhope out of town. Tonight—before any of Gruel's gunny pards show up. They'll kill you for sure if we don't!"

CHAPTER 14

Cam and Stanhope rode into the Stretch B at midmorning the next day. Both looked a good deal the worse for wear, and the fact did not escape Stacy for a moment.

She met them at the corrals along with Jaz, Jozie, and old Miguel. Only Juana, the Navajo girl, was not present; she had remained at the main house. "Dan Stanhope! I'm glad to see you again, but I never thought I'd see you looking like this! And Cam . . . your face and your hands! Have you been in a fight?"

One entire side of his face hurt when he tried to smile. "Sort of," he said and then went on to relate to her what had happened. "We are going after the cattle, Stacy," he added as he finished. "Stoddard stayed behind to arrange for someone to take care of his forge and stable, but I expect him here by tomorrow noon at the latest."

"Blake Stoddard." She repeated the name thoughtfully. "Always a good man and a good friend to the Stretch B. But somehow I hate to drag him into this. Mala is not going to react kindly toward us if we manage to get those cattle back. And certainly it may be dangerous trying . . ."

"He's not being dragged, Stacy," Cam said. "He insisted. Said it was about time folks woke up to the fact that it could affect them as well as the Stretch B."

"Well, about time is right! But even so, he and Dan here make only two more men. Will that be enough?"

Cam and Stanhope exchanged glances, and Cam said, "We talked about it all the way here, Stacy. We've decided it will."

She looked at Stanhope. "Dan?"

"Actually, it's more my contention than it is Cam's," he admitted frankly. "I know that valley like the back of my hand. It's made to order for an easy gather—one of the few places in that country that is. It's a slight upgrade coming west until sometime after you leave the box, but from there on it's all downhill to the plains. And if there's any direction those Stretch B cows will wanta go on their own, it's toward the plains. Believe me, I think we can do it, if we can just get them beyond the box."

Stacy still looked a bit skeptical. "Cam says the box has been fenced, Dan—that it is guarded night and day. What if you're discovered?"

"There's that risk, all right," Stanhope acknowledged. "But it's also the one thing a few can avoid better than a lot. We'll be forced to do our work at night, to do everything we know how to do to get those cattle out before the Cross Arrow knows what's happened, to avoid a confrontation rather than to cause one."

Stacy frowned, puzzled, and Cam said, "Stacy, Blake Stoddard thinks, now that the Terhunes' scheme is in the open, that we can enlist the aid of the other ranchers to help us. He may be right, although Dan's experience trying to get some of your old riders to come back wasn't that good. But the point is, if we go in with an army, we invite the other side's army to assume we mean war. Men would be killed on both sides, good men as well as bad. And no telling what would happen to the cattle in the process. We've got to do everything we can to get them out first, then see what happens."

"A war anyway, don't you think?" Stacy observed.

"Maybe not. After all, they are your cows. What can the Terhunes do? Their scheme will be busted and maybe so will their will to continue."

Stacy wagged her head doubtfully, but only said, "When would you go?"

"Anytime the next few days will be best. There'll be a moon out. All we're waiting for is Stoddard. When he's here, we'll go."

She looked from one to the other of them dubiously. "Are you sure either of you is in any shape for it? I mean . . ."

Dan Stanhope's eyes were both sunken and bloodshot, but the look in them was alive. "I can't speak for anyone but myself," he said, "but the shape I'm in is no one's fault but my own. I feel awful and I've got the shakes so bad I almost can't stand here. If anything, I'll probably feel worse tomorrow. But now's my chance to make up for what I've done, and someone'll have to kill me to stop me. I don't ask forgiveness, just the chance to make it up. Nothing more."

Stacy was clearly touched. "Oh, Dan . . . you don't have to be forgiven! I never blamed you for what happened!"

"No, I don't reckon you did," he said. "But that don't matter. I should've stayed and that's that."

She didn't try to argue. She turned hesitantly to Cam instead. "And you, Cam? I can't believe you tangled with Max Gruel and he didn't break half the bones in your body."

Cam once again forced a pained smile. "I don't think he broke any. I've got some sore ribs and a bunch of bruises, and I'm so tired I can hardly stand. But I'll be ready when the time comes, you don't have to worry about that."

She turned to look at Jaz and Jozie, now leaning against the corral fence in almost identical poses. They shrugged in unison, but quite obviously were not against the plan. Even old Miguel nodded affirmatively when Stacy's eyes met his.

Finally she said, "All right. I guess I'm convinced. I just don't want anyone getting hurt or killed, do you hear?"

She was looking at Cam, and all he could say was "We'll do our best, Stacy. I promise you that."

A short while later, after she had gone and as the rest of them were getting ready to leave the corral, it was the normally silent Jaz who took Cam aside and asked, "You whip that Max Gruel good, Stallings? You whip 'im real good?"

A little surprised, Cam said, "I did my best, Jaz. Why?"

"Did you kill 'im?"

"Why, no . . . I don't think so. Of course not."

The Indian's eyes were dark and inscrutable as he said, "You should have, Stallings. He gonna hate you now, like Guerrero and Emory. Somebody gonna have to kill 'em all or they gonna kill you . . . Don't matter what happens with them cows, Stallings. Someday them men gonna try to kill you."

It was late the following day before Blake Stoddard showed up, and to everyone's surprise he was not alone. He and two young Mexicans dismounted in front of the main house and were met there by Cam, Stacy, and Dan Stanhope.

"You know these boys, Stanhope," the blacksmith said as he came up to the porch to shake hands. "Maybe you, too, Miss Stacy. They've never been Stretch B riders, but they're outa work just now and they're good hands, believe me. Francisco Luna and Pablo Navarro. They've agreed to ride for us, if you'll have them."

Stacy looked in uncertainty from Cam to Stanhope, then back to Stoddard.

The blacksmith seemed to sense her quandary and said quickly, "They understand about being paid, Miss Stacy. All they ask for now is a place to bunk and their grub. Otherwise, they're like me, they just wanta help."

"We can use them, Stacy," Stanhope said. "I don't know how Blake got them to come, but he's right. They're good boys and we can damn sure use them."

Stacy went over to the two lithe young riders, neither of whom was probably a day older than her two Navajos, and said, "Then I am very proud to have you both. Please go on over to the bunkhouse and tell Miguel to find you a couple of bunks. He'll show you where to put your horses. And thank you. Thank you so very much for coming."

As the two led their horses beyond earshot, Blake Stoddard said, "Well, it's a crying shame they're the only ones I could get to come, but maybe they'll be enough for what we have in mind—eh, Stanhope?"

"I'd say just about right," Stanhope replied. "We're lucky to have them."

"What about the other ranchers, though?" Cam asked. "I know we're not looking for any more help on the drive out of the valley, but what about after that? Eventually we're going to have to have the support of our neighbors, and to get it they're going to have to know exactly what's going on."

"Don't worry about that part of it," Stoddard said. "One reason it took me this long to get here: I wanted to make sure everything you told me about the Stretch B herd got spread around and spread around good. I don't reckon you can look for much real help from the townspeople, and I don't know how much you'll get from the ranchers just yet. But I can tell you this: the word is being spread. Everyone between here and the Arizona line will soon know what the Terhunes have tried to do. It's low-down as hell, and in the long run I don't think folks'll stand for it. I think soon as they get to talking to one another they'll get mad, and when that happens, well, good old Gerd and Mala might just as well leave the country for good!"

Stacy looked as if this might be the most heartening thing she'd heard in months, and the gratitude in her eyes immediately settled on Cam.

Quickly he warned, "Don't count us a winner yet, Stacy. We're still a long way from having got that Stretch B herd back. When we do that, then you can congratulate us—okay?"

"Okay," she said agreeably. "But I still want you to know that whatever happens now, I appreciate all of you, and especially you, Cam. Without you, I'd never have had a chance. I know I wouldn't."

Cam smiled self-consciously. "Like I say, when we get those cows back, we'll celebrate. And when we sell enough beef to balance your books again, you can even pay us all a bonus or something. Meantime, I think we better do some planning." He looked around. "Anybody disagree?"

No one did, and within moments all had trooped inside the house to see what they could come up with.

Much of what it would be, they had already discussed. Their assault on the valley of Red Creek would take place two nights hence. Barring cloudy weather, a full moon could be expected to make its appearance on the eastern horizon about dark, and every advantage would be taken of its light to attack and neutralize the guards at the entrance to the box canyon. The fence would come down. They would ride the valley to its eastern extreme, then begin the gather, moving the herd west, back toward the box.

It would not be easy; there would be only six of them—the two young Mexicans, Jaz, Stoddard, Stanhope, and Cam—but with any luck at all, by daylight they would be clear of the valley and by noon would have the leaders of the herd within sight of the plains and their Stretch B home range.

Between the Stretch B and the valley, each man would lead an extra horse. Once there, they would change to the fresher mounts and release the ones they had ridden till then to return home. They could not risk being astride spent horses when they might need them the most. Likewise, they would go well armed—rifles, six-guns, and ammunition aplenty for each man—despite the fact that they hoped to avoid the need for gunplay. They knew they must be ready for almost anything and were determined not to be caught unprepared.

All in all, it seemed a good plan, especially since it even gave Cam and Stanhope—both pretty well used up at this point—plenty of time to become rested before they went. A good plan indeed . . . with only one point of strong contention among its makers: Stacy wanted to go along and none of the men thought it a good idea that she should.

She finally relented only in the face of complete and combined opposition, but she did not do so happily—a fact Cam was to attest to later as the two of them stood on the porch of the main house after the others had retired to the bunkhouse.

"They are my cattle, Cam," she complained mildly. "I just hate so not to play a part in getting them back. Surely you can understand that."

"I understand," he sympathized. "But what we're doing is just too dangerous. Anybody who has ever worked cattle at night knows that. Even without the Cross Arrow to concern us, it would still be too big a risk. Believe me, Stacy, it would."

"But to just wait here, not knowing," she moaned. "That part will simply be horrible."

"I know. Jozie won't like it either. He's probably up to the ride now, but I need someone to stay with you besides Miguel. The three of you and Juana will just have to handle things here. With any luck, we'll be back late day after tomorrow, your cows will be home where they belong, and it'll all be over. You'll just have to look at it that way, Stacy, and accept it."

"All over, Cam?" She voiced the same concern she had earlier. "I still can't believe you think that."

"I'm just trying to take it one step at a time," he said simply. "We won't go looking for trouble, believe me, we won't."

"But even if you succeed. Even then, all won't be over. They won't take it with a smile, Cam. I know my sister and I think I know what kind of men she has working for her. Gerd Terhune might not have the backbone to do much himself, but Mala will never let it rest. I know she won't."

"No, I guess she won't." It was a disturbing thought, and he knew that here in this country of little or no law, anything might be possible. The Cross Arrow would not go down without a fight, and if it came to that, the Stretch B was likely to find itself seriously outgunned. Depressed a little, he frowned.

"I'm sorry, Cam," Stacy said intuitively. "You are trying so very hard and things *are* looking up for us now. I shouldn't be so negative. Please forgive me. I do have faith in you—honestly I do."

He didn't know if it was what she said or the way she said it, but it caused him to regard her suddenly in a different manner than he had. She was standing there, half in and half out of the porch shadows, her hair blowing lightly in the afternoon breeze, her fine brown eyes locked on him and holding within their depths something that never failed to move him whenever he really looked. Quite honestly, it was a moment in which he didn't know whether to be inspired or humbled . . .

There was something new there, too, something in her eyes that was more than just faith or gratitude, and in the face of this he felt momentarily tongue-tied.

She went on. "Anyway, I'm just trying to say that I want you to be careful, all of you. Don't ever let your guard down, Cam. Don't you ever!"

He promised that he would not, that he would not forget her warning no matter how successful their venture with the cattle turned out to be. He promised now and he promised again a day and a half later as the six of them prepared to ride out on their way to Red Creek. He promised it and he meant it and he would not forget.

But what he remembered most as he rode was not her words. It was that look that had been in her eyes.

CHAPTER 15

The early evening sky was clear. A bright creamy moon had risen at the expected hour and was slowly making its way upward from the eastern horizon. At the mouth of the canyon, now resting in moon shadows cast by the towering walls of the box beyond, a campfire flickered. Over the fire a man stirred a pot of beans; nearby two others lounged. One of these two had just poured himself a cup of coffee from a steaming pot sitting next to the beans; the other, a fellow called Hank, grumpily fumbled around in his bedroll for a flask he had been keeping there. After a moment he found it, but even this did little to relieve his grumpy mood. "As if it wasn't bad enough to have to stay out here all week," he mumbled, "now my relief don't show up when he's supposed to. Just my damn dumb luck!"

"Just be patient, Hank," the man at the fire said. "He'll show."

"Yeah—when? Hell, it's dark already. When?"

"He'll show, Hank," the man repeated patiently. "You just wait and see."

"Fine for you to say, Jess," Hank retorted. "You only been here two days and Bill, here, four. It's been a full week for me, and if there's anything I hate, it's sittin' around a goddamned camp with nothin' to do, all day every day, but guard a goddamned fence!"

Jess was unperturbed. "Might as well relax and have some supper," he said. "The beans are hot and the coffee's boiled. Your man will come when he comes. Here, take a plate."

Grudgingly Hank pocketed his flask and accepted the plate. Bill moved over to do the same, and for about ten minutes the three of them were silent while they ate. Hank shoveled his beans impatiently down, finished mopping up his plate with a day-old biscuit, then deposited the plate by the fire. Pouring himself a cup of steaming hot coffee, he retook his position a few feet away.

A moment later he drew up alertly, listening. "What was that? I thought I heard something."

"Aw, come on, Hank," the one called Bill said. "You're hearin' things . . ."

"No, I'm not. Listen!"

All three did and for several moments they heard nothing other than the normal night sounds. But then, somewhere out in the darkness, a horse snorted. One of their own mounts, hobbled on the other side of the camp, responded with a soft nicker. Soft footfalls sounded, and presently the vague form of a rider appeared.

"Who is it?" Bill asked, not particularly concerned, but a hand on his six-gun just the same. "Speak up, man! Who are you?"

"Stan Wilson," came the reply as the man drew up and dismounted. "Christ, you fellows sure are nervous. I'm only here to relieve Hank . . . That is you, ain't it, Hank?"

"Damn right it's me. Where'n hell you been, Wilson? I been lookin' for you ever since noon today!"

Wilson came up to the fire. "Nobody told me that. Fact is, I wasn't even supposed to be your man. Roy Crow was, only he took sick and Terhune sent me instead. I didn't even find out till after noon that I was comin'."

Hank looked around at his companions. "Sick! You hear that? Roy Crow, sick! Jesus!"

"Well, it ain't all that big a deal, Hank," Bill said. "What's one more night out here, anyway?"

"One more night, hell!" Hank muttered, striding across camp toward his saddle. "I ain't puttin' in another damn minute o' this duty. Nossir! I'm goin' in tonight." He took up his bridle and stalked off into the darkness toward the horses.

Presently he was back, leading a chunky bay. As he moved toward his saddle, Jess called out, "Hey, since you're leavin', how about passin' that flask around? Stan, here, says he didn't bring a bottle and we're all out otherwise."

Hank looked around, considered it a moment, then said, "Aw, what the hell," and reached inside his vest for the flask. He tossed it over to Jess, then went back to saddling the horse, his mind quickly back at his bunk at the ranch and the two days he had coming in town as a bonus for his week spent at the guard camp.

A few minutes later he finished tying on his bedroll and mounted up. It was a two-hour ride to the ranch, and he was anxious to be on his way. "Watch these boys, Stan," he said, in a much better mood now. "They're both hell on bad poker players, if you know what I mean. Be seein' you, fellows."

He rode out across a land now bathed in moonlight, on a trail he knew like the back of his hand and amid murky landmarks that threw distorted, almost eerie shadows across his path. He rode along at a leisurely but steady walk, thinking mostly of those two upcoming days in Vera Velarde, of McKenzie's place and a dusky little Spanish lass who sometimes came to sing for the customers there. He was no longer in a grumpy mood; he rode now with the light, jaunty air of a man who had no worries and didn't expect any.

He had gone a little more than a mile when suddenly he remembered the flask. He had left his flask with Jess. Damn!

For a moment he considered just leaving it. He didn't care about the contents: the thing was no more than half full anyway; and for sure he didn't begrudge Jess or Bill or Stan what was left. But the flask . . . his old man had given him that, and it had been his grandfather's before that. He'd hate like hell to lose that flask. And if there was anything wrong with good old Jess, it was the man's almost infamous propensity for losing things. Lariat ropes, pocketknives, hats . . . hell, he even lost a saddle once!

Hank hated to retrace his steps, but his fondness for that flask was strong and he hated like crazy to think about losing it. And it was only a mile back there; he was going to be late getting to the ranch anyway . . . so what the hell! With a shrug, he reined the horse around.

It seemed a longer mile going back, but in reality it didn't take all that much time to cover it, and presently he came once again upon the grassy flat that stretched between him and the camp. The campfire still twinkled against the dark background of the box, and he was certain that by now the three men would be deeply engrossed in a hand of Mexican monte or poker around the fire. He reached the creek and rode along it toward the camp.

It wasn't until he was within a hundred yards of his destination that he realized something was wrong and pulled up abruptly. There was some kind of disturbance within the camp. He heard voices, yelling, then saw figures dashing between him and the campfire. Then came more yelling and finally the dim shapes of horsemen descending out of the darkness.

He froze. *Someone was attacking the camp!*

For several moments he just sat there trying to sort out in his mind what might be going on. Who was it and what could they possibly want? It came to him with a jar. The Stretch B! Jesus . . . it had to be!

So what should he do? He didn't know how many of them there were, or exactly what they had in mind. So far, there had been no shooting . . . but what was going on?

He knew, seconds later, when he heard the first cedar post snap, then another and another. He could hear hoofbeats, more voices but less yelling now. They were pulling down the fence to the box. They were after the Stretch B herd—they had to be!

Desperately he calculated what he should do. What had happened to Jess, Bill, and Stan he had no idea, but he knew there was very little he could do alone to stop their attackers. Not here, not now. Too, it could take all night for them to work the entire valley and begin to move the cattle out. There was time for him to ride for help—four hours minimum, probably more, for him to get to the ranch and for a crew to be rousted out and brought back here. But time enough, he decided. Plenty of time. . .

Quickly he reined his horse back in the direction of the Cross Arrow, setting out at a much faster pace this time, and forgetting all about the flask he had just minutes before been on his way back to get.

The crew from the Stretch B were aware that one man had come and another gone, and they guessed correctly that it was a matter of one relieving the other of his duty. They gave the one who left plenty of time to be well on his way and had no reason to believe that he would return. They gave him the time, then moved in on the remaining three.

Surprise was their weapon—that and Jaz. The young Navajo and one of the Mexican boys, the one called Francisco, slipped in so close without being seen that they were almost in the poker hand being dealt beside the fire before anyone knew they were there. They leaped forward, weapons drawn, with orders for "hands up" and "guns dropped." The three unsuspecting guards never had a chance. They found themselves disarmed, dragged aside and out of harm's way, then tied hands and feet and left so they could not interfere later.

Then Jaz, the two Mexicans, and Blake Stoddard were lassoing posts and pulling down the fence, laying it flat all across the mouth of the canyon, then cutting its wires near the center and pulling the ends to the side as far as each would go, hoping to avoid tangling a good horse in the hated barbed wire later on.

When this was done, the six of them splashed single-file up the creek and into the box, not once suspecting that their presence had been detected by someone other than the three guards they left behind.

Cam and Stanhope rode side by side through the night, the herd building steadily ahead of them, calves bawling here, cows answering softly there. They brought up the drag end, while Stoddard, the two Mexicans, and Jaz rode a loose flank and swing somewhere to either side and just a little ahead. The cattle had been nervous and jumpy at first but seemed to settle down as the herd grew and became used to being quietly pushed up the valley. The sky was alive with countless stars; the moon was at its brightest; visibility was almost as if it were day. So far, things were going even better than they'd hoped.

"You know, Stallings," Dan Stanhope said presently. "I guess I never really thanked you for what you did for me in Vera Velarde the other night. I figure Max Gruel might've killed me if you hadn't come along."

"And he might've killed *me* if you hadn't jumped in when you did," Cam responded. "I'd say we owe each other about equal on that score."

"But there's more to it than that," Stanhope insisted. "You gave me a second chance to come back, to be doing this. I failed the Stretch B twice otherwise. I won't do it again, but it's only because of you that I can say so. I want you to know I appreciate it."

Cam was silent for a moment. The man deserved some admiration. He'd sworn off the bottle on top of everything else and had been half sick ever since. Everything about this deal had been hard for him, yet at no time had he faltered. "Well, I'm glad you're here. None of the rest of us knows this valley the way you do. It's made a difference already, believe me."

Stanhope seemed to shrug. "It's no big deal now. We've got these cows on the move in the direction we want them to go. We should have it made—if we don't have trouble at the end . . ."

Cam frowned. "What do you mean, 'trouble at the end'? What end? What trouble?"

"The end of the valley—the box. It's possible they'll balk at the box."

Cam frowned even more deeply. "That box is seventy-five to a hundred yards wide. Why should they balk?"

Stanhope shrugged. "It narrows down suddenly when compared to the rest of the canyon, and it's a good five hundred yards long. You can never tell about cattle; anything that looks like a restriction can turn them. And in the dark like this, well, there's just no telling."

Cam thought about this with growing concern. He knew now that there were more cattle in the valley than he had first thought; they would constitute quite a large herd by the time the first of them reached the box. If the leaders turned or would not enter it, disaster could occur as hundreds more piled up behind them. Calves and even cows would be trampled and a stampede back down the valley might occur; the Stretch B mission would then be a failure and no telling the consequences of that.

He looked at Stanhope. "Bad business if it happens, all right. What do you think are the odds?"

The other man shook his head. "I dunno. But as I think about it, bad enough we oughtn't take chances; bad enough we can't afford to just tag along and hope."

Cam nodded. He could see what Stanhope meant. "Someone's gotta ride point, is that what you're saying?"

"That's my opinion, yes."

"It could be dangerous, in the dark like this."

Stanhope seemed to smile. "No worse than being back here if they turn on us. You know that, I think."

"Yes," Cam acknowledged. "Yes, I do. Just the same, I think I'd choose drag if I were comparing the two . . ."

Again Stanhope smiled. "Good. That means it's decided. I'll take the point—"

"You know I didn't mean it that way," Cam protested immediately. "I wasn't trying to dodge the thing."

"I know, I know," Stanhope said. "But it still oughta be me. I know the valley best, and it'll take some doing to get ahead of the herd now. I am the only logical choice."

Cam knew he was right. It wasn't a case of who was better between them; it was a matter more of who was familiar with the surroundings, who could best lead the way not only through the box but beyond to the plains as well—Stanhope, of course.

"How far is it to the box from here?" Cam asked. "How long will it take you to get into position?"

Stanhope considered his surroundings. "I'd say four, maybe five miles from here. An hour for me to get where I need to be. Two, three hours for you, riding drag—no less than that, but more if things go slow getting the leaders to start through. Chances are it'll be well past midnight before we clear the box."

"We'll be riding blind back here," Cam warned. "We won't have any way of knowing until too late if you're in trouble."

"I know that. And we probably won't see each other again until the herd reaches the plains. Just push them easy and don't worry. If they don't get excited, we'll be all right. I'll send Jaz and Pablo back to ride flank, Blake and Francisco to help you with the drag. The canyon will pinch in enough we won't need any swing riders, so long as everything keeps moving like it's supposed to."

"Just don't take any more chances than you have to," Cam said, fully aware that the man was downplaying the hazards of it. "Okay?"

"Don't worry!" Stanhope laughed softly. "No bunch of cows is gonna do me in, you can bet on that."

"I hope you're right," was all Cam could say.

A few moments later, Stanhope urged his horse forward and began making his way carefully through the herd. He waved back once, and Cam returned the wave; then the other man was gone in the darkness, and Cam did not see him again.

The air thickened steadily with the smell of dust and cows. No matter how carefully the herd was gathered, or how slowly it was allowed to move, the sounds of bawling calves grew until the noise approached a din; hundreds of horns clacked constantly; the drag riders became as if drugged from staring at the swaying sea of moonlit backs that stretched before them. There just was no way a thousand head and more could be brought together without these things happening. Seldom before, in fact, had it been done so successfully by so few riders, and Cam was quick to credit the skill of his companions for every bit of it. Certainly he did not know what he would have done without Stanhope, who by riding point had taken on the loneliest, most difficult job of all. And he must be succeeding, for by now the leaders must either be at or passing through the box, and there were no signs whatsoever at the rear of the herd that all was not proceeding smoothly up ahead.

Still, Cam was only cautiously optimistic. Cattle were funny creatures; they could be just as stupid in a herd as they could be cagey when operating as individuals. They could yet bunch up, even halfway through the box; calves could be trampled; and almost any loud or sudden noise might stampede them—especially at night. The bright moonlight was of course a help, but in many ways it also posed hazards—revealing things the animals otherwise might not see, casting shadows, some moving, which might at any time spook an already spooky cow, steer, or bull. One never knew what it might take to set them off; sometimes it was next to nothing.

Cam thus rode easily but alertly, talking constantly in a soothing voice to the animals nearest him. To his left a short distance was one of the Mexicans—Francisco Luna, he thought. Beyond Francisco, riding flank, was Jaz. To Cam's right rode Blake Stoddard, and beyond him, Pablo Navarro commanded the other flank. Cam knew that all four men were proceeding just as he was—slow and easy, always alert.

Now and then an animal tried to fall back, and in a few instances it was a small calf and its worried mama. These Cam let go, knowing full well that the calf might not make it anyway if forced to keep the pace. But most of the calves were old enough and large enough to continue, and for that reason were pushed relentlessly onward.

The moon was almost directly overhead by the time Cam discerned the walls of the box looming dead ahead. The cattle were bunched tightly and moving slower now; doubtless many had already pushed through the narrowed neck of the canyon and had begun to spread out beyond. He could only hope that they continued to move in a herd, that Stanhope's lone point would be enough to lead them the way they were supposed to go. If it was not, Cam knew there was nothing immediate that he or any of the others could do to help out. It must go well now or not at all.

The progress of the herd soon slowed almost to a crawl, and presently all five riders found themselves relegated to the drag. The box was squeezing them in, forming a bottleneck, disrupting what had been the calm of the trailers and causing them to react impatiently now to the pressure of the drag riders. Increasingly, the pressure was on the riders to hold them. Time and again Cam found himself spurring to turn a cow or a yearling that was trying to break back, splashing back and forth across the creek, yelling, taking chances in the dark of forcing his horse into a hole and a fall, but knowing that he had to do so or risk a major breakaway by the herd. He could hear his fellows yelling also, off to his either side, and he knew they were having to do the same.

It seemed to take forever, but gradually they drew upon the box entrance. The walls loomed straight above them and the herd had begun to move freely again. Somewhat in relief, the five riders found themselves riding almost side by side now.

"I think we've got it made, Cam," Blake Stoddard called over as the tail end of the herd entered the box. "We're gonna make it through."

Cam nodded, mostly to himself since Stoddard couldn't see him that well. "Step number one. Now all we have to do is see if things are still together on the other side."

"Yeah," Stoddard mumbled. "The other side."

Perhaps it was intuition, perhaps not, but each rider must have felt the same little unexplained flutter of apprehension then. No telling what caused it, but Cam knew he felt it. And he would remember the feeling for a long time afterward, for it was only moments later, when they were still but halfway through the box, that the first shots rang out up ahead.

A chilling few seconds after that they heard the first low rumble, then roar, of thousands of stampeding hoofs racing away from them into the night.

CHAPTER 16

They emerged from the west end of the box only to be met by more gunfire, and this time it was aimed at them. The bright moon was suddenly no asset at all. Bullets spanged off rocks around them, and they were forced to retreat back inside the canyon.

"Who in hell is that?" Blake Stoddard called out, dismounting to take cover.

Cam's first thought was of the three guards they had left bound and gagged outside the box entrance. Somehow one of them must have loosed himself from his bonds, freed his fellows, and then set out to spook the herd. But as he thought about it he realized that the muzzle flashes he had just seen had come from at least half a dozen weapons; there was no way three men could have been responsible for all of that.

"Trouble," he finally said, also dismounting. "Big trouble, if it's who I think it is."

"The Cross Arrow, you think?"

"Who else?"

"Jesus."

Cam almost smiled. "Yeah," he said, then turned. "Jaz, Pablo, get over here. Francisco, you hold the horses back a ways and out of sight."

"What're we gonna do?" Stoddard asked.

Cam was looking around, mostly at the rocks and boulders that formed the base of the canyon wall. "Take cover and see if we can hold them off for a while, I guess. I don't know after that."

"What about the cattle? What about Stanhope?"

Cam shrugged. The rumble of hoofbeats had died away now; the cattle were gone, although where to or how scattered they had become he had no idea. As for Stanhope, well, they would just have to hope he had managed to get out of the way, that he had not been the target of any of those first shots . . .

Cam started as someone came quietly up behind him. He turned. It was Jaz.

"I don't think we better stay here, Stallings," the Indian said softly. "I think we gonna get trapped if we do."

"Trapped?" Cam once again looked around.

The Indian shrugged and pointed toward the east end of the box. "There ain't no way out if they get behind us, Stallings. They already got us penned in on this end, and we can't climb these walls." He looked straight up as he added this last statement. Enough said.

"Christ—he's right!" Stoddard said, looking east. "How hard would it be for some of them to get around there?"

"I don't know," Cam said. "If it occurred to them ahead of time, probably not hard at all. And I agree—Jaz is probably right. We better make a move to get out of here now, if we're going to make one at all."

They made it to their horses; they made it halfway back down the length of the box . . . only to realize they weren't going to make it any farther. Muzzle flashes shone brightly as guns barked all across the eastern opening of the box; bullets ricocheted off rock and thudded into the ground all around them; the dark shapes of horsemen hove into view. Desperately Cam and his men fired back, hoping to at least slow the attack until they could regain cover.

But where to go? Where they had just been was inadequate at best; where they were now was even worse. The whole situation was clear: the Cross Arrow wasn't just out to stampede the cattle, they were after the Stretch B riders who had gathered them. And they had their quarry trapped perfectly, with no way out of the canyon and maybe nowhere to go within it.

Cam was already contemplating a desperation charge to break free when suddenly he recalled something he'd seen earlier on the far side of the box, the north side. A break in the wall—not a way out, more likely a cul-de-sac from which escape might be difficult—but maybe, just maybe, a place to take cover.

He looked around. His horse danced nervously, wanting to run; Stoddard and the others fired wildly on Cam's either side. Their adversaries were advancing from both sides now, effectively cutting them off and catching them in a crossfire.

Quickly he decided. "Over here!" he called. "Follow me this way!"

Mala Terhune dismounted her horse well back from the west box entrance and the fighting. The gunfire in the canyon was intense; the Stretch B riders were trapped; their herd had been stampeded into the night; the three guards had been freed. Mala had Gerd and twenty men on this end of the box and ten more had circled around to the east, thus blocking all hope of escape for Cam Stallings and his fledgling crew.

At least she assumed they had Stallings boxed up in there. Gerd had assured her it would take at least half a dozen men on the drag end of the herd to even hope to push the cattle through the box. And even the most ambitious count gave the Stretch B no more than six or seven men altogether. Of course one of them might have ridden point. No one had been able to tell in the dark. But if there had been someone, he would have to have been the luckiest man alive to escape the stampede. The balance of them had to be bottled up in the canyon, and Mala Terhune's hopes were that one of them was indeed Stallings.

It was true: she wanted him dead. Gerd and Pit had thoroughly convinced her of that need even before tonight. And when Hank had come pounding into the ranch a few hours ago on a lathered horse to report that the guards to the canyon had been overpowered and the fence pulled down . . . well, they all had known it was Stallings and his upstart crew who were the perpetrators. They all had known it would be no holds barred from here on out. Even Mala knew: Cam Stallings and his men must die!

Too bad, too, she told herself. She could have liked Stallings; from the moment she first saw him, she knew she could have liked him very much. She had given him a chance to hire on. But he wouldn't, and now he had become a liability much too great to tolerate further.

Naturally it would have been better if Pit or Lizard had somehow put an end to him before now. It angered Mala no end to think that the Stretch B herd had been scattered as it had. No telling what it would take to regather them now; it might not even be possible. But Stacy's crew was doomed, and without them, younger sister would have nothing. All would still be Mala's in the end. It would.

And the circumstances—the one good thing about this whole miserable affair: the killings would be justified. The story would be carefully told. Stallings and his riders had been caught red-handed in the midst of Cross Arrow range, driving off Cross Arrow cows—for who would know the difference whose they were now—dying to a man during a pitched battle brought about in an effort to apprehend them for their crime. Justified . . .

A footstep sounded just to Mala's right, startling her. It was Fern Carty. "You all right, ma'am?"

She nodded impatiently. Her bodyguards: Carty, Emory, Guerrero, Gruel. Gerd wouldn't let her leave the ranch, wouldn't let her stay here now, without them. Carty was the only one she could really stand, and she wasn't sure about him. Bodyguards!

Of course they didn't relish their duty any more than she did. The shooting had slowed some now but was still going on over there; the battle apparently had not yet been won. And these men, killers all, probably resenting every minute spent nursemaiding their lady boss on the sidelines, must want in on it.

She wondered if they would go on over and join in if she ordered them to. Thinking about it, she decided probably not. They were Gerd's killer dogs, not hers. Gerd had told them to stay here; they minded Gerd.

She looked around. They were located on a hillside covered with juniper and piñon. Guerrero and Emory were nearby, loosening their saddle girths. Gruel, his features still a black-and-blue mess from the beating Stallings had given him, was sitting on a rock, staring balefully in the direction of the shooting. Carty, the moonlight glinting strangely off his seldom-smiling face, was likewise gazing toward the west entrance to the box canyon, from this point perhaps half a mile away.

Suddenly it occurred to Mala why the unsaddlings and the faraway looks. All four of them were expecting something of a fairly long wait. "The shooting hasn't stopped," she said suddenly. "Why hasn't the shooting stopped, Fern?"

He wagged his head. "I dunno. We got them trapped in there, looks like, but for some reason we can't get to some or all of them. They must be holed up somewhere."

"You mean it's settled into a siege? That it could go on all night?"

"All night and all day tomorrow, if they're holed up good enough. No way to tell from here."

Mala's face fell. The one thing she'd wanted: to get it over with. Now this!

She turned once more to Carty. "But that means we could be out here all night waiting. All night and tomorrow!"

He looked at her tolerantly. "Yes, ma'am. I suppose that's what it could mean, all right."

For a moment she just stared off into the night, her thoughts churning. She considered her situation now something of a predicament and wondered how much she could really trust the four men who were supposed to be her protectors. Well, it was a bit late in the game to be asking that, she had to admit. She had wanted to come on this expedition, and she was doing to have to endure what went with it. If problems arose, she would just have to handle them the best way she could.

She turned back to Carty with a steely look. "Very well. If that's the case, then there will have to be an understanding."

He gave her a puzzled look in return. "What understanding is that, ma'am?"

"If you four are going to stay here with me tonight," she declared firmly, "then we are going to have two camps. One for me, one for the four of you. And I am armed, don't forget that. I'll trust none of you any further than I think is safe. Do you understand?"

For what seemed a very long time, he just stared at her. Then he said, "Yes, ma'am. I know my job, ma'am. I understand." And he turned and walked away as if that was all he ever again intended to say on the subject.

Mala watched him go and could not help the funny little chill that ran up her spine as she realized how little control anyone ever had over a man like that. Still, she wondered how much luck she herself might have with him if she were to really put her mind to it. She wondered quite seriously.

A few moments later she found a comfortable spot beneath a large juniper tree to settle into, and thus began the long wait for the first light of day.

The shooting stopped altogether for about an hour just before dawn. Both sides, it seemed, had discovered at about the same time that they were only wasting ammunition. Each knew where the other was; each knew there was nothing that could be done about it at night. Cam and his companions had indeed found the break in the canyon wall to be a large cul-de-sac, with only one way in and the same way out but with plenty of cover for both themselves and their horses. The Cross Arrow, on the other hand, enjoyed two general positions—in the rocks at either end of the box—and were likewise well entrenched. The problem was, only open space existed between these positions and the cul-de-sac, with just enough moonlight to make it all but impossible to attack without being seen and cut down in the process.

Thus the firing had become nothing but a holding game, each side letting the other know it was still alert and on the lookout—until that hour before dawn when it stopped completely. One side, then the other, simply ceased shooting, causing the uncertainty as to what each was doing to grow and grow as the next hour passed.

With sunup came long shadows and even a slight chill in the air; then came full daylight at last, as the sun rose above one corner of the canyon rim, bathing the cul-de-sac in bright light for the first time that day.

Cam and Jaz were on guard, having taken the last watch of the night while the others caught a couple hours' sleep before daybreak. They had a good view of the entire canyon, and to some extent the scenery extending beyond the box opening on either side. What they saw was not a happy sight. It had the grisly appearance of a battlefield.

About fifty yards directly in front of them lay a dead horse, shot from beneath Francisco Luna before he could reach the cul-de-sac last night. Beyond this, and stretching beyond the canyon into the grassy flat to the west, were strewn the bodies of dead cattle, mostly calves trampled in the stampede. A few were older animals; a few were even still alive, but were either dying or were injured so badly they could not rise and walk away. Unhappily, Cam and his men could not spare the bullets it would have taken to put these latter unfortunates out of their misery, and the other side, for whatever their reasons, had not chosen to.

"What d'you reckon the losses were, Jaz?" Cam asked as he took in the scene. The Indian was behind a large boulder less than fifty feet away and had plainly been taking in a similar view.

"Dunno, Stallings. Lotsa calves out there, but mebbe not so bad. Mebbe coulda been lots worse."

Blake Stoddard, having just shaken out of his bedroll, came crawling up behind Cam. He stared. "It damn sure looks bad to me," he said solemnly.

Cam gave a grim nod. "Yeah, but I think Jaz is probably right. Fifty, maybe even a hundred head, but only peanuts compared to what it could have been. In fact, if they stopped the run soon enough, it may not be very bad at all."

Stoddard looked at him quizzically. "You figure there's much chance of that—them stopping the run like you say?"

"In this country, yes. Hills, trees, canyons. The herd would split and scatter, then slow down, and eventually stop altogether."

"Well, maybe we got one break, then. But what about Stanhope? Do you think he's lying out there somewhere too?"

Cam wagged his head. "I don't know. I sure as hell hope not."

Stoddard was silent for a moment. "And our friends, the Cross Arrow—any sign of them since sunup?"

"I saw some movement in the rocks over by the west entrance a little while ago. And around first light I heard some yelling on the other end. That's about it."

"What d'you reckon they're up to?"

Cam shrugged. "Waiting us out, I guess. Who knows."

Stoddard looked around worriedly. "I don't suppose there's some way they can get behind us—from up above?"

Cam followed his gaze, which was about as straight up as one could get. It was a rugged view that greeted him, where canyon rim met with bright blue sky and left one almost dizzy for having looked at it.

"They'd have hell, Blake. They could never come down that thing, and most places on top they'd have to expose themselves long before we would in order to fire down on us." Then he thought more conservatively about it. "Better keep an eye out anyway, though. Are Francisco and Pablo awake yet? Maybe they could cover the rim while we watch the front."

"Good idea," Stoddard said, then turned immediately to make his way back toward the bedrolls.

Cam had only half swung back to the fore, however, when Jaz said, "Hey, Stallings—look!"

"Where?"

"Over there. See 'em?"

He saw eight or ten riders formed in a group just beyond the west entrance—gathering for an attack, perhaps?

"And over there," the Indian went on calmly. "The other end of the box—more yet."

Cam switched his gaze quickly. Another eight or ten men, only this time on foot and spread out about evenly across the downcanyon opening, made tiny figures three hundred yards away.

"They gonna come get us, Stallings. They gonna come slow an' easy, make us shoot a lot, mebbe take all day . . . but they gonna try real hard to get us. We better have lotsa bullets, Stallings. We gonna need 'em bad."

Cam, a grim, set look on his face, reached down and picked up his Winchester "Yellow Boy." He laid it within handy reach on the flat top of the boulder in front of him, then called back to the rear, "Blake, I think we may have to get along with just one man to watch the rim. The way things are looking, we're going to need at least two of you up here."

CHAPTER 17

There was no all-out attempt to storm the cul-de-sac. Surprisingly, the attackers came on foot, the line of men to the east advancing individually at a crouch until cover was reached, then dropping out of sight until one man at a time they were ready to make their next move forward. Meanwhile, those to the west had also dismounted, leaving their horses somewhere out of sight outside the canyon, and were proceeding to pursue the same tactic.

Watching, it was all Cam and his companions could do to hold their fire. " 'S what they want us to do," Jaz cautioned. "Shoot while they're still long range. We can't do that, Stallings. We gotta wait."

It was a cat-and-mouse approach all the way. For several minutes all of the attackers would be entirely out of view. Then, suddenly, one man would jump and run, maybe ten, maybe twenty yards, only to drop out of sight again. Each time, it was pure agony for Cam and his men not to shoot. In fact, it was almost impossible to get off a shot. As yet the nearest Cross Arrow man had not drawn closer than 150 yards on the west or 200 yards on the east; and no matter how hard the defenders tried to be ready when it happened, they never knew where the next runner was going to come from. At no time was there any real opportunity for aiming; seldom was there a good target even if there had been time to sight in on one.

Only Jaz was not discouraged. "When they get closer," he said patiently. "Then we pick out two or three up front and watch 'em. We make 'em think about that runnin'. You watch."

Cam nodded agreeably. "Good idea. You and Francisco watch the west side; Blake and I'll take the east. Holler if you need help, okay?"

The Indian nodded, and both he and Francisco settled in among the rocks, rifles rested in firing positions, eyes keen.

It wasn't very long before Jaz squeezed off a shot. This was quickly greeted by return fire from at least half a dozen rifles. Everybody ducked as bullets ricocheted above their heads and whined viciously off in unpredictable directions. While this was going on, another runner on Jaz's side suddenly sprinted twenty yards and was down again before anyone could recover and get off a shot. The Cross Arrow had thought of everything—including what to do when their adversaries started firing at the runners. One man runs, the others cover him with fire of their own, and all hands duck at the cul-de-sac. Simple but slick, Cam thought. Slick.

"We gotta hit one of 'em," Jaz said grimly. "Nothin's gonna help till one of 'em goes down. We gotta hit one, Stallings."

"Okay," Cam said. "Pick one out and next time we'll all give him a try. Maybe that'll work."

Jaz nodded. "Behind that little bush over there. The closest man is behind that bush. I figure he'll run pretty quick. Watch 'im."

The bush was a good hundred yards away; three other men ran forward and dropped from sight, and shots once again spanged wildly off the rocks around the cul-de-sac, before finally the designated target sprang to run.

This time, all four defenders were ready; their rifles cracked almost in unison. Cam even got off two shots and he was pretty sure Jaz did too. The man cried out, spun in midair, and went down, perhaps not killed but hard hit beyond a doubt. Firing erupted in earnest from both east and west then, and all heads went down within the cul-de-sac.

"We got 'im," Jaz said with a near smile. "Now they gonna think a minute before they run. Watch both sides now—we'll get another one."

It was nerve-wracking business, but fifteen minutes later another runner went down, screaming and with at least two bullets in him, and for a good half hour after that no one ran at all. The attackers fired a lot, sometimes sporadically, sometimes in regular fusillades, but they did not run. This lasted until finally three jumped up at once and two of them made the mistake of running toward the same place—an old driftwood pile less than seventy-five yards from the suddenly erupting muzzles of Jaz's and Francisco's rifles. Both went down halfway there and lay writhing ten yards from anything that resembled cover.

Another fusillade followed from the Cross Arrow positions, but the attack had lost its steam completely now and the next man to run, it turned out, was running away from the cul-de-sac rather than toward it.

"Well, we broke that up," Blake Stoddard said proudly as the firing died completely a few minutes later.

Cam was less than ecstatic. "Yeah. But they're still out there and we're still trapped in here—five men with only four horses, fifty yards from a creek we'd get killed for sure trying to reach, with only so much ammunition and damned little if anything to eat. We broke it up, all right. But they've still got us where it's no fun being pinched and I don't think they're aiming to let go."

Stoddard's mood dampened noticeably. "What are we gonna do, then—surrender?"

Cam shook his head. "I don't think so, Blake. Fact is, I doubt if we could if we wanted to. I think they want us dead, and I doubt if they'll settle for anything else."

"You mean kill us in cold blood? Christ, they can't get away with that!"

"Maybe not. But look at it the way Terhune probably does. Dead, we can't tell anybody what we were doing here. He and his men caught some cow thieves on their range and had it out with them. The cow thieves lost, and that's that. Alive, on the other hand, we tell our side of the story and what we were really doing here comes out. Terhune can't allow that, and I don't think he'll be taking any prisoners because of it."

"Then what *do* we do?"

"I don't know," Cam said wearily, thinking. "Try to make it till dark, I guess—and hope like hell there are some clouds to cover that moon. Maybe then we can make a run for it. Maybe then . . ."

They sat and watched and waited. Once in a while someone from the other side fired a shot and the bullet ricocheted off rock, then whizzed harmlessly into the distance or into the ground close by. Otherwise, the action had ceased and the attackers had withdrawn to their original positions.

Overhead, the sun beamed fire; the rocks in the cul-de-sac became blistering to the touch; the men had to be careful to set their rifles in the shade lest they become too hot to pick up when needed. They grew thirsty listening to the unattainable waters of the creek trickling past within rock-throwing distance of their positions; and as the sun cooked down upon the canyon, the smell of death began to permeate the air.

It was mostly the dead cattle dotting the canyon bottom that smelled, but it was impossible for those inside the cul-de-sac to forget that at least three men lay out there in much the same shape. Four had been shot, only one that they knew of was still alive, and he had crawled behind the pile of driftwood and had not been seen nor heard from for some while now.

"How long has he been there?" Stoddard asked from where he rested in the shade nearby.

"I don't know," Cam said. "It's past noon now. About one o'clock, I figure. He's been there several hours already, that's for sure."

"You reckon he's still alive?"

Cam shrugged. "Could be, but I haven't seen him move anymore. And he won't answer when I call to him. Probably doesn't believe we'd let him go without shooting him again. Either that or he's in no shape to go."

"Jesus," Stoddard said unhappily. "What about his buddies? They doing anything?"

"Not much. A couple of riders showed themselves over near the wall on the west end a few minutes ago, but they disappeared again, and I haven't seen anyone since. Did you see them, Jaz?"

The Indian, like Stoddard, had retreated to what shade he could find behind a nearby boulder. He nodded affirmatively. "I saw 'em. One of 'em was a woman—Miz Mala, I reckon."

Cam stared at him. "Mala? Are you sure? That's a long way off, Jaz. Can you be sure?"

"I'm sure."

Cam looked back at Stoddard. "Blake, did you hear that? Mala Terhune is over there! Jaz saw her, and I guess so did I!"

"Does that surprise you?" Stoddard asked simply.

Cam met his gaze. "Well, no, I guess not. She's not the sort to sit back at the ranch and wait, I guess . . ."

"No, she's not."

"Still . . ." Cam shook his head.

He thought about Stacy then—she wasn't the sort either. The thought made him more glad than ever that he'd made her stay behind. He shuddered to think about her being trapped here like this with him and the others. He didn't really know if the Cross Arrow would shoot a woman, but at the same time it was hard for him to truly gauge the depths of Mala's hatred for her half sister. And Jaz, good old keen-eyed Jaz, was probably right: Mala *was* out there; Mala and Terhune, Emory, Guerrero, Gruel, Carty—they were all out there, Cam would bet on it. And if ever he entertained any illusions about mercy, he had none upon this realization. There would be no lack of the killer instinct in that crew. None whatsoever.

Stoddard had just gone back to check on Pablo and the horses, and Cam turned once more to the canyon. Not much was happening. Across the creek, two turkey vultures had landed and were feeding on a dead calf, and overhead at least three more were circling. On either end of the box not a soul was in sight. Even the occasional firing had all but ceased, for it had been a good thirty minutes now since the last shot had rung out. Off to Cam's right, Jaz leaned against the cooler side of his boulder, relaxed but watching, always watching. Francisco Luna, a few feet away, had finally succumbed to the long ordeal and was asleep. Thirst and hunger gnawed at each of them, Cam knew, but neither sensation was any worse than the fatigue they all must feel. He himself was sleepy, for he had slept almost none at all before his watch in the wee hours of the morning and less yet since. He wished to God something would happen, yet he was glad for the respite, too. They did not have an endless supply of ammunition with which to hold off an attack, he knew.

He began to wonder if the Cross Arrow had suspected this yet. Would they try another assault? If not, why hadn't they at least tried to come in on them from behind, from the rim of the cul-de-sac? He thought about this and decided unhappily that it was because they didn't have to. All they have to do is wait us out, he told himself silently. They know we've got little or no chance of escaping, even after nightfall, but they also know that we must at least try. Even if they don't know that we are without canteen or food or enough ammunition for a prolonged fight, they must figure that even short one horse we will eventually have to try.

And they'll be ready for us; God, how they'll be ready!

Wearily he leaned back to rest his eyes from the merciless glare of the sun, thinking vaguely now how poorly cut out for this sort of thing was an orphaned cowhand from Colorado. Then, for a few moments at least, he let it slip from his mind and just dozed.

Dimly he heard someone calling his name. ". . . Hey, Stallings! Wake up, Stallings!" It was Jaz, rifle in hand, peering over the boulder a few yards away.

Cam blinked his eyes at the bright sun, then jerked upright. "What's the matter? What is it?"

"Somethin's happenin' over there," the Indian said. "I heard some hollerin' a minute ago, then a couple of guys come runnin' down outa the rocks and some others come around with horses for the two that was runnin'."

He was looking across the canyon toward the west entrance. Cam followed his gaze. A little dust cloud rose from around the bend, just outside the box. There was more yelling.

"What's up?" Blake Stoddard asked, coming to take up a position beside Cam. "What are they doing?"

"I don't know yet," Cam said. Then, noticing the sun and the shadows it threw from off to his right now, he added, "Good grief! What time is it?"

"About three," Stoddard said. "You fell asleep. Nothing was happening so we just let you alone. Pablo and I took turns watching the rim while Jaz and Francisco kept an eye on the canyon."

"Jesus," Cam said, still concentrating on the situation across and up the canyon. He said to Jaz, "Anything happening on the other end?"

The Navajo just wagged his head.

Nevertheless, Cam was still looking in that direction when the first shot rang out. It came from the west, from beyond the mouth of the box. He whirled to look that way and in the process of doing so heard half a dozen more shots come in staccato succession. Suddenly a regular din of shooting erupted, some coming from outside the canyon in the general direction of the Cross Arrow's position but at least as much or more coming from somewhere farther away. He looked around at the other men and was greeted with expressions as perplexed as his own. All apparently had the same question in mind; none of them had the answer.

They didn't have time to speculate, either. Shooting erupted to the east now. All heads turned just in time to see half a dozen riders come tearing into view, headed upcanyon toward the opposite end of the box. It didn't take much study to figure out that they were Cross Arrow riders and that they were being pursued, but who they were running from was completely unclear. In fact, the men in the cul-de-sac were so puzzled by the whole thing that not one of them thought to raise a gun. To a man, they just sat there and watched.

A couple of riderless horses appeared next, running from east to west, and behind them came perhaps a dozen riders, only these men were neither riding desperately nor in fright. They were undoubtedly in pursuit of the first six riders.

"Well, I'll be damned," Blake Stoddard said. "Can you believe this?"

On the west end now, riders appeared in two groups—one milling in confusion, the other encircling the first aggressively. The six men who had fled the east entrance pulled up, whirled back, pulled up again, and finally just stopped forlornly where they were. Moments later, they too were surrounded and apparently being disarmed. There was no more shooting, and after a few minutes it occurred to those in the cul-de-sac that not only had friends arrived but that it was probably safe now for them to leave their retreat.

Blake Stoddard crawled out atop one of the boulders and waved both arms high overhead, and presently two riders broke away from the melee across the way to ride in his direction. In both relief and amazement, Cam recognized Dan Stanhope and Reece Crawford. As they rode up and stopped, he saw that both were astride Railroad Slash horses.

"I wouldn't ordinarily be glad to see someone ugly as you, Stanhope," Blake Stoddard said, half leaping, half falling down from the boulder, "but man, right now I'd sure like to shake your hand!"

Cam, too, made his way down and was followed closely by Jaz and the two Mexican boys. He put his hand up to each rider in turn, just as Stoddard had before him, and said to Stanhope, "We were afraid you'd become some kind of meat under all those hoofs last night. I guess it's the understatement of all time to say I'm glad to see you weren't."

Stanhope smiled. "It was a horse race, let me tell you. And don't think I didn't worry about you guys. I heard the first shots and then the herd coming behind me, and I didn't have time to do much more than get out of the way. Next thing I knew I'd damn near run my horse to death and was halfway to the plains. The herd scattered and quit running, but I just kept on going. I knew it was the Cross Arrow doing the shooting because there were so many of them. I couldn't think of anything but going for help, and that's what I did. I went to the Railroad Slash first partly because it's the biggest neighbor the Stretch B has and partly because I figured we could make a pass by the other outfits on the way back here."

Reece Crawford looked at Cam. "He didn't have to ask us twice, Stallings. None of us are proud of how long we've stood by in this, and we'd already got the word sent by Stoddard about the Stretch B herd being held on Cross Arrow range. We were organizing to be at the Stretch B by tomorrow anyhow to offer our help, so it wasn't hard for Dan to bring us together for this. We came just as soon as was possible, believe me."

Cam glanced back across the canyon. "Well, I hope you don't mind my saying you weren't any too soon. We were in a lot of trouble here, as you can see."

The rancher straightened in his saddle. "As I say, none of us are any too proud of our earlier inaction, but we're here in force now—my outfit, the Circle R, the Dot M. And you can bet we'll be helpin' you with those cows. We won't go home till they're all back on the Stretch B plains where they belong. You've got my word on that."

"What about them?" Cam asked, gesturing. "The Cross Arrow—what do we do with them?"

The man studied on it only briefly. "We send for the law. We'll have to hold 'em till someone can get here, but that's no problem. We got Terhune and it shouldn't take long to scare up Mala and the others—" The sudden change in Cam's expression stopped him abruptly. "What's the matter? What'd I say?"

"You said 'Mala and the others.' Do you mean Mala's not over there?"

"Why, no . . . no, she's not. We didn't really expect her to be, though—"

"And the 'others'? What others are you talking about?"

"Well, those damn gunnies, mostly," Crawford said. "We kind of looked for them first off, you know, but we didn't see a thing of Emory, Guerrero, or Gruel . . . and what's that other fellow's name—Carty?

Yeah, those four. They and Mala are not in the bunch we rounded up."

"He's right, Cam," Stanhope confirmed. "Unless they're still hid out somewhere, the ones he's named are not here. Anyhow, Mala probably stayed back at the ranch, and Gerd could just as well have told those gunnies to stay with her . . ."

Cam's eyes were but thin slits and his voice coldly serious as he said, "I don't know about the gunnies, Dan, but I'm sure about Mala. Jaz says he's sure he saw her not two hours ago. I'm convinced that she definitely *was* here."

CHAPTER 18

Cam didn't know how concerned he should be that Mala was not among the captured Cross Arrow crew, but it didn't take him long to confirm that indeed she was not. And just as Reece Crawford had said, neither were Carty, Emory, Gruel, nor Guerrero. Somehow that did worry him. It worried him a lot.

· They tried to question Gerd Terhune, but the man was extremely sullen and would only say that he did not know where his wife and the four men had gone. They weren't in on the fight, they weren't here, and that was that. Most of the Cross Arrow crew members—disarmed to a man now and being carefully held under guard—knew little or nothing. One man said yes, the boss lady had ridden out with them last night but had stayed back from the fight throughout, and apparently the four gunhands had stayed with her. Another man confirmed this, but neither had seen her since last night. A third man was discovered who admitted that he had been the fourth guard at the entrance to the box last evening, and that it had been he who had reported the Stretch B's presence to Terhune. He also confirmed that Mala and the four gunmen had been on the scene—not only last night but during the afternoon, briefly, as well. He had seen them talking with Terhune about the time Cam and Jaz thought they saw Mala, but all five had disappeared after that and he had no idea where they had gone.

"It's those gunnies still running around loose that bothers me," Cam told Crawford and Stanhope a few minutes later. "Do you suppose they and Mala know yet what's happened?"

Mitch Ressler of the Circle R had just ridden up and apparently overheard Cam's remark as he did. "If they don't, they will soon enough," the rancher said, dismounting. "Word of something like this spreads overnight in this country. The Terhunes are through here and I reckon even Mala will know that, soon as she hears."

"You mean she might fly the coop?" Stanhope asked.

The man nodded. "Wouldn't you?"

"I dunno about that," Reece Crawford said. "I been thinkin'. I know that girl pretty well, and I know how bad she wanted the

Stretch B. I say there's no telling what she'll do—her and those gun-hands of Gerd's. No telling atall."

Cam frowned. "Maybe we better try to find them, then. Any idea where they'd go?"

"Well"—Crawford mulled it over—"my first and only guess is back to the Cross Arrow. That's assuming they left before we got here for some reason and don't know what's happened. Which is possible. Who knows."

"But what if they do know? What if they saw and sneaked off while the fight was going on?"

"Then the Cross Arrow is probably the last place they'd go. And I don't know where otherwise. Like I said before, I don't figure there's any telling about Mala Brightwood Terhune."

"My suggestion, then," Mitch Ressler said, "is let's send some men to the Cross Arrow and find out."

"And if she's not there?" Stanhope asked.

Ressler only shrugged. He did not know.

"I'd go along with his suggestion," Reece Crawford said. "Only don't send any more men than are necessary. We'll need a fair group to es-cort the rest of these fellows to town and to hold 'em while we send for the law. What's left of us can help you Stretch B fellows regather the herd and move them onto the plains. If Mala's not located by then, well, we can take it from there—assuming anybody even cares that she's found."

"That sounds reasonable," Dan Stanhope concluded. "What say, Cam?"

Cam, vaguely troubled by the whole conversation, did not manage to sound very convinced as he said, "Yeah . . . that's okay. Sure . . ."

One group, led by Lester McNaab of the Dot M, headed out in the direction of town with Gerd Terhune and his crew, including three dead and one wounded, in tow. There was no longer any resistance among the captured men, mainly because they sensed it was Terhune who was most in trouble and not themselves. Terhune didn't resist mostly because there was precious little he could do alone. He didn't even seem to want to do anything. His whole world had collapsed around him, and because of this he looked both broken and defeated in every sense of the words. He went silently and did not even look back.

A short while later, a second group headed by Mitch Ressler and composed mainly of Circle R riders, struck out for the Cross Arrow to look for Mala. A third group, of which Cam was a member, remained behind and because it was late in the day decided to set up camp and rest their horses overnight before beginning the regather of the herd tomorrow. Cam, Dan Stanhope, Blake Stoddard, and Reece Crawford sat around a campfire discussing the events of the day—at least, three of them were. Cam sat mostly in silence, and the worried look on his face at last came within the notice of his companions.

"You're awful quiet, Stallings," Blake Stoddard finally observed. "What's the matter?"

Cam smiled weakly. "I dunno. Just a bit uneasy, I guess."

Dan Stanhope eyed him perceptively. "You've still got Mala and them gunnies on your mind, I bet."

Cam only shrugged, and Stanhope said reassuringly, "Well, I wouldn't worry if I was you. Chances are Ressler and his bunch will be back in a couple of hours with all five of them. Then you'll know it's over and we can all go back to full-time cowpunchin' again."

Cam stared at him. "You really think that?"

"Why sure." Stanhope blinked. "You mean you don't?"

"No, I don't."

"But why, man?"

"Because I don't think they'll find Mala and her men at the Cross Arrow. I don't think they're there."

Stanhope looked around at the others, then back at Cam. "How do you figure that?"

"She was here. And so were Carty and the rest of that bunch. They had to be. And I don't figure they'd just leave in the middle of the fight. I think they saw what was happening and escaped."

Blake Stoddard leaned forward. "And?"

"And even if Ressler and his men found them," Cam went on, although not exactly in answer to Stoddard's question, "do you think the likes of Carty or Emory or Guerrero would let themselves be taken just like that? Not much! No, I think they're still to be dealt with and I suspect so is Mala. And it bothers hell out of me, if you really want to know."

"But what can they do now?" Stoddard persisted. "The Cross Arrow is busted. Terhune and Mala tried to steal Stretch B cattle and they tried to kill Stretch B hands. Everybody will know, and even if the law doesn't deal with them they're still through around here. So what can Mala and four men do now?"

Cam rose. "That's the trouble. The more I think about it, the more I have no idea what they are liable to do. Maybe it's nothing, maybe it's something. And who is busted around here is Gerd Terhune—not necessarily Mala. I'm not sure the law or anyone else will be able to pin the sins of the Cross Arrow on her. Maybe she doesn't know that, but I don't think she's just going to give up and go away. What she wants is the Stretch B and what's still in her way is Stacy. That's what bothers me most just now."

"Stacy," Stanhope repeated a little stupidly. "Christ—I all but forgot about Stacy!"

"Yes, you did. And I didn't do much better, till a little while ago. I was just so proud of myself for making her stay home and out of all this I forgot that she's there with only Jozie and old Miguel to protect her." He paused, thinking. "Look, I'm sure she's in no real danger yet, but I'd sure feel better if she were here. I know she'd wanta help with that gather, to see her cattle in a herd once again. Why don't I go on in to the ranch tonight and bring her back tomorrow? I'll even bring Jozie, too. What say?"

"Are you sure you wanta go alone?" Stanhope asked. "You don't want anyone to go with you?"

Cam shrugged. "I don't see any need. You fellows will need all the help you can get here, especially if Ressler's crew doesn't get back. It won't be like rounding them up in the canyon, you know. This is going to take a lot of men."

Stanhope looked around, then said, "Well, your horse hasn't done anything but stand around all day, and you're the boss. Whatever you say is fine with me."

"Good." Cam was already turning toward his saddle. "Look for me back by noon tomorrow." Ten minutes later he was saddled up and on his way out of camp.

As he rode off, Jaz walked up to the group and stared after him. "Where's he goin'?"

"To the Stretch B to get Stacy," Stanhope answered, a little surprised. "Why?"

"Alone?"

"Yes. Alone. Why do you ask?"

The young Navajo shook his head stolidly. "Dunno. Just wondered." But not long afterward, he, too, saddled up, and without a word of explanation rode off in the same direction as Cam had gone.

Full dark claimed the land well before Cam left the wooded foothills and reached the plains. The moon rose at his back and immediately flooded the scene with soft light. He rode easily, saving his horse, and turned almost due north as he came fully into open country. A few small, fluffy clouds floated lazily in the sky; it was warm; there was almost no breeze. In some ways, the air actually seemed heavy, as before a storm.

Cam figured he was an hour and a half easy riding time from the Stretch B now, and because it really wasn't all that far, he for a while resisted any urge to hurry. He would be there soon enough, he kept telling himself; there was no use abusing his horse. Nevertheless, he presently allowed the animal out of its steady walk into a brisk little trot, and after about a quarter of a mile of this spurred it into an easy lope. This continued for another half a mile, after which he returned to a walk to let the animal cool. He wasn't really hurrying, he told himself; it was a nice pleasant night and certainly the horse wouldn't hurt from a little light galloping now and then . . .

But maybe because he was trying so hard to convince himself not to be apprehensive, he stayed with the slower gait this time and presently managed to occupy himself with counting the dim shapes of cattle that were scattered here and there. He hadn't been too surprised at the number he had seen closer to Red Creek; he had fully expected to see quite a few Stretch B cattle throughout the foothill portion of his trip. To find so many already out on the plains was an added bonus he had not anticipated, however. Which was just fine. Any break at all would be welcome in the attempt to regather the herd and move them away from Cross Arrow range for good.

Still, he could not put himself fully at ease; he just could not say to himself that all is over and the only thing left now is the cowboying. Despite Mitch Ressler's foray to the Cross Arrow headquarters, Cam was convinced that Mala would remain loose somewhere with those four goons of Terhune's. And he couldn't help remembering what Jaz had once said: ". . . *Someday them men gonna try to kill you.*" And Stacy: "*I know my sister and I know what kind of men she has working for her . . . Mala will never let it rest. I know she won't.*"

He tried not to think about it; he went back to trying to count cows; he thought about Stacy and worked to picture how happy she would be to hear that the herd was being recovered and that Gerd Terhune would not trouble her again; he breathed deeply of the clear night air and thought how much better things seemed now than they had just a few days before . . .

And then he saw in the distance the first ruddy glow of flames—and knew with sudden alarm that not only was something big on fire up ahead, but that he was looking directly toward Stretch B headquarters and Stacy Brightwood's store.

He came pounding into the ranch yard, his horse lathered and its sides heaving, only to be faced with raw havoc and destruction. Not only the house and store, but the barn as well, were consumed by flames. The entire scene glowed orange-red, and eerie, white-looking smoke billowed upward in dense clouds all around. A calf bawled and horses were running around loose in the yard, and from the barn a desperate neighing indicated that at least one animal was trapped there. The entire area for two hundred yards around was lit up crazily, almost like day, and the only thing not on fire was the bunkhouse—which, for that reason, was where Cam went first.

He dismounted at the porch and charged up to the door, which he found ajar. A lamp glowed inside, but a quick inspection found no one there. Outside again, he searched the yard desperately. There was no one in sight. His eyes locked on the main house just as the roof crashed in and embers leaped high in the air. He thought of Stacy and cried out her name and knew as he did that there was little chance anyone would hear over the roar of the flames. But then he did see someone . . . someone running near the house, falling, then rising to run again.

He turned to his horse but the animal had disappeared, probably having whirled to run the instant Cam had dismounted and left it only moments ago. He whirled back and started to run toward the main house, toward the figure he had seen running away from it. He ran wildly, hoping and praying it was Stacy and that she was all right. He stumbled and fell but got up again. He ran blindly. He saw the figure running in front of him, away from him, and he called out, "Stacy! Stacy, it's me! Jesus . . . wait! *Wait, will you!*"

The figure fell and did not get up, and then as Cam drew near another figure suddenly materialized, this one on horseback and coming out of the darkness and into the firelight seventy-five yards away. The rider drew up, but Cam didn't know, almost didn't care, what to make of it. He just kept running . . .

But then came the muzzle flash and the report of a gunshot; something hit Cam hard, causing one leg to go out from under him in midstride. He spun around. He fell. He hurt. He tried but could not get up.

And then he heard: "*I got him! I got the bastard dead in his tracks!*" And there was more gunfire and someone else yelling and a crazy-wild screech from behind him that sounded frighteningly like an Indian war cry, and then more firing, and suddenly he felt numb and weighted down and he could not move. He felt more helpless than he had even that day on the malpais when he was pinned beneath his horse.

When he passed out, seconds later, it was with the distinct feeling that the dead horse was there on top of him all over again.

CHAPTER 19

What he awoke to was the acrid stink of charred wood and a terrible blur all around him. He was sick and in pain. It took several minutes for his vision to clear. It was daylight, but he was no longer outside. He was in a bed—a bunkhouse bunk—and a window was open just over his head. There was very little breeze, yet it was not hot. It was morning, probably not two hours past sunup. Coffee was boiling on the stove at the cookshack end of the bunkhouse. Someone else was there.

A voice said, "You awake, Stallings? Hey!"

Jaz. Dear God, it was Jaz.

"You awake, Stallings?" the young Navajo repeated, coming over to stand beside him.

"I've been shot," Cam announced stupidly. "Someone shot me last night . . . was it last night? Dammit, Jaz, you tell me it was two days ago or something like that, and I'll shoot you!"

The Indian smiled. "You awake," he concluded simply.

"Jesus. What's happened? The fire, the shooting, Stacy . . . is Stacy all right?" Cam rattled it off so fast it made him dizzy. God, how his stomach churned, how he hurt . . . But where did he hurt? All over? Yes . . . but no, it was his leg, his left leg mostly.

Jaz sat down on an adjacent bunk. "Dunno ever'thing yet. Miz Stacy gone. Jozie gone. Old Miguel, he dead. Shot in the back out by the corrals. I bury him already. Juana, she's okay. She's cookin' breakfast. She run from the house and you chase her. Two men come and shoot you. I shoot and yell and scare 'em off. Think 'em Gruel and mebbe Guerrero. They ride off in the dark and don't come back. Think 'em pretty scared of Indi'ns." He gave a little laugh that was really more of a grunt, then didn't say any more.

"But where? Where did Stacy and Jozie go? What about Mala and the other gunnies? Did they set the fires?" Again he was rattling off things faster than he could think. Of course they set the fires . . . but where *was* everybody now?

"Dunno yet," Jaz repeated patiently. "You gotta get up from there, get dressed, eat, get some coffee. I gotta go see. Think Jozie took Miz

Stacy into the malpais. Think you told 'em one time to do that. If them gunnies and Miz Mala chase 'em there, I gotta go see."

"But what about Gruel and Guerrero, if that's who they were? What were they doing without the others?"

Jaz shrugged. "Stay behind, set fires, I reckon. Dunno."

Cam tried to rise. "Well, you can't go after them alone. Am I shot anywhere besides my leg? Did you catch my horse? Surely I can ride . . . oh, Christ." He collapsed back on the bunk as pain shot up his leg.

"You can't go," Jaz said sternly. "You wouldn't be no good help. Juana take care of you. Just me go."

"Jesus," Cam said, but he could see there was no use arguing. Jaz helped him get dressed and over to the cookshack end of the bunkhouse, where he then sat him down at the table. For a moment Cam thought he was going to pass out before they reached the table. But he didn't, and although he could stand to put very little pressure on the leg, he was able to hop along with Jaz's support and still not cause the leg to bleed. The wound had been very expertly wrapped and Cam suspected even cauterized.

"Is the bullet still in there?" he asked as Juana came around with a cup of coffee and a plate of fried eggs and ham. The smell of the food caused his stomach to churn wildly, despite the fact that Juana was an excellent cook and there was nothing wrong with either the eggs or the ham.

"Nope," Jaz said. "Me cut 'im out. You never wake up. You just don't make 'im bleed, you hear?"

"I don't think I have enough strength to even do that," Cam said despondently. "I never felt this weak before in my life."

"You be all right. Get some food. Rest a little bit. You be all right," Jaz assured him, then turned. "I gotta go now."

Cam watched him out the door and listened as the young Indian trotted his horse beyond earshot of the hoofbeats. Then he turned to stare at the plate of eggs in front of him. After a couple of deep breaths that helped his stomach some, he picked up a fork and began slowly to force some of it down. Several minutes later, when he had finally finished, he reached across for his coffee cup and looked up at the girl still hovering nearby.

"Did he catch my horse, Juana? Is the horse out there?"

The girl stared at him. "He catch it," she said hesitantly. "It down at the corrals. But you not goin' nowhere, Stallings. Jaz said you gotta stay here."

Cam took a tentative sip of the coffee, then said, "Like hell I do!"

* * *

Stacy Brightwood stared out across the lava beds. Here, farther in on them than she had ever been in her life, they were even more stark and treacherous than she had imagined they would be.

They stretched for miles. They undulated endlessly, their jagged rock surfaces broken only intermittently by the scattered basins of good soil and grass and low-growing bushes and sometimes a few trees. One could drop off into one of the basins now and then, but they never led anywhere and you always had to top out upon the rock again to proceed. And Jozie didn't seem to like either situation: the former left too many tracks while the latter was high ground on which two riders could perhaps be skylined and because of the rocks was unbelievably difficult going for the horses.

But they had no choice. They were going to the place Stacy's father had told her about, and Jozie said there was no other way there. They had left the ranch just before sundown yesterday, only a few minutes after Jozie had raced in with the news that he had just been shot at from a distance by five riders out on the range. This was alarming news in itself, but when he added that the distance had not been so great that he could not identify who it was, that it had been Mala and the four gunnies headed toward the Stretch B with apparent fire in their eyes, Stacy had known there could be no hanging around to get shot at further. Reluctantly, they had left Miguel and Juana behind, mostly because there was no time to organize any greater exodus than Jozie and Stacy were able to put together, and because Jozie had insisted that four riders would leave too many tracks and slow them down.

They entered the malpais just at dusk, at a point where Jozie said they must, and rode until full dark was upon them. There they made a fireless, cold-supper camp for the night, for Jozie said to go farther in the dark would only get them lost, and no one alive could trail them on the malpais at night anyway. Hopefully no one could in daylight, but Guerrero was back there, and Jozie said that if any of the five could, that shriveled little Mexican who could ride any horse, follow any trail, and was so quick to kill would be the one.

They saw the rich orange glow of the fire and its smoke rising two hours after dark, and they knew with sinking hearts that only the Stretch B ranch buildings could make such a fire. They also knew there was no use going back; there would be nothing they could do. Stacy cried and worried about Miguel and Juana and wondered how Mala could do such a thing, but after a while she turned her eyes from the blaze and did not look at it again that night.

Come first light, they were up after a fitful sleep. All they could see now of the fire was a lingering plume of smoke rising in the distance.

They did not spend much time looking at it. By sunup, they were on their way again. That had been several hours ago.

"How can you possibly tell where to go?" Stacy asked dully, now, as she viewed the endlessness of the lava beds. "It all looks so much the same to me."

"Not the same," he said. "We're on the trail now. We gonna go there pretty straight from here on. You gonna see."

To Stacy, the "trail" seemed so indistinct she almost couldn't tell there was one. "Is it still far?" she asked.

He shrugged. "Not so far now. Mebbe take a few hours, mebbe more. Can't hurry too much. We gotta not leave no good trail or they follow us. Gotta ride 'round in the rocks lotsa times and stuff."

Well, Stacy thought, there was indeed plenty of rock, if that was going to help. But it was so hard on the horses; even shod, their feet were taking a terrible beating.

"Jozie," she said presently. "What's going to happen to us out here? Even if we get there, we only have provisions for a few days. And if they find us . . ."

Again Jozie shrugged. "Dunno. Dunno what's gonna happen. Mebbe Stallings come, mebbe we get help." He shrugged once more.

Stacy thought about Cam and Stanhope and Jaz and the others. What had *happened* at the Cross Arrow? Certainly something must have, for Mala and her men had shot at Jozie without provocation otherwise, and they had burned the ranch. This remained something Stacy almost couldn't believe. What indeed had happened at the Cross Arrow? What had set Mala off so? What did she now have in mind? Was it murder? Was that her last resort, her last hope now of obtaining the Stretch B? The death of its only heir? Had Mala gone completely mad?

They rode on. The sun had drawn well up in the sky now, and the black lava rock absorbed its hot rays like a sponge absorbs water. Stacy grew thirsty, but they had brought only one canteen. Jozie said they must conserve until they got there. There would be the ice cave and water there, but they must reach it first. And it would get hotter. Much hotter.

They looked back constantly. Not once did they see anybody coming, but Jozie said no matter: their pursuers were back there someplace, he knew they were. They must not stop until they found the place Stacy's father had showed him; they must hide there and hope that eventually help would come.

Fern Carty didn't cotton much to "woman huntin'." He hoped it wouldn't come to a killing and told himself he'd have nothing to do with it if it did. But still, here he was, square in the middle of the hunt and nowhere close to turning back. Why?

Well, it was just that he'd never met a woman like Mala Terhune before. Never. A woman who might actually be his, if he would just play the hand she seemed to have dealt him. A woman who needed him just now and knew that she did, for who among those other three goons could she trust even for a moment? Carty smiled inwardly. Any fool could see the gleam in Pit Emory's eyes whenever he looked at her, and the same was true, to only a slightly lesser extent, of Gruel and Guerrero. Only Carty kept them off her, for it was Carty alone that all three were afraid of.

So it was the woman, this beautiful, fiery woman, who was after the other woman; it was the woman who offered them each money, a lot of money, if they would help her; and it was the four men who—at least for the moment—submitted themselves to her beck and call, albeit for anything but the most loyal of reasons.

They had camped at the edge of the malpais overnight and entered the lava flow at daybreak, following tracks that dark had forced them to abandon the night before. Even in daylight, it was not easy. Guerrero was a good tracker, but this malpais stuff was a case of its own. Not once had they lost the tracks completely, but at best the going was agonizingly slow and uncertain. Just now, Guerrero was on foot and leading his horse well ahead of the others, studying the ground carefully and refusing to let anyone proceed until he was sure of what he saw.

Carty and Mala had stopped and were sitting their horses about fifty yards back, waiting. Gruel and Pit Emory were two dozen yards farther back yet.

"Do you think Lizard and Max really shot Cam Stallings last night?" Mala asked, after a bit.

"They say they did."

The woman twisted impatiently in her saddle. "And do you think he's dead?"

"I have no way of knowin', for sure. If you'll remember, Lizard and Max weren't all that clear with their story. They said somethin' about that other Navvy showin' up and them clearin' out. Stallings may be dead, he may not. I don't really think so, because that's what brought Lizard and Max here as much as anything. They hate him and they want him dead. It's their hope that if he's not dead, he'll at least come on after us so they can get him for good this time."

"And even if he doesn't come, Jaz is back there. Always Jaz. He will come after us, won't he?"

"He might, yes."

"And what will happen if he does?"

Carty shrugged. "Someone'll get killed, I reckon. Maybe him, maybe the other Indian—the one with your sister . . ."

Mala's eyes suddenly flared. "Don't call her my sister! She has ruined me, caused me to lose everything I ever wanted. Don't ever call her my sister again, do you understand?"

Carty gave her an uncomfortable look. "And you wanta kill her, is that it? You actually want to kill your own sister?"

"*I said don't call her that!*" Mala hissed, keeping her voice down only so Emory and Gruel would not hear. "Yes, yes, yes! I do want her dead. It is the only way now. I want her dead, and I want to do it myself. I must, don't you see?"

Carty shook his head. No, he did not see. He had killed his share of men; it had been his way of life for years now. He was neither proud nor ashamed of it. He had done what had been his lot to do. But the killing of blood kin, such hatred evidenced by a woman—he understood none of that.

Suddenly the woman's expression changed, as if she had seen something in his face that frightened her or made her unsure. "Don't look at me that way, Fern—please. I need you, and you must help me. I'll make it worth it to you afterward, believe me, I will."

It was Carty's turn to twist in his saddle. He still didn't like this, but he had never known the joy of a woman this beautiful before; he had never been rewarded with a promise such as she offered. There were things about a man's world he was damned tired of, and what he had missed in the way of fine women was one of them. It was about time he made up for some of that.

He glanced up at the sun beginning to beat down on them now, then looked back at Gruel and Emory. They did not seem to have been listening. He turned once more to Mala.

"Just do what I tell you," he said in a low voice. "If you want my help, first thing is, I've got a notion you and me would do better without them others. I got a notion we sure as hell would."

How Jozie did it, Stacy had no idea, but he never once lost the trail. It was dim, almost never used nowadays, and in many places seen only because it had been worn in rock by countless moccasined footsteps in days gone by. But Jozie stayed with it until, along about midafternoon, they finally found the tiny valley with the ice cave.

What they saw was just another of those basins, less than a mile long and half a mile wide and rimmed at least in part by abrupt lava walls that sometimes rose to as much as twenty feet in height. Where the walls were not abrupt, access was no more difficult than any of the other basins they'd seen but in all cases required care in locating the best route. Here the trail wound down among the rocks and brought them to the basin floor not two hundred yards from a small clump of junipers, and the ice cave.

"Are you sure this is the right place?" Stacy asked, nevertheless, as they reached the cave. "I mean, all places look so alike here. Just rock, rock, rock. Everywhere."

Jozie dismounted in front of the cave. A steady trickle of clear water fell into a glassy pool at his feet. "This is the place. The cave, ever'thin' . . . just like I remember it. C'mon. Get a drink before the horses. This water's good 'n' cold. You'll like it pretty good."

Stacy gladly did as instructed and was instantly rewarded with the sensation of having her lips nearly frozen by the water while one hand was being burned by the nearby rock she had placed it on. But this did not stop her from drinking. She cupped her other hand beneath the trickle and sipped greedily until the hand, her lips, and her throat were all three almost numb from the cold. She had never enjoyed a drink of water so much before.

When she finally rose, wiping her mouth with her sleeve as she stepped back, Jozie laughed lightly.

"What's the matter?"

"You drink plenty much. You drink 'im almost dry." He laughed some more.

"I was thirsty," Stacy retorted, although also smiling. "Aren't you?"

"Yeah, but I'm gonna leave some for the horses," he said, still laughing as he bent down.

Stacy, deciding the joke had had its run, turned her attention to the cave. It wasn't a terribly large one, its mouth measuring perhaps no more than four feet by four feet. But it *was* an ice cave. She had heard of them for many years but had never seen one, mostly because the Stretch B lay on the wrong side of the lava flow to visit one handily. She didn't even know what caused them, although her father had told her once that it had something to do with the way the lava had cooled all those eons ago. But regardless of its cause, there was ice in there, even on a hot summer day like today. And whatever the water source, ice formed, thawed just enough near the entrance to bring about the trickle of water, and thus formed the little pool at the base of the rock in front of the cave.

"I'm gonna unsaddle the horses," Jozie said, rising. "Gonna hobble 'em and go back up the trail to see if I can see anybody followin' us. You stay here, make camp. Okay?"

"Can we build a fire later—so I can fix some supper?"

He looked around. "Mebbe a little one. Mebbe after dark. We'll see."

There were three fair-sized junipers growing almost together a few feet from the cave, and once Jozie had gone, Stacy went over and sat in the shade cast by the larger of the three. The horses grazed on coarse galleta grass about twenty-five yards away, and but for them and Stacy and a few birds there did not seem to be any life within the basin. She had both a rifle and a small-caliber pistol with her, and laying the rifle within comfortable reach at her side, she leaned back to rest her eyes.

She did not intend to fall asleep, but time passed sort of dreamily as if she indeed were dozing, and when she next stirred, the shadows had lengthened noticeably around her and Jozie was still gone.

She began thinking about making camp for the night. There wasn't much in the way of wood for a fire—even a small one—and possible shelter consisted almost solely of the small clump of junipers. She wondered if she and Jozie really were being pursued, if their trail could possibly be followed. If so, how far back were their pursuers? How soon might they come? And if they caught up, what then? Was this a good place to be, or would she and Jozie be forced to run once more? And if they ran, where would they run to? On and on into the malpais? Forever and ever? Or would Mala finally catch up and have her way . . . ?

Stacy shivered at this thought. What better place for a murder than the malpais—where a body almost certainly would never be found? Perhaps coming here had not been such a good idea after all. It was what Cam had advised her to do, and in the hurry of the moment she had not thought any further than that. Well, there were risks in everything. Certainly not many places would be any harder to find than this one, for if they were going to get run to ground here, they would probably get run to ground anywhere they went. And if Cam should come to the ranch looking for them, he would know immediately where they had gone. He would know, for here on the malpais was where he had told them to go. Of course, he himself had never been to the place, and to find it he would need Jaz along for a guide, or perhaps be an even better tracker than the likes of Lizard Guerrero and all those others already back there trying. And to expect either Cam or Jaz to come at all was to presume that either or both had not been hurt or killed while at Red Creek on the Cross Arrow—there was always that terrible possibility!

Stacy shuddered, for this line of thinking only served to disturb her. It was no good worrying over things she could do nothing about. She rose and decided to busy herself by trying to find some firewood, and to wrest some comfort from the situation by telling herself that at least she was not alone here. She had Jozie with her . . . at least, she had Jozie.

But even this small bit of solace was due to be shattered a few minutes later when she heard shots and knew instantly that the reports had
come from somewhere beyond the rim of the basin—in almost precisely
the direction Jozie had gone.

CHAPTER 20

It took Cam nearly half an hour to get his horse saddled and then figure a way to get himself mounted. His left leg would carry almost no weight at all and it finally became clear that he would have to ease the horse up to the corral fence and crawl aboard from there. This proved no easy task, as the animal plainly had never been mounted from a fence before. But somehow Cam managed, and despite the problems was quick to see that he did have an advantage or two as he rode north toward the malpais.

First, there were at least eight sets of tracks for him to follow rather than just one, two, or three; quite a trail had been beaten out, and this would make things easier here and perhaps possible once the lava beds were reached. Second, no one up ahead knew he was coming. Even Jaz didn't. Whoever had shot him last night, whether it was Gruel and Guerrero or someone else, might even think him dead. The others would either think the same thing or would not be aware of his presence on the scene at all.

But that was about it, as far as advantages went. His leg wound was above the knee, and in addition to the pain and relative immobility it caused him, he rode in constant fear that the wound might reopen. He did not feel very strong and assumed he had bled a good deal before Jaz got to him last night. More bleeding yet could be serious indeed and certainly could cut his already questionable effectiveness to none if it started up again and could not be stopped.

Fortunately, there had been no recurrence so far; he was able to keep pressure off the leg by keeping his weight slightly shifted in the saddle, and the horse—a long-legged blue roan—had an easy walking gait that did not jar him significantly. He was both alert and hopeful, and he had no intention of getting himself into a jackpot he could not get out of. He carried both rifle and six-gun, a replenished supply of ammunition, a freshly filled canteen, and all the beef jerky and cold biscuits that he could cram into his saddlebags. He figured he was an hour and a half behind Jaz and no telling how far behind the others. He had no idea what he would ride into or what he might do when he got there; he just hoped he would be able to help out, if needed, and that Stacy would be found rescued unharmed.

He had no trouble following the several sets of tracks between the ranch and the edge of the malpais. He even made good time, considering the pace he was forced to set for himself, and presently was surprised to come upon a spot where someone—at least four or five persons—had made camp the night before not three miles from the ranch. He did not require lengthy speculation as to who those four or five persons had been.

He reached the edge of the malpais before noon, and this time was not surprised to find signs of a second camp a little farther in. Jozie and Stacy, he was sure—most likely having been halted by nightfall. He wondered if they had known that they were no farther from their pursuers than they had been, if they had seen the fire at the ranch. He decided they probably had on both counts and knew how discouraged that must have made Stacy.

But they had gone on, nevertheless. The tracks of all parties moved out to the north, onto ever-rockier ground over which Cam knew tracking would become next to impossible. He scanned the scene ahead all the way to the horizon. He scanned it again and again. It was an awful backdrop against which to see anything or anybody not skylined. He saw nothing move. He rode on, following the tracks.

He no longer made good time. Several times the tracking became so difficult he had to retrace his steps and begin again from the last known point of the tracks. Still he did not see anyone up ahead. Once his horse almost stepped on a rattlesnake; it was coiled, and its rattles suddenly whirred, causing Cam's horse to jump almost out from under him. The reptile was almost black, the color of its surroundings. It struck at but missed the horse, and Cam, not wanting to shoot or waste the time it would take to flay it to death with his lariat rope, reined around it and passed on by.

The sun was very hot now; his leg throbbed, but luckily still did not bleed. He rode on, tracking carefully. He ate a few pieces of jerky and drank water sparingly as he rode. He did not stop even to rest. He knew he had everything to spare but time. He grew light-headed, but still he did not stop.

And then a somewhat startling realization struck him. He was no longer following eight sets of tracks. Somewhere back there in the rocks, at least two, perhaps three, riders had departed from the trail being followed by the other four or five. Somehow he had not noticed, and now he was completely unsure how far back the separation had occurred—and certainly he had no idea which two or three had cut away. Quickly he looked all around. Nothing moved; he could spot no one.

He followed the tracks around a small grassy basin where someone had worked very hard not to leave a trail and someone else had labored equally hard not to lose one. The sun was well to his left now; midafternoon had come and gone. He began to worry that nightfall might catch the lot of them still out here like this; he wondered what had become of Jaz. Was the young Indian still with the trail or had he been one of those who had split away? Certainly the Navajo knew where Stacy and Jozie were going; he knew of the place Amos Brightwood had told his daughter about. But would he try to circle around and get ahead? And if he had done that, where were the other tracks going? Had Mala and her group missed something too?

Cam had no way of knowing. He had no choice but to continue on. The sun continued to drop. Four o'clock now, at least. He rode on for another half a mile, then a mile. It seemed to take forever, and but for the occasional tracks he would not have known anyone other than himself was within fifty miles . . .

He would not have known—except it was then that he, too, heard the shots being fired somewhere up ahead.

Stacy didn't know what to do. The gunfire hadn't stopped with just one or two shots; it hadn't stopped at all, in fact. Instinctively she had grabbed up her rifle and ducked for cover behind the nearest rocks. The shooting continued, and after several minutes she had become convinced that more than one or two rifles were involved. She counted at least four different-sounding reports and was convinced also that some were coming from farther away than others. The idea that Jozie might not be involved never crossed her mind. She knew he was out there and was certain that it was he, primarily, who was being fired upon.

The question was: What should she do? She couldn't see anybody and was certain that all of the firing was taking place beyond the south rim of the basin. Should she go there and try to help out, or should she saddle up and run? Or should she simply stay where she was? She did not like the idea of running, rejected the notion entirely, in fact. But of the other two choices, she had no idea. Indecision assailed her, and for the moment at least she did nothing but sit and listen.

The shooting slowed some but did not stop completely. It became desultory. Someone was pinned down out there, but who? Jozie? Or was it the other side? Could she be of help if she went, or would she simply be in the way?

She continued to wait. Five minutes passed, then ten, then fifteen. It seemed forever. Shots were fired less frequently now, but never was there a complete cessation. What should she do?

She looked around the basin. The horses, hobbled, had at first thrown up their heads at the shots and had even acted a bit nervous over them. But now they had gone back to grazing and were not far away. Should she catch them and saddle them back up—have them ready in case Jozie should somehow slip away and wish to make a run for it?

Again she was unsure. Where would they run to? How far could they possibly get? They would have to leave the basin, but could they? Was there any direction they could go without being seen? In broad daylight, she doubted it. Perhaps they could slip away after dark, but how soon would that be? She looked at the sun; three hours from sundown at best, three and a half till dark—a long time to hold out, she was sure.

And the question kept nagging her: Was there anything more immediate she could do to help Jozie? Shouldn't she try to slip up there and at least see if she could locate him?

She thought about this for several moments, then decided. Yes, that's what she would do: she would go to Jozie.

Pit Emory sat crouched behind a great jumble of malpais rock, thinking to himself: "Christ—what a helluva deal this is!" It was that damned Indian up there, he knew it was. And he had all three of them pinned down—Lizard, Max, Pit—all three of them. Like fools, they had ridden to within a hundred yards of him and never knew he was there—until Max spotted him jumping from one rock to another and for the second time in two days, without waiting to see what was what, had fired on him—and, of course, missed! That chump, Max!

And now it was them in trouble, for despite the fact that they had him outnumbered three to one, he had position on them. And in this case, position was everything and numbers almost nothing. They were holed up within a low swale surrounded by jagged outcroppings and low bluffs and really had nowhere to go but straight back or straight ahead, either of which would put them in the open for one of the Indian's deadly shots. And of course it was he who had the high ground, which made it just that much more difficult for them to try to make a move.

Not that it was completely hopeless, however. For some while now, Pit had been trying to figure a way to circle around the Indian. He thought he had such a way spotted, too—a way with plenty of cover—if he could just make the first fifty yards or so. Trouble was, it sure did seem a wide-open fifty yards, and the more Pit studied on it, a damned long fifty yards as well.

So, thus far at least, he just had not been able to bring himself to try it. He was even beginning to wonder if he gave a damn about the Indian or the girl, either one. After all, where were the Terhune woman and Carty? They had hung back to let the woman rest and hadn't been seen since. So where were they? Pit, Max, and Lizard could sure use a little help just now. Yes they could.

Pit looked around. Lizard was about twenty yards away, to Pit's left, crouching similarly behind a large rock. Beyond Lizard, another twenty yards, Max hugged an outcrop that rose straight above his head. About a hundred yards back, their horses had wandered to the far end of the swale. It concerned Pit that the animals would get completely away if they went much farther. At least they must be beyond the Indian's view, for Pit never doubted that the Navajo would put a bullet in each of them if he could. Nothing he'd like better than to have his adversaries on foot, Pit knew. That was only smart.

· Pit shifted his weight and a bullet spanged off rock above him. Guerrero fired back, as did Max. Pit only cursed. Some of those bullets were coming too close, and who ever knew when a ricochet might hazard into a target as big as a man? Of course, if they could make it till dark . . . but Christ, how long till then? Too long, that's how long.

Once again he eyed the fifty-yard stretch to his right and the cover beyond. It was then that he caught sight of a slight figure moving in the rocks, about two hundred yards to the right of the Indian's position but only half that far from Pit's. He squinted hard, even though he knew already who it had to be.

For a moment the figure was skylined. There could be no mistaking the small-brimmed hat, the dark-colored divided riding skirt and vest, the lithe grace of the body. She was moving uncertainly, as if momentarily lost, but it had to be Stacy Brightwood.

Pit Emory, more seriously than ever now, began to eye that fifty-yard stretch next to him. He thought if he could cross it he might get to the girl before she could reach the Indian. He considered the odds carefully. After a moment, he decided. If he could get Lizard and Max to cover him, it would definitely be worth the risk.

With the sudden, almost violent re-eruption of shooting from below, Stacy quickly took cover. She knew now that she had badly miscalculated Jozie's position; he was to her right at least 175 yards, and was obviously the target of the renewed fusillade. She did not think whoever it was down there had seen her, for none of the bullets seemed to come her way.

Too, as far as she could tell, there were only two guns firing, although there might as well have been ten for all the lead being thrown. Quite plainly someone was intent on keeping Jozie so hunkered down behind cover that he could not even raise his head to look back. But why? Why so all of a sudden would they want to do that?

She removed her hat and very carefully peeked out around the mass of rock she had hidden behind. Little white puffs of smoke rose lazily above the rocks at the head of the swale below. From her angle she could just see one man crouched low against a rock face, firing every few seconds up at Jozie. The other man she only glimpsed as he rose and fired and then disappeared again all in one quick movement. Neither would make any kind of a target for Stacy to hit, but she was considering taking a few shots just to take the heat off Jozie—until suddenly a third man shot into view to the left of the other two, and she realized why all the covering fire.

The man was racing across an open stretch of ground toward good cover not seventy-five yards from Stacy's position. And as she sat frozen for those few seconds it would take him, it became clear that he would make it, too. Almost before she knew it, he was diving out of sight behind a huge rock slab and she could see him no more.

"Dear God," she breathed through a dry throat and trembling lips. "Oh, dear God!"

But even before she got a chance to panic completely, something else happened. A fourth figure appeared in the rocks above and behind the two who had remained at their first positions. A slender, catlike figure who had a good view of the backs of all three men at the head of the swale. For a moment, Stacy was sure it was Jozie, somehow having slipped around. But it wasn't, for suddenly a shot rang out from Jozie's original position and she knew he was still there. So who . . . who was this new man? Jaz? Could it be Jaz?

She watched, fascinated as the figure achieved the top of a rock bluff and quickly knelt, rifle brought to shoulder in an aiming position. Two quick shots rang out and Stacy heard a bullet whine viciously off into the distance after striking rock somewhere below her—a miss, of course. But the second shot had not been a ricochet. A much duller sound accompanied the report. Had he hit someone? The man who had only moments ago raced across the open stretch in Stacy's direction, perhaps?

Suddenly one of the other two men jumped and ran desperately. Jozie fired at him and so did the figure atop the bluff. The man disappeared in the rocks well to Stacy's left and below the open area. He did not appear to be hit. The third man hugged the rock face he was hiding behind even closer and tried to fire back at Jozie, seemingly unaware that the figure atop the bluff was moving at a crouch to a point just above him now. The figure leaped down and suddenly the two were grappling, one much larger than the other but also much slower. They fell into the the shadows of the rock face. A hoarse scream went up—a scream of fright and then pain. Then came another scream, followed by abrupt quiet. There was no more shooting, no more screaming, no movement anywhere.

For several moments Stacy was as if mesmerized. She simply sat there, staring down, wondering what to do next. Should she call out to Jozie and whoever her other apparent ally was, or was it safe yet to reveal herself?

Her concentration was jarred rudely as a foot crunched gravel behind her. Startled, she tried to turn but got only halfway around before someone clapped a rough hand over her mouth.

"Don't try to scream, miss," Fern Carty told her gruffly. "I can damn well assure you it won't do you any good!"

CHAPTER 21

Cam shifted his left foot from the stirrup and slid painfully to the ground. He hated to dismount, for his leg had stiffened considerably and he was constantly unsure, once on the ground, if he could remount the horse.

But he'd ridden up on a dead man, and he felt it necessary that he at least get down and have a look.

It had been a full half hour since he'd heard any shooting, but still he had approached the scene with care. Just because he couldn't see anyone at the moment, didn't mean there weren't plenty of places to hide in ambush up ahead. A man was obliged to be leery if he wanted to stay alive, Cam was convinced of that.

The body lay face down, half in, half out of a shallow crevice, and because of its size, identification was made all but academic. Nevertheless, Cam hobbled stiffly over and turned the body face up, then stepped back in revulsion. It was Max Gruel, all right, and either Jaz or Jozie had finally got his chance at the man's gizzard! For just a second, Cam actually felt sorry for poor Max, his throat cut like that and all. People might joke about such a thing . . . until they'd seen it done. Cam almost threw up, but somehow he stifled the impulse.

He looked around. So, now the enemy was down to no more than four: Guerrero, Emory, Carty, and Mala. He wondered where everybody was, and it gave him a chill to think about one or all of them being nearby with a rifle trained on his back.

Well, no one had shot him yet, and for some reason he felt pretty certain that most, if not all, had gone somewhere else. Trouble was, where?

He looked around further, found a lot of empty rifle shells scattered about, foot tracks, even horse tracks. But he found no signs that anyone other than Gruel had been hit or knifed—no more blood, primarily— and certainly no sign of anyone or their horses having remained in the area.

He expanded his search slightly, took note of the open area off to the right, and finally found what looked like a running footprint leading across it. Leaving his horse ground-reined where it stood, he decided to try to follow the tracks for a ways and painfully began hobbling along in the direction the first track had taken.

, Nothing about the situation looked very hopeful. Where the ground was not rocky, it was covered with gravel and finding additional tracks was no small chore. After about thirty yards, he figured he'd found one for about every fourth step the man had taken and was lucky to be doing that good. The next twenty yards found him faring no better—if anything, worse. He was about to give up and go back . . . and would have, except it was then that he saw the second body, lying about twenty-five feet away at the base of a jumble of rocks.

He wagged his head; the body lay in the shadows and he almost hadn't seen it. With rifle held in a ready position, he limped on over to the spot and found Pit Emory twisted grotesquely in the final position of his death throes, a single bullet hole in the chest and blood all down his shirt.

Once again, Cam looked around, a little less certain now that he was alone. His leg throbbing, he looked back toward his horse, the distance between them now seeming twice as far as he knew it really to be. Feeling a sudden urgency to get back there, he spotted a fallen yucca stalk a few feet away and wondered if it would serve as a crutch. It wasn't much, but it might do. He was just bending down to pick it up when the shot came, kicking up dust and pebbles frighteningly close to his feet.

A second shot careened off a nearby outcrop and buzzed wickedly off into the distance. Without waiting around, Cam hit the ground then rolled and squirmed his way toward the nearest cover—a jagged piece of lava that jutted into the air about five feet and was no less than that across. Two more shots ricocheted behind him as he went, and for a few moments he simply lay there trying to catch his breath and gritting his teeth against the renewed pain in his leg.

But he knew he could ill afford to relax. Whoever was shooting at him was not far away and might at that very moment be moving closer. Somehow he pulled himself around, into a half-crouching position and levered a shell into the barrel of his rifle. He then attempted to peek over the rock to see if he could spot his adversary.

Another shot greeted him, whining overhead and causing him to duck quickly back down. Whoever it was had Cam and his cover zeroed in; if there were to be many surprises, they weren't going to come from this end, that much was for sure.

A voice called to him. "Hey, gringo! I got you pinned down good, no? Do you hear me, gringo?"

Guerrero! Cam gripped his rifle tightly. He did not answer.

"I thought we got you last night. Too bad for you, eh, gringo? Now I gonna make it worse for you—you hear me?"

Still Cam did not answer. He had moved slightly, hoping to achieve a position from which he could see around the chunk of lava rather than over it. Tentatively, he scanned the area before him. All he could see was lava rock and late afternoon shadows. There was no sign of Lizard Guerrero.

"Come on, señor. I know you are not hit. Are you scared? Are you scared of what's gonna happen to you now, gringo?"

Cam moved stiffly around to the other side of the rock. His leg hurt terribly with every movement, but somehow the bleeding had not resumed. Again he searched the scene with his eyes. Nothing. Still nothing.

"I'm coming to get you, señor. Better be ready!"

Cam jerked. The man had moved; the voice had not come from the same direction this time.

"I know you're hurt. I saw you walk. How about I shoot your other leg this time, for what you did to me in Vera Velarde?—eh, gringo?"

Off to the right . . . he was moving right, circling, coming closer. Cam shifted his position once again, watching intently. Two minutes went by that seemed like twenty. Somehow he had come to expect Guerrero to call out every now and then. Three minutes, four, still nothing.

Then, suddenly, a pebble bounced off rock nearby. Cam whirled around. The rock had been thrown, not dislodged by foot or hand. Guerrero was trying to be tricky. Cam was not fooled. But where was he? It made no difference not to fall for the trick if he did not know where the man was.

"Put the rifle down, señor." The voice was right on top of him now. "Don't turn around. Just lay the rifle down, then you can look. I want you to see me when I kill you."

A dull, sick feeling in the pit of his stomach, Cam quickly gauged his chances. If the man was going to kill him anyhow, why lay down the rifle? Trouble was, Guerrero was almost directly behind him and was very, very close.

Cam cursed himself silently. Even though he had not been fooled by that rock he'd heard, he had still let it distract his attention. And now Guerrero had the drop on him for sure. But should he discard the rifle or not? Or should he try to whirl and shoot? It would require almost a 180-degree turn—could he do it quickly enough? And what kind of target would he have if he made it? The odds were not good, he knew.

"You ought to at least give a man a chance, Guerrero," he said, stalling for time. "I never took you for the kind to gun an unarmed man."

The Mexican laughed, but his voice was deadly cold. "You took me for a fool in Vera Velarde, gringo! I gun you down now like a dog and never blink an eye!"

He knows I've got to try it, Cam thought. *He's making it so I do. He knows he won't be shooting me down unarmed. The little bastard knows!*

Very slowly, Cam took a deep breath, drawing his muscles up for the effort he knew he must make. His rifle was cocked, but bad leg and all, he must whirl from an awkward crouch, and he knew that all he could really hope for was a miracle. Yet he must do it; he had no other choice. And he must make it quick, for the Mexican might just go ahead and shoot . . .

Somehow he was not surprised that the left leg gave on him as he turned, nor that because of this he fell backward as he whirled and fired. He had made his try; he could do no more. He was fully prepared to have missed, to feel immediately the harsh impact of the other man's lead striking him. He even expected to hear the report from Guerrero's rifle coming before that of his own.

But it did not happen that way—not quite, at least. There was another shot, but Guerrero did not fire it. Surprisingly, it came from behind Cam somewhere, perhaps some distance away. Cam's first glimpse of Guerrero was of the man standing atop the lava chunk, looking down, aiming . . . but suddenly staggering back—Cam had no idea if from his own shot or the other one—firing finally but with an aim that was ruined now, then losing his balance and falling backward, disappearing beyond the rock.

And that was all that happened, except for Cam just lying there, stunned, thinking he should do something but not knowing what. And then someone was coming to stand over him, and someone else said, "Hey, Stallings, you pretty damn lucky, you know that?"

Jaz! And Jozie! One of them was already scrambling up over the lava chunk, checking on Guerrero, the other bending down to see about Cam.

"Jesus—where did you fellows come from?"

Jozie smiled. "We waitin' for Guerrero to come out. We know he's hangin' around in the rocks somewhere. Just had to wait till somethin' brings 'im out so we can see 'im good."

"Yeah, well, you damn near waited too long," Cam mumbled as he struggled to get to his feet. "But I'm glad you didn't wait any longer, believe me. Is he dead, Jaz?"

"He's dead," the other Indian said, coming around the rock from the other side. "Break'um neck when he fall. Gunshot just graze'um ribs."

Cam just stared at him. The man must have lost his balance atop the rock when he got hit. But for that, and the fall, he probably would not have been hurt badly enough to keep him from getting off a well-aimed second shot.

"Well," he breathed, "whatever it takes, I guess. But the main thing now is Stacy. I figured all along if I could find you boys, I could find Stacy . . ." He looked around expectantly. "Well, where is she?"

There was something wrong in the two young Navajos' expressions then as they exchanged looks but did not say anything.

Cam frowned in sudden apprehension. "Jaz, Jozie . . . where *is* she?"

It was Jaz who finally answered. "We dunno, Stallings. We dunno where she is."

In simple distance, Stacy was less than a mile away, but in this end-less mass of lava where everything so looked like everything else, it might just as well have been ten miles.

They were on foot, she and Fern Carty, and apparently they were lost. He had disarmed her and discarded her weapons, then dragged her down through the rocks, his hand over her mouth so she could not scream, into a depression in the lava beds, then out across more rocks until they arrived at another of those grassy basins similar to the one with the ice cave. Except here there was no ice cave, and apparently there wasn't anything else Carty was looking for either. They had heard distant shots just a few minutes ago, but all was quiet again now, and the direction of the shooting had been indistinct. It did noth-ing to help Carty locate himself.

"Damn," he said as they reached the basin floor, speaking almost for the first time since he'd captured her.

"What is it?" Stacy asked. Obviously the man no longer worried that she might be heard if she screamed, for he had ceased to hold a hand over her mouth some while ago. He did not release his iron grip on her wrist, however. "What are you looking for?"

"Your sister, for one thing," he mumbled in a gruffly concerned voice. "The horses I left her with, for another."

"And you thought they would be here?"

"I would've sworn it." He looked around in exasperation. "How in hell could I have got so damn mixed up?"

Stacy didn't know whether to be apprehensive or hopeful. "You mean you're lost? We've walked all this way, and you are lost?"

He bent an impatient scowl on her. "It wasn't all that far," he said. "We've gone in circles . . . that's what we must've done. I would have sworn this would be the place."

Stacy switched her gaze to the horizon. The sun was very low there now; not much daylight remained. For reasons she felt now were too obvious to ignore, she was in no hurry to find Mala. But then, what would happen to her even if they did not find Mala! A night alone with Fern Carty? This possibility didn't cheer her very much either.

"Well, obviously this isn't it," she said, in response to his last statement. "I mean, there are no tracks here. Even if she had been here and left, wouldn't there be tracks?"

His scowl turned even harder. It was a simple thing a man like him should not have overlooked. His mood not helped by the realization, he yanked her half off her feet and started dragging her along in a new direction.

"Where are we going now?" she called, trying to keep up without falling.

"It's gotta be over this way," Carty said, glancing at the sun as if for a bearing. Still, she thought his tone more hopeful than confident. "It's in one of these basins. I'll find the right one yet."

Stacy had no choice but to allow herself to be dragged along, tripping and stumbling but never quite going down because he wouldn't let her. She went like a child being hauled out to the woodshed by an angry father—except this man was not her father, and there was nothing as innocent as a woodshed around here.

"Can't you just call out to her or something?" she asked breathlessly as they crawled up through rocks and out of the basin. "You *could* be going the wrong way, you know."

He stopped and looked back at her exasperatedly. "You'd like that, wouldn't you? Have me yellin' and whistlin' all over the place. Bring those Navvies of yours runnin' like a pair of hounds on a scent trail, wouldn't it? Yeah, you'd like that all right." He sneered, and although Stacy had once considered him the most decent of the Cross Arrow gunhands, she realized now that wasn't saying much. Frightened by what she saw in his expression, she vowed not to make any more suggestions.

They trekked across quite a large expanse of jumbled lava outcrops and boulders before dropping off into the next basin, and almost immediately it was plain that Mala and the horses were not here either. Carty was almost beside himself now. He made Stacy sit down on a rock—which she was more than glad to do by now—while he stormed around looking for tracks and found none. Finally he calmed down and presently sat down a few feet away.

"We've come too far," he said, as if talking to himself. "We've come too damn far."

Stacy regarded him silently. He had carried with him a rifle and six-gun, but nothing else of substance—no canteen, probably no food, certainly no bedroll. And the sun was down now; dusk was upon them. She shivered, but not from cold. It was over seven thousand feet in altitude here on the malpais, but the heat of the day was well preserved in the dark-colored rock. It would not be cold or even very cool until perhaps the wee hours of the morning. It was from the thought of being out here alone overnight with Carty that Stacy shivered, not from cold.

"Why do you want to find my sister so badly?" she asked after a few moments. "Are you going to help her kill me? Is that what you want to do?"

He looked suddenly uncomfortable and would not meet her gaze. "That's my business, girl. And if it is what I want, then that's just the way it has to be."

"But why? What could she possibly give you that makes it worth my death? Money? Herself?"

Even more obviously than before, he still would not meet her gaze. He even appeared a bit stung, as if the remark had somehow hit home in a very painful way.

"My God," Stacy breathed.

"Don't be holier-than-thou with me, girl," he said sternly. "I ain't claimin' to be anything better'n what I am. And as far as your sister goes, right now I'm mostly worried about findin' my horse. A man could die wanderin' around out here on foot. More'n anything just now, I ain't wantin' to wind up dead over this deal."

Stacy eyed him. "You know Jaz and Jozie are out there, don't you? You heard those shots a little while ago. That might have been them; you know if they find us they'll kill you. And Cam Stallings and the others . . . they could come looking too. You know that, don't you?"

He met her gaze this time, and there was a returning hardness in his eyes as he did. "That's one thing about me havin' you, girl. Them Navvies—yeah, I know they're out there. And the shots—could be one of them gettin' it, could be Guerrero or someone else. Who knows? But whatever, as long as I got you, they're gonna hesitate to shoot. And for sure, I ain't worried about Stallings. Nossir! That one's bought it, I figure. Max and Lizard got him last night. Got him good, they did . . ."

Something inside Stacy suddenly was as if stopped then; she didn't even hear the rest of his words. She just stared at him with a feeling of having been hit where least expecting it. "You lie! I know you *lie!*"

His smile twisted grimly. "They told me they got him. He showed up at the Stretch B while they was settin' the fires last night—I reckon you saw the sky light up—and they shot him. One of the Navvies showed up and run 'em off before they could make sure, but they both said he went down and didn't get up—"

Almost without warning there was a rage within Stacy, a sudden, intense, almost blinding rage that was the culmination of all that had been heaped upon her. All she could think was: *Cam ... they've killed Cam!* And the desire to strike out was so powerful within her that there was no longer any caution about her, nothing to stop her or to make her care what happened now. She looked at Carty, and with an angry scream leaped at him, swinging, scratching, clawing. The abruptness of this caught him off guard, knocking him off balance. The rifle he'd been holding clattered on the rocks, and both he and Stacy went to the ground.

There was never any doubt that the man's strength would prevail, once he'd gathered his wits and set out to regain control. Even in the midst of her frenzy, Stacy knew she could not compete with him physically. But she didn't care. Her fingernails ripped at his face and drew blood; she slapped and punched and tried to kick. At first he defended himself somewhat passively, trying to cover his head with his arms, then grabbing at her and trying to push her off of him. But she was no weakling; her muscles were trim and tough, and her fury gave her strength she would not normally have had. She did not relent and it took only a short few moments for Carty to realize that she was not going to. It was then that he began to fight back in earnest.

Stacy, who had actually achieved a position on top of her opponent now, suddenly felt herself being shoved violently backward and away from him. She landed hard against a large, upright chunk of lava and her breath went out of her as blinding pain shot up her back and caused her to feel that she might pass out as a result. She slid unceremoniously to a sitting position, and for a moment just sat there in a daze while Carty got slowly to his feet.

He stood looking down on her, a strange expression beginning to claim his features, which to Stacy was suddenly very frightening. It was as if something dreadful within him had been loosed—a violence he now had decided not to even try to control.

"W-what are you going to do?" Stacy asked tremulously.

He stepped toward her. He did not need to explain and they both knew it. He reached down and grabbed her by her blouse front, yanking her upright, encircling her with his other arm and bringing her tightly against him. Slowly but with determination, he forced her head back and put his mouth roughly on hers. Sickened now as well as frightened, Stacy tried desperately to twist away, but he cupped her chin with one hand and would not let her go. She struggled even harder, and somehow this time did break partially free.

But not completely. A hand caught her vest, tore it, and cost her her balance. She fell back against her attacker, hands against his chest, her face looking up and once again close to his.

He smiled lewdly. "You're almost as pretty as your sister, you know that?"

Once more she tried to twist loose. "Let me go! Let me go, *you animal!*"

"Not a chance, girl," he said. "Not now. I'm gonna have it my way, and, say, pretty one—you may even like it! Ha! Ha!"

Somehow this not only sickened her further, it infuriated her. Very suddenly, and without thinking, she spat in his face. Not just once, twice.

"*Why, you . . . you . . .*" he sputtered furiously. "*You little bitch!*" And then he hit her—hit her so hard she virtually left her feet before staggering back to land on her side a full five yards away, her ears ringing and the entire left side of her face feeling as if it had just exploded.

She lay there stunned, her head spinning—or was everything else spinning instead—unable for the moment to even move. She knew only vaguely that Carty still stood where he had been when he hit her, that he was saying something.

". . . Nobody spits in my face, you hear—nobody!" There was more she did not understand, then, ". . . Not gonna mind killin' you a bit now, by damn. When I'm through with you . . . won't mind a damn bit . . ."

Cold fear entered her consciousness, cleared it. He was going to kill her. Degrade her and kill her. She groaned and tried to turn over . . . and as she did, felt something cold and metallic beneath her—Carty's rifle!

Had he seen it? It was covered now by her body, but had he seen or remembered it being there from before? Could she get to it and bring it to bear quickly enough? She would have to jack a shell into the chamber, she was sure. Could she do that too?

She moved just enough that she could look up at him. He was still standing there, his face bleeding where she had scratched him, his eyes glaring. She felt around with one hand for the lever mechanism on the rifle. She grasped it. Carty took a short step forward.

"Don't . . . please don't!" she called out.

He took another step. Stacy rolled and came up in a crouch with the rifle, levering the action in one quick motion, raising the barrel so that it was trained on her antagonist. He stopped, surprised, even took a step back. Stacy quickly struggled to her feet, keeping the rifle leveled all the while.

"Why, you . . ." he started, then broke off. He took another step forward.

"Don't do it," Stacy warned, her finger trembling over the trigger. "Don't come near me, Carty! Don't you dare!"

Ignoring this, he took another step, forcing her to back away. But she could only go so far, a matter of a few feet, before backing into a boulder. Trapped, she could neither get past him nor back away farther. Carty took another step.

"I'll shoot," she warned. "I will. You'll leave me no choice."

He extended a hand to arm's length, reaching toward the barrel. His fingers were less than three feet away. He started to take another step. Stacy screamed, "No!" He suddenly swiped at the rifle barrel. He missed. The weapon boomed and bucked in Stacy's hands even though she never would remember having pulled the trigger. Carty's face went blank with shock and surprise as he was catapulted backward and off his feet, dead perhaps even before he hit the ground, blood already spreading across his shirt front and the bullet surely having destroyed his heart.

Stunned, Stacy just stood there and watched. The man was in his death throes and she knew there was nothing to be done for him. She felt sick. She was on the verge of throwing up. She also felt faint and sensed that she was very close to passing out. She looked around for something to sit on, and was moving toward the rock she had sat on earlier when a sound in the rocks somewhere on the near rim of the basin startled her and caused her to halt in midstride. It was a sound like a horseshoe striking rock—followed closely by a voice calling out:

"Fern . . . was that you down there? Answer me, Fern! I've been trailing you for an hour . . . *Fern!*"

Stacy whirled, tension gripping her. The light was bad now and she could not see anyone up there, but there was no question who it was. The voice was Mala's.

CHAPTER 22

Stacy stepped quickly back into the shadows. It had been foolish for Mala to call out like that; it was as much a warning to foe as friend. But there had been a note of fear in her voice, probably born of the anxiety of being left alone and lost, and in that fact probably lay the explanation for her lack of judgment. It also served to worry Stacy just that much more about her own situation.

If there had been anything at all rational in Mala's nature of recent days, it certainly couldn't be counted on to be there now.

Almost surely she was armed. She would not even be here if she did not want Stacy dead. This whole crazy situation could culminate in only one thing if they came face to face now: two women, blood related, rifles in hand and shooting it out like two hardened gunmen—a scene and a circumstance heretofore, in Stacy's mind at least, reserved only for the cruel, hard world of men . . .

The unavoidable images her mind conjured up while trying to picture it were nightmarish and very frightening. She had just killed a man, and even though it had been done in self-defense the thought that she must carry that fact with her forever was horrible enough; but to be forced to fight Mala, to kill or be killed in a battle with her own sister—could she do that?

Well, she could if she had to. The animal instinct to survive would dictate if it came to that. The thing she must do otherwise was to avoid the confrontation. But how and for how long could she do so?

The fast-settling darkness would help her—she could of course more easily slip away without being seen at night than in daylight—but it might also hinder her. The two of them might stumble onto one another accidentally, even with the bright moonlight that Stacy knew could be expected later. She must be careful. She must hope to somehow come upon Jaz and Jozie before running into Mala or whoever among the Cross Arrow gunhands might still be out there. She must get back among friends . . . somehow.

She thought of Cam, of what Fern Carty had told her only minutes ago. It caused her to feel at first a dull, inner emptiness, but then came anger, a sudden desire to strike out again, just as she had done with Carty. But then she heard Mala's horse moving down among the rocks, coming closer, and she told herself: *No! You must not think that way. Maybe what Carty said was a lie. Dear God, please let it be a lie!*

She looked around, calculating which way to go. Very carefully she began moving farther back into the shadows. Mala called out again: "Fern! Answer me, Fern! Are you still there?"

A chill went up Stacy's spine. Mala was much closer now. And there was still some light. The next few minutes were paramount; she must be very, very careful not to be seen. She made her way up among the rocks, trying not to be hasty, trying desperately not to make any noise, carrying Carty's rifle cautiously in one hand and using the other to steady herself as she climbed.

From behind her now, there came a little shriek, and she knew that Mala had finally discovered Fern Carty's body. There was quiet after that.

Mala stared down at the body, clenching and unclenching her fists in helpless rage and frustration. "You stupid jackass!" she exclaimed beneath her breath. "You had her! You had Stacy and you let her get away!"

She knew he'd captured the girl; she had waited and waited and finally had gone looking for him when he didn't come back. She rode one horse and led the other, and somehow had stumbled across his and the much smaller bootprints she knew could only be Stacy's. She'd trailed them, saw how they were wandering, and realized that Carty had somehow become lost. The idiot!

So now what was she supposed to do? Had Stacy done this? Had she somehow got a gun and killed the feared Mr. Carty? Or had she had help? God, how many people were wandering around on this godforsaken malpais piece of hell, anyway? Those two Navajos, for sure. It had to be one or both of them responsible for all the shooting earlier. But where were they now? Where were Guerrero, Emory, and Gruel? Where was Stacy? Where was *anybody*?

She looked around anxiously. Clouds were forming on the western horizon; it was almost dark. She could barely see tracks anymore. She left the horses ground-reined as she tried to study the footprints. After a few minutes she decided it was hopeless. She could find only two sets of prints, the two she had been following. But so much of the ground was covered with rock, even here on the edge of one of the basins, that she just could not be sure. It had been that way all along; pure luck that she had not lost the trail on a dozen different occasions, just enough soil here and there that she could pick up the tracks when she had to. In fact, she had just about concluded that the trail was lost for good when she heard the shot and, like a fool, shortly thereafter, called out to Carty. Jesus. How foolish that had been! And now, the last light of day rapidly vanishing, there just was no way . . .

Once more she surveyed her surroundings. It was up to her now; she was all alone. And maybe Stacy was too. If so, it would be just the two of them, a fitting way to end it. Mala herself might never have the Stretch B now—she admitted it, at last—but she could still exercise her revenge. She could make certain that Stacy didn't have it, either.

But where was Stacy? She couldn't have gone far. How long was it since the shot had sounded? Five minutes? No more than that. She continued to search the area with her eyes, thinking hard about the situation as she did.

Stacy must be armed, but would she fight? Mala grinned. Probably not, unless she had to. Mala knew her half sister well enough to know that she would avoid it if she could. But where was she? Where to look with night approaching? Should she even try to look at all?

She was still debating this a few seconds later, when suddenly she caught sight of the barest movement not a hundred yards away on the basin rim.

For the first time in a long time, the night sky did not remain clear. A million brightly blinking stars became gradually obliterated as a massive cloud bank moved in from the southwest. A great golden moon rose like a giant prop against a stage sky, only to be blotted out an hour later by the fast-moving clouds. The malpais, for a short while bathed in moonlight, was now cast almost pitch black. In the west, lightning brightened the clouds and intermittently broke the blackness on the ground. And the air smelled fresh and moist and good as conditions built plainly for a good rain.

Stacy simply watched and waited. She was tired and hungry and thirsty, and although the coolness of the night air was invigorating, she felt she must conserve what energy she had left for when she really needed it. Too, she knew she could not just go wandering endlessly across the lava beds; Mala or no Mala, Stacy had to guard against becoming hopelessly lost, for to wander too far could take her miles from where anyone might look for her, and to track her that far across this rocky waste might eventually become impossible for friend as well as foe.

So she had finally come to a place among the rocks, a place she could hide within and see from in all directions, a place well removed from where she had last seen Mala, a place in which she hoped she could somehow survive the night.

She gripped Carty's rifle tightly, and wished disconnectedly that she had food and water and perhaps even a slicker in case it really rained. She looked skyward. How she had waited for this first good rain of the season. How welcome its coming should have been. But right now she dreaded it. Somehow it even frightened her, as if being out here alone on the malpais with her own half sister stalking around wanting to kill her was not already bad enough. The thunder rumbling now in the west, the lightning, the whole eerie atmosphere that was one moment dark and the next light, deepened her gloom and made her question even the worth of survival. There had been plenty of times in the past year when she had felt alone, but never like this. Never.

A large drop of rain splattered on her hand, another hit rock beside her, another struck her in the middle of the back but did not soak through her vest and blouse. The land was suddenly alive with temporary light and thunder cracked overhead so loudly she almost jumped straight up. The smell of ozone mixed with moisture filled the air. And out on the malpais something moved. Stacy got only one brief glimpse, but she would have sworn it was a horse and rider. The land went black again and she could not see to tell for sure.

Heart pounding, she straightened and waited tensely for the next flash of lightning. Drops of rain continued to fall. It seemed like forever before she could see anything again. The entire world lit up as lightning streaked from horizon to horizon and an earth-shaking clap of thunder split the sky. And Stacy saw again—the horse and rider, closer now and possibly two horses instead of one, the second being led. But then they were gone again, and she did not know what to think or what to do.

Was this Mala? Was she coming this way?

The rain began pelting down harder now; water dripped from the brim of Stacy's hat; her clothes were becoming wet. She shivered slightly and shifted her weight. It would be but a matter of minutes before her vest and blouse were soaked through. The rifle, too, was getting wet and there was nothing she could do about it.

She waited for the next lightning flash. It came but did not last long. She could not see the rider this time, even though she was certain she had looked in the same place as before. It had to be Mala, of course. But where had she gone? Where was she now?

Stacy gripped the rifle even more tightly. If she kept coming, she would soon be very close. Was it possible Mala had located her? Had she somehow seen her? It hardly seemed possible . . . but so did a lot of other things that had been happening lately.

Somewhat nervously, she surveyed her surroundings. It wasn't a bad place, as long as she hadn't been seen, but it could almost be a trap if she had. Maybe she should move—under cover of the darkness and between lightning flashes—just in case . . .

The thought didn't appeal to her much. The footing was treacherous enough in daylight; at night it could be disastrous. Already she had cut one hand and a knee on the rocks, she had twisted an ankle slightly, and she had almost taken a headlong fall more than once. It was why people avoided the malpais. It could chew you up, defeat you, reduce you to a groveling, helpless child. Some had surely died trying to cross it, and they had been fools. Perhaps there were more fools out here yet . . .

Lightning streaked and a heavy clap of thunder rolled across the sky. The rider was there again, coming very slowly but coming directly toward Stacy, nevertheless. Darkness regained the land. Grudgingly Stacy rose, shivering now as the rain came harder; she started to move away. Lightning flashed long and unexpectedly. A shot rang out and a bullet ricocheted nearby. Stacy almost fell.

"You shouldn't have moved, Stacy! I saw you then! I am going to get you now!"

Mala's voice chilled her almost more than did the rain. It was dark again. She felt her way along, slipping time and again and almost dropping the rifle each time.

"It's no use to run, Stacy. I'll get you anyway."

Stacy stopped in her tracks. Mala's voice seemed to have come from a different direction this time. The rain and the darkness, her inability to see the moon or stars or anything else that might give her a bearing must have disoriented her. But was she *that* disoriented? Could she wind up moving *toward* Mala rather than away from her? Hesitantly she stumbled off in a new direction.

She had gone fewer than twenty-five yards when lightning once again raced across the sky. Instinctively she stopped and went to her knees, crouching to present a lesser target for both the eye and the gun. Through the rain she saw again the forms of rider and horses. They were in front of her. She had been going straight at them again! But how could that be? She stared into the utter darkness that followed the lightning and wondered.

It's useless, she told herself. *To run is useless.*

She felt around in the rocks, which she already knew were sharp and hazardous, until she found a place where there was more soil than rock. She inched her way there and settled herself into as comfortable a position as she could achieve. The soil was almost clay; it made very sticky mud. But she did not care. All that mattered now was that she would run no more. Mala had taken the thing too far. She would crouch there waiting; she would fight. Her only advantage now was to be stationary, to be alert and ready when the time came.

Very slowly she jacked a shell into the rifle's firing chamber, hoping the steady patter of the rain would drown out the sound. She had no extra ammunition for Carty's rifle—a different caliber altogether from her own—only what was in its magazine. If she took any shots, she would have to make them count.

She crouched and waited. Mala did not call out anymore and hadn't for some time now. It was a matter of who had the most patience. They were both waiting . . . waiting for the momentary light to flash in the sky once again.

It seemed to take forever, and when it finally did come, it came almost too quickly. As hard as she was trying to be ready, Stacy was caught off guard. The horses and the rider were there still—only closer, much closer than before—but Stacy rose and brought the rifle to her shoulder much too late to get off a shot before the scene went black again. She relaxed, swearing uncharacteristically beneath her breath, but she did not crouch back down.

Next time, she thought. *Next time.*

But could she really? Had being slow been the real reason she hadn't fired just now, or was it because she couldn't? Mala was her sister, after all. Her own flesh and blood. Could she do it? She gripped the rifle tightly. *She was going to have to . . . If she wanted to live, she was going to have to shoot . . .*

Lightning flickered across the sky, which erupted suddenly with a particularly violent roll of thunder. And there was Mala, less than twenty yards away, still astride her horse, her rifle trained.

"*This is it, Stacy! I have you now!*"

To Stacy, everything after that happened either too fast or too slow. Mala's words came fast, while Stacy's own instinctive raising of her rifle seemed terribly slow. And the lightning seemed suspended, as if things would never go dark again. As Mala had said, this was it. Two fingers squeezed triggers, two rifles bucked. And at the same instant a tremendous bolt of lightning struck down upon them with a deafening crack that seemed to shake everything, drowning out the gunshots as it hit.

When it was dark again, Stacy Brightwood lay collapsed where she had stood.

CHAPTER 23

The rain had long since ceased and the sky had fully cleared by the time Cam found them next morning. It was about nine o'clock, and he had been searching since sunup. Jaz and Jozie had been with him half an hour earlier when they had found Carty's body, but they had since split up, somewhat in desperation at this point, to look for Stacy. The two Indians were probably not far away now, but Cam suspected they were beyond shouting distance, and when he came upon Mala first, then saw Stacy twenty yards away, he grimly raised his rifle and fired off three shots.

It took only a limited examination to see that Mala and both of her horses were gruesomely dead. The horses lay sprawled one atop the other, legs atangle, paunches swelling and necks twisted. Cam knew instantly what had happened to them. He had seen what lightning could do many times in his years on the range, even though admittedly he had never seen anything quite like this. Mala lay a few feet away, back arched strangely where she had landed atop a chunk of lava, mouth open and body stiff, her rifle lying in the mud and rocks beside her. She had been shot once in the chest, and it was anyone's guess whether that or the lightning had got her first.

Stacy on the other hand was curled tightly in a fetal position, and her condition was much less clear. Cam was on one knee beside her a few minutes later when Jaz and Jozie rode up.

"She dead?" Jaz asked solemnly, after surveying the scene.

Cam looked up. His voice cracked as he said, "I can't find a pulse or tell if she's breathing. And she's cold . . . I can't see where she's been shot or anything, but God, she's cold!"

Jaz dismounted quickly and came to conduct his own examination. Cam watched silently, knowing already what the Indian would find. The girl's clothes were still damp from the night-long soaking they had received, her skin a deathly blue-white—yet no serious outer injury was to be found. There were a couple of minor cuts, a bruise or two, but nothing that could kill her. Just nothing.

After a few moments Jaz looked up in puzzled sadness. "I'm sorry, Stallings. She musta got too wet and cold. I dunno."

Cam, a gigantic lump caught in his throat and a dead feeling growing inside, stared down at the bedraggled body of the girl. "She's not as stiff as Mala," he murmured half hopefully.

Jaz shook his head. "Don't mean nothin'. She prob'ly died after Mala. Mebbe not too long ago."

This really shook Cam. If they had only arrived sooner, or if they could have found her last night, before darkness had forced them to quit looking . . . maybe . . . maybe they could have . . .

He looked away, fighting tears. *Jesus. Can this really be? After all we've been through, this?*

For several moments he just knelt there in stunned silence. Then, finally, he squared his shoulders and looked back at Jaz. "Break out my bedroll," he said. "Get me a blanket to put over her. Come on, hustle up, man! I can't just let her lie here like this."

Jaz hurried to do as he was told, and presently Cam had Stacy covered, then as an afterthought wrapped her tightly in the blanket.

"What're we gonna do with her, Stallings?" Jozie asked.

Cam looked up, startled. "Why, take her back to the ranch, I guess. We'll . . . bury her there—beside her father."

"How we gonna take her?" Jaz asked with a practical air. "You don't wanta throw her over a saddle, do you? You gonna carry her?"

"No, I don't want to throw her over a saddle," Cam said. They had brought her horse with them from the ice-cave basin, but the idea of handling her in that manner was completely repulsive to him. "We'll probably have to take turns, but I'll take her first. Here, let me get mounted, you hand her up to me."

Stiffly, he rose and hobbled over to his horse and led it over to a rock large enough for him to mount from. Once aboard, he looked back at Jaz. The Indian reached down and collected the small, curled-up form in his arms and brought her over to where Cam sat. He handed her up carefully, as if he was afraid he might hurt her even though he knew that was impossible now. Cam shuddered as he took her, but then cradled her head against his left shoulder and scooted back some in the saddle so he could rest her hips in front of him. This promised to be awkward, so he lifted her left leg and hooked it stiffly across the pommel so the body would not constantly be trying to slide away. This done, he rearranged the blanket to cover her fully.

He looked at Jaz and Jozie. "I'm ready. Let's go."

Jaz looked over toward Mala. "What about her?"

"We'll send someone back for her," Cam said, unable to hide the bitterness that welled inside him. "Otherwise, right now, I just don't care."

They rode for nearly two miles across the malpais before Cam pulled up and asked Jaz if he would take a turn carrying the body. "My arms are dead," he said. "And the blanket's slipping. Here, you take it. We can rewrap her after you've got her."

The Indian reined his horse up beside Cam's and took the blanket. Cam shifted his weight and thus that of the dead girl, and was just bunching his muscles to hand her over when suddenly a sound escaped the body, almost like a low moan. For a moment it gave him an eerie chill, but then he shook it off. He had never fooled with a dead body before; he didn't know what all stages one went through, or if one might or might not make sounds. He looked down at the face, the closed eyelids, the lips, slightly parted now—pale but not as blue as before . . . or was he imagining that? His eyes somehow moved to her chest, where her blouse was partway open but not enough so to actually expose a breast. He even imagined he detected a slight rise and fall, but of course he could not have. An illusion, that's all . . . But somehow he couldn't quite leave it at that. And besides, it wasn't the only thing wrong. With the blanket removed, there even seemed to be a slight warmth passing through her still lightly damp clothing to his shoulder and chest. The body had been so cold before, and much more rigid—she was practically limp now!

He jerked as if stung when once again there was a sound, only this time he was convinced it had passed between the slightly parted lips—a moan, it was definitely a moan! And the lips had become more parted, he'd swear to it. He looked quickly at Jaz. "Did you hear that?" he asked hoarsely. "Did you?"

Jaz reacted in pure puzzlement. "What? Did I hear what, Stallings?"

Suddenly Cam's heart was pounding so hard he thought it would burst. The girl's lips had moved for certain this time. And as if this wasn't enough, there then followed a minute little flicker of expression across the face, a flutter of the eyelids, a weak stir of the body, another moan . . .

"Jaz . . . Jozie!" Cam almost screamed it at them. "*Help me get her down!*"

They arrived back at the burned-out ranch late that afternoon, and found the place surprisingly alive with activity. There were maybe eight or ten cowboys down at the corrals, unsaddling their horses, and among them were Dan Stanhope, Blake Stoddard, and the two Mexican boys, Francisco Luna and Pablo Navarro. The others were apparently members of the neighboring outfits, just come in off the range from working the Stretch B herd, and to attest to the success of their efforts, cattle could be seen spreading out all across the plains for as far as Cam could see—a rewarding sight to be sure.

His first priority, however, was Stacy. Somehow, miraculously perhaps, she was alive. But she was still highly lethargic and it worried him a good deal that although she had long since regained what seemed to be full consciousness she had yet to respond to anything they said to her. Again and again Cam had asked her if she hurt anywhere, if she was still cold, if she even recognized him or either of the two young Navajos. But she only stared, zombielike, either through him or past him, and would not say a word.

They took her directly to the bunkhouse and carried her inside where she could be given warm clothing and be put to bed, and were immediately ushered back outside as the girl Juana took over from there.

Dan Stanhope and Blake Stoddard met Cam on the porch as Jaz and Jozie headed off toward the corrals with the horses.

. . "Man, are we ever glad to see you!" Stanhope exclaimed, looking around at the ruined ranch buildings. Adobe walls still stood at least in part where the main house and store had been, but the interiors and roofs were obviously destroyed and the barn had been reduced to nothing more than a pile of charred timbers and ashes. "Stacy's girl in there told us some of it, and we were about set to go lookin' for you when you rode in. What happened out there? What's wrong with Stacy?"

Cam flopped tiredly down on a bench that rested against the front wall of the bunkhouse and proceeded to try to relate the story to them. When he finished several minutes later, his deep concern for Stacy was so overriding that all else paled beside it.

"I never heard of anybody near freezing to death in summertime before," Blake Stoddard commented thoughtfully. "Or acting like that when they came out of it. Are you sure she's not hurt somewhere?"

Cam shook his head. "She's got a bad bruise on her face, but somehow I don't think that could do it. And we sure couldn't find anything else. She must have fainted or been knocked out when the lightning hit, then lay there in the wet and cold all night. I do think keeping her warm and quiet might help. That's what's brought her back this far, I think—the fact that one of us had to hold her and that we kept her warm all the way here."

Stoddard shook his head. "Too bad it's so damn far to the nearest doc. Maybe one could help . . ."

Cam shrugged and did not look or feel hopeful at the suggestion. Somehow he doubted it; he doubted it very much.

Stanhope came over to sit beside him, then leaned back to stare out across the plains. "Well, at least the Terhunes are out of our hair, what with Mala dead and Gerd waiting in Vera Velarde for the sheriff to come and cart him off for trial. And we got the cattle back—most of them, anyway. I figure seventy-five percent at least and more yet to show up before the fall roundup. Which is pretty good, if you ask me—huh, Blake?"

"That's right. And that's not all either," Stoddard responded encouragingly. "Stacy's neighbors will come through bigger than ever now, Cam. Ressler and McNaab themselves are down at the corrals, and they're already talking about sending into Vera Velarde for some lumber. I figure they'll shoot for everything the sawmill can provide and have it here by late tomorrow—three, four wagonloads at least, and enough men to rebuild this place in a week. Barn, house, even the store, if Stacy wants it—"

"If Stacy will ever want anything again," Cam said glumly. "Have Ressler and McNaab thought about that?"

Stanhope jerked, then shot him a stern look at this. "Come on, man —don't talk that way. Of course she will. You gotta believe that. She's got to now, she's just got to!"

Cam met his gaze and wished he could be so positive. "I hope you're right," he said. "I hope to hell you're right."

A few hours later he sat alone on the porch. The sun had long since disappeared and full dark had settled. A gleaming gibbous moon was just rising and laying the grassy plains light gray in contrast to all that was around them. A camp had been built over near the store and a fire blazed, the cowboys surrounding it, joking or playing cards, 'or laying out their bedrolls, since the bunkhouse had been reserved strictly for Stacy and Juana.

In a little while Cam would go down there. Just now, his mood one of unease and depression, he felt more like being alone. Long ago it had dawned on him that working for Stacy Brightwood meant something more to him than just "riding for the brand." But so much had happened so very fast that he just had never had the time nor the opportunity to realize *how* much it meant to him, how much *Stacy* meant to him.

He looked out across the softly moonlit plains and saw in his mind's eye places like Bell Cow Cienaga and Loco Creek and Paint Horse Mesa; he thought of Vera Velarde, of the mesa country and the malpais; he idly felt inside his vest pocket for the now well-worn maps Stacy had drawn for him what seemed so long, long ago. He thought of Jaz and Jozie, of Dan Stanhope and Blake Stoddard . . . of loyal old Miguel, who had given his life.

He thought again of Stacy. She had been asleep a little while ago when he'd gone in to see her. She still hadn't spoken and she hadn't eaten. She was as if in a trance, and neither he nor Juana nor anyone else seemed to know how to bring her out of it. Knowing nothing of such things, Cam was afraid she might never come out of it.

The lamp went out inside as he sat there—Juana going to bed. He sighed. Not much use hanging around further, he told himself. Still he sat there for perhaps ten minutes more before drawing himself stiffly erect, the idea in mind to hobble on over to the camp across the way.

He had gone but a few steps when the sound of the bunkhouse door opening behind him caused him to stop.

He turned. A lone figure stood in the porch shadows just outside the door. "Juana?" he asked. "Is that you, Juana?"

The figure moved toward him, out of the shadows and into full moonlight. Her hair was down and hung billowing about her shoulders, and was light, not dark. It was *not* Juana. Alarmed, he all but forgot about his bad leg as he started back toward the porch steps. "Stacy! What are you doing out here . . . ?"

For a moment she just stood there, wobbling slightly, but regarding him nevertheless. She wore one of Cam's old shirts and a pair of Jozie's breeches rolled up at the ankles, because nothing extra either of hers or Juana's had survived the fire at the main house, and she had a blanket from her bunk wrapped around her shoulders.

"Stacy," he repeated, coming halfway up the steps. "Can't you answer me? Can't you please just say something?"

At first she only continued to stare, and he feared that she was no more than sleepwalking, that nothing had changed. But just as he had decided this, her expression changed, her eyes widened with recognition, she trembled noticeably. Then, almost without warning, she cried out and the blanket fell and she was in his arms, crying:

"Cam! Oh, Cam—I thought I would never see you again! I thought you were . . . Carty told me that you . . . And then I . . . Oh, Cam—what has been *happening* to me?"

For a long time he just stood there and held her while she cried, and he almost cried too. But he wasn't sad; somehow he could tell by the feel of her, by the way she cried, that she was going to be all right now. He thanked God silently for the tears.

CHAPTER 24

About noon the second day following, Jaz and Jozie brought Mala's body in off the malpais. Cam cursed himself for not having brought her in when they came with Stacy, for it had taken that long just to find her again and to bring her back. Needless to say, it was not a very pleasant task. The body was placed almost immediately in a grave already dug, next to that of the girl's father and not far from where Jaz had buried Miguel.

Cam, standing on makeshift crutches nearby, watched as Stacy herself placed a temporary marker at the head of the grave, and he marveled openly at her demeanor. If there was any antipathy or rancor in her, it was well concealed.

"You think it strange that I put her beside him, don't you?" she asked as she finished.

He shrugged uncomfortably. "A little, maybe. Yes."

"He wouldn't begrudge her her place, Cam," she explained in a steady voice. "She was a grave disappointment to him, but he didn't hate her. He could never do that."

"And you? You don't hate her either?"

She shook her head. On her face there was only sadness. "It's enough that I must live with the fact that my bullet may have killed her before the lightning hit; I don't have to live with hatred too. Anyway, it's pointless to hate the dead, Cam. You should know that."

After supper that evening they sat on the bunkhouse porch. The sun was just down and a few fleecy clouds hung pink-orange and purple above the horizon. The cowboy camp across the way had grown to over twice its original size now, and the beginning structure of a new main house was already in evidence about halfway between the old house and the store. Nearby to this, three wagonloads of lumber had been stacked neatly and all three wagons had gone back to town for more. Money would have to be borrowed to pay for the materials, but the house would soon be rebuilt completely, as would the barn. There would never again be a store.

"My father built it as a service to the people settling here," Stacy had said on that point. "Vera Velarde is growing now and our store really isn't needed anymore. Besides, this is a cattle ranch; that's all I want it to be from now on: the biggest and best around."

Cam was glad to hear her talking this way. She had been pretty subdued for the past two days, and understandably so. They lacked the medical knowledge to explain what had happened to her, just as they could only guess at what had so miraculously brought her out of it. Cam was just thankful that despite all else, she was recovering, and her present reflection of optimism had to be viewed as just one more good sign.

They had talked a lot these past two days about a lot of things. Much had been a filling in of what had happened, for both of them. Some had been about themselves, their future together—too much in some ways for a forty-a-month former grub-line cowboy to handle just yet . . . but there would be plenty of time for that, they both knew. Plenty of time.

Tonight they talked less than usual. They were tired of talking. But they didn't leave the porch. It grew late. Even the cowboy camp had become quiet and only the barest flicker of its campfire could still be seen. The lamp inside the bunkhouse went out, signifying that Juana, too, had gone to bed. A mild breeze blew across the ranch yard. Somewhere out on the open plain a calf bawled. Cam, Stacy, that calf out there, and a few crickets could have been all that were left alive on earth.

Stacy let herself sink comfortably within Cam's arms. They watched the night, the stars, a few thunderheads putting together on the horizon. An owl hooted from somewhere, the crickets chirped. The breeze had momentarily died. A distant bolt of lightning flickered among the clouds. And behind them, outside their view, sprawled the malpais. Dark and quiet and immutable. A reminder. Forever.